Also by Daniel Finn

Two Good Thieves

MACMILLAN CHILDREN'S BOOKS

First published 2012 by Macmillan Children's Books
a division of Macmillan Publishers Limited
20 New Wharf Road, London N1 9RR
Basingstoke and Oxford
Associated companies throughout the world
www.panmacmillan.com

ISBN 978-0-230-73800-3

1 3 5 7 9 8 6 4 2

A CIP catalogue record for this book is available from
the British Library.

Printed and bound by CPI Group (UK) Ltd, Croydon CR0 4YY

For Patrick, a poet in the sun

The grace and shadow of a single tree in bloom
settled in me like gentleness

From 'Shade' by P. Daly

CHAPTER ONE

It was like this.

Reve's skiff, a small open-decked fishing boat, was in close to a ragged cliff that butted like a boxer's nose out into the sea. In hard weather this was a bad bit of coastline. There were rocks and shallows and eddies that would pull and twist a small boat about and smash it up against that cliff when a sea was running. It happened. But today the sea was glass, and anyway Reve reckoned it was worth the risk coming in this close; you could net good jackfish here, if you were patient.

The sea barely moved, just a faint sigh as it breathed against the cliff, and Reve was patient.

He could see every twist of weed and strip of white sand tucked up between the rocky gulleys; he could see sunlight flashing as shoals of sprat twisted in and out of shadow. Six metres down right here, but everything looked so close he could almost reach out and touch it.

The sun scored down the back of his neck; he wiped the sweat from his eyes, squinted against the glare. Concentrate.

The rest of the fishing boats were far out, nailed to the horizon. It was usually the way, him fishing on his own like this. It was Tomas's boat, and not every fisherman was Tomas's friend. Reve didn't mind one way or the other. In fact he liked to fish alone.

There!

Maybe five metres away, on the ocean side of the skiff. And again.

The sea boiled as a big fish turned rapidly, just beneath the surface. Reve shifted his grip on the coil of net. One end was fixed to the stern, the other he gripped in his left hand, the belly of the net he held in his right, ready to throw.

Up in the bows, tucked into the shade under the folded sail, a scruff mat of a dog opened one eye and murmured a growl. Best fishing dog in the village – only fishing dog in the village – lazy as hell, but he loved it up there in the bow, keeping an eye on Reve. Like he was the boss.

There it was again, a little closer. A twist and slash on the surface. Big! Feeding on sprat, must be. He hoped it was a jackfish, something bigger than Tomas had ever caught, a giant fish, deep and strong, a fish to put dollar in their pockets.

Come on, a little closer. A little closer.

Tiny white fish shrapnelled out of the water, instantly followed by a wide splash of silver. He flung out the net. Perfect. It uncoiled in the air and then sank fast. He counted: one and two. And then his hands blurred they were hauling so fast, sweeping in the net. Any second he would feel it, that weight, and then the bang and tug of the tangled fish.

But there was no weight, nothing. The net slithered in around his feet and Sultan didn't even bother to raise his head, just yawned and pushed his nose down into his paws.

Reve grimaced. He had been so sure.

He splashed seawater over his face and head, then shook the wet from him just like Sultan did when he came out of the sea and up on to the beach. Then he leaned out over the side, willing that jackfish to swim right up to him. 'Come on,' he urged. 'I know you there, you fat old fish. Come on an' I snatch you up in my hand.' He leaned over further, pushing his face down into the cool surface, squeezing his eyes tight and then opening them slowly . . .

Hair like flame burning around her face, lips a little apart, like she was about to say something. A smile that had no happiness in it and a hand held up to beckon . . . or maybe to wave goodbye.

So close he could almost touch her, except he couldn't move. He couldn't breathe. He couldn't think. It wasn't possible. It was his sister, it was Mi. And it wasn't her at all. Long dark strands of weed reached up and stroked across her face, criss-crossed, as if tightening like a net . . . He stared so hard his eyes felt as if they were about to tear out of their sockets and every tendon on his neck was bunched up tight. His heart was hammering in his chest. He couldn't believe what he was seeing and yet there she was.

He jerked back, spluttering.

Sultan, suddenly alert, was up, paws on the side, barking and barking. Reve didn't even hear his dog. He took a big breath and dived overboard and swam fast, straight down, eyes wide, staring this way and that.

He reached the bed, lungs bursting, grabbed a fistful of thick weed and twisted round on himself, half expecting her face to be right there, her cold hand reaching for him.

A black crab the size of a human skull waved his claws at him and then backed down into a crevice.

Where was she?

Like the cursed fish. Nothing.

His head pounded, a mallet banging his chest. He let go and kicked hard, bursting through the surface with such force that his head, shoulders and chest came right up out of the water. He gasped for breath and clutched at the side of the boat, barely aware of Sultan whining and scratching and licking at his hand.

He let go and dived again, steadier this time, looking this way and that. Maybe a freak current had pulled the body down into a rock gulley, maybe . . . He surfaced again. The tide was slack. There was no current.

He dived again and again and then, exhausted, hauled himself back on board and slumped down in the stern. He must have imagined her.

Mi never went in the sea. Never. Never stepped in a boat. No one get drowned if they don't go in the water, she used to say.

So it couldn't have been her. Maybe someone else who looked like her? No. No one look like Mi. No one got that red hair. No one got her looks.

The sun could make you see things . . . give you waking dreams. He knew that all right, but it'd never happened to him. He didn't even dream in the night-time. Never had. Mi was the dreamer – half lived in a different world from the rest of them. But not Reve. He worked. He fished. He cooked. He minded Tomas. He minded Arella. He minded Mi. What time did he have for dreaming?

Sultan sniffed his hand and then put a paw on Reve's leg.

'I'm all right,' he said, more to himself than to the dog.

Sultan tilted his head, as if he understood perfectly well what the boy's words meant, and then retreated to his shelter in the bows.

Reve didn't move. Maybe this was one of those things that had meaning, like with Mi and the way she could tell when a storm was coming; the way her spirit voices told her things, like when she stopped in front of old Baufice and told him he needed to take two nets because he was going to catch more fish than one net could swallow. And that's what happened. No one else caught a thing that time, not even Tomas.

Or the time she stopped in front of Elena's and told her she was going to birth two babies and that her sow would birth piglets on that same day. She hadn't been joking. Mi didn't joke. It happened like she said.

Maybe he had caught this from her somehow, the seeing of something that carried meaning. Maybe Mi was in trouble again. Maybe worse this time.

The village, Rinconda, was more than five miles up the coast, and a long hard row, but maybe he could pick up a scrap of breeze away from the shelter of the shore. Quickly he poured seawater into the battered plastic box where he had the jackfish he had caught earlier, covered them up again, pulled out the oars, set them into the pins, then sat on the centre thwart and rowed. He dug the blades in and pulled, heaving the skiff out from the cliff. He dug, and pulled and feathered the blade and tried not to imagine the trouble she was in. He rowed steady but hard, putting his back into it, trying to keep the worry down in its hole, but every time he pulled on the oars that face floated into his mind.

The sweat poured down his back and his hands burned against the wood but he pulled hard and ignored the pain. He had seen a drowned body one time, all snagged up in a net. He'd got that memory sharp and clear. He saw it all again right now as he rowed: the skin gone grey and puffy, the eyes dead like the eyes of a shark-fish, the fingers poking through the net, and when the body was laid out they'd all seen the little hole in his chest, all puckered up like a belly button. The whole village had seen that, been made to see it.

He had been five and Mi had been eight years old the day their father was dragged up out of the water and on to the harbour wall; the day their mother had stepped out of their lives; the day Tomas the Boxer took them into his home.

He rowed hard but steady, and as soon as he felt the touch of wind on his cheek he shipped the oars and scrabbled up the sail and sat back in the stern, his eyes fixed on the hazy blur that was Rinconda, willing the skiff to cut through the water and bring him home quick.

CHAPTER TWO

LoJo was on the beach when Reve sailed the skiff in. There was a little harbour at the foot of the village that they all called 'the wall' because that's about all it was: a wide stone wall that hooked out into the sea and gave some shelter in the stormy season. The real reason it was there was because it was for unloading the fast boats when they slipped in at night, and it was all sweat and fear and hurry in case the coastguard or police came poking their nose. Most fishermen, like Reve, kept their skiffs up on the sand and used the harbour wall for mending nets, passing time. The village itself stretched back from the harbour almost as far as the north–south coast highway. It was not much more than a straggle of shacks, mostly clad in black plastic, with patchwork roofs, rickety porches and sandy yards pegged out with driftwood and wire fences. A few men with money had more substantial places: Theon, Reve's uncle, had the cantina and Calde had a block-stone house, workshops and a builders' yard and a factory where some of the Rinconda women were lucky enough to work.

As soon as LoJo spotted Reve he ran down the beach and waded in. 'Seen you comin in,' he called, grabbing hold of the bow. 'You ahead of everyone, Reve. Done any good?'

'Some,' said Reve, letting the sail go and jumping over the side. 'You seen Mi?' He was anxious to hear she was all right; the whole strange business of the young woman in the water nagged at him worse than a salt sore. But then the truth was he worried about Mi all the time anyhow.

'That's what I come tell you,' said LoJo, taking the other side of the skiff and helping Reve to drag it inshore. 'I seen her coming back from Theon's, walking fast, like she get bee-stung.'

Sultan had his front paws up on the bow and was barking, as he always did, wanting the boys to hurry and pull the skiff on to the sand, so he could jump down without getting wet.

'Go on!' said Reve impatiently. 'You nothin but noise. Get down!'

Sultan barked again and jumped, skipped ahead of a little wave and then, without a backwards glance, trotted off along the beach, away from the harbour and the village, heading for Mi's place.

'What happen with Mi?' asked Reve. 'She start shakin, falling down . . . ? Someone throw bad talk at her?'

'Maybe. I seen Hevez and Ramon try to stop her on her way out from Theon's, but she just push by, came down the track half running she was going so fast, and she was talking to herself, real angry, and she pass me an' my mother like we wasn't there. My mother call to her but she just kept on, smoke lightning. Bet she was haulin a curse on Hevez, bet that was what she was at. Everybody know she can call down a curse bette'n anyone on the coast, shrivel up the devil and push him down in the hole – that's what I hear.'

LoJo spat on the sand. For a boy a year younger and almost a head shorter than Reve he sometimes seemed like one of the old fishermen. Only difference maybe was that he had more talk in him than a radio station.

'Hevez getting worse all the time, Reve. Reckons no one touch him for anything.'

Of all the bad things in Rinconda, Reve thought, Hevez and his friends, or maybe Hevez and his uncle Calde, were the worst. Hevez was a swagger boy with a dirt mouth, who liked to pick fights and give hurt, but only when he had his friends at his back, and only when the boy he was picking on was half his size. LoJo got knocked around a fair bit.

Hevez's uncle, Calde, ran the village and owned most of the skiffs in the fleet. Tomas was quite unusual having his own boat. LoJo's father, Pelo, a quiet, hardworking fisherman, owed Calde all the time. Most of anything a body wanted in Rinconda, then it was Calde that got paid. If he got his fat fingers in you, he'd squeeze your gut tight till you paid whatever dollar you owed him: fishermen like Pelo paying off loans on their boats, boats that Calde's yard fixed and built; families who had to go burying up on the hill and wanted a coffin, that got made in the yard as well.

And he had other business: he was hooked up, smuggling for the Night Man. That was business that no one breathed a word about, not unless they wanted to end up beaten, maybe get an accident happen to them, maybe get tangled in a net.

That was why Hevez felt he could do just what he

wanted. He never did a spit of work, just showed off his new jeans and thought any girl in the village lucky if he let her bend down and kiss his foot. Some did, but Mi never gave him the time of day, looked right through him every time he stepped in her path.

Reve said, 'They didn't follow Mi out of the village, did they?'

LoJo shook his head. 'They up on the wall.'

Reve put his hand up to shade his eyes. He could make out one or two figures working on their nets, which meant it wasn't Hevez and his friends. 'They're not there now, Lo. You sure they didn't cut along the beach?'

LoJo looked worried. 'I don't know. I don't think so, Reve. I didn't see them go that way. They never gone out there, have they? That's her place. Everybody know, you don't go out to Mi's place unless she hold a meeting . . .'

'They touch my sister, I swear I do some bad thing.' Reve hurriedly finished wrapping the sail, yanking the cord tight so the canvas wouldn't come loose. And then checked his catch. He should take the jackfish straight up to the cold store, but they would be fine for a little while. He'd see Mi was all right first. He scooped fresh seawater over them and covered them again.

'What you goin do, Reve? My daddy says your Tomas the only man who can face down Calde. But I reckon you need me if you goin pick a fight with Hevez.'

Even though he was anxious to get going, Reve couldn't help smiling. LoJo had more talk than muscle; a strong wind would blow him over. 'Your daddy won't want you getting in fights with anyone, LoJo, not with a baby coming.'

'I can throw a punch good as anyone. I got whipcord and steel in my right arm, Reve.'

'You got so much muscle, maybe you carry up the sail for me?'

'Sure I carry it for you, but you goin teach me to box, the way Tomas teach you?' He stabbed his skinny fist into the air, once, twice, and puffed out his cheeks, like he was doing some real hurt. 'Then we pull down anyone who push their weight. See!' He snapped an upper cut and almost hit himself on the nose. 'Like that, eh! Land one in Calde's belly.'

'Then you'd be the king of Rinconda. Here –' he passed him the boom and sail – 'you take this now.'

'I'm serious, Reve, hey, you teach me some moves. Hevez don't push you like he do me – him an' Ramon an' Sali.'

'I'll teach you, Lo, but not now. You try keepin out of their way.

'My daddy say everybody in this place got their head tuck in the sand. You tellin me that's what I got to do?'

'No. Just take this up for me. I'll see you later.'

'OK Reve.'

So they split: LoJo shouldering the long boom and sail, hurrying up the beach towards the little harbour, while Reve started to run along the hard sand to the right, heading the same way as his dog had gone. The real burning heat had gone out of the day, but the breeze was warm and sticky in his lungs and his body ached from the hard rowing, but he was used to that. He ran grimly. He didn't have his head in the sand. He reckoned he could see what was happening.

Mi was getting a name that stretched out beyond Rinconda. People brought her things so she would make a prayer or go step in the spirit world for them. But there were others who didn't like having her anywhere near the village, a few sour-faced women mainly. She didn't care 'bout them. Didn't care what people said. Never had, but maybe that was because she was the one who had her head 'tuck in the sand'.

Part of the trouble was that with her flame-red hair there wasn't anybody looked like her in Rinconda, not even Reve; and then she took herself off to live on her own in a busted-up old car. Asking for trouble, Tomas said.

Hevez was trouble, him and his pack, dogs always sniffing round her. Only way to stop a dog sniffing was to give it a hard lesson. Reve bunched his fist as he ran.

A third of a mile along the strand he could see the acacia tree that gave a bit of shade to her car. But he couldn't see her sitting in her usual place, crosslegged up on the roof of the Beetle, staring out to sea.

'Mi!'

He ran up from the shore, pushing himself to go fast through the soft dry sand.

He heard Sultan barking and then he heard Mi scream, shrill and angry, 'You come another step I tear a hole in you!' She never yelled at Sultan. It was the boys.

Reve tore past her crazy little sand garden of fishbone, stick and sea-washed glass bottles and there they were on the far side of the car. Mi down on her knees, her face twisted up with rage, spitting curses at them, her red hair like a storm cloud round her head, the sleeve half torn off her shirt, a little trickle of blood on her shin. It looked like she'd fallen or been thrown, but she had a broken bottle in her hand, and whether it was the cursing or the sight of that sharp glass, the three boys facing her were keeping their distance.

Hevez with his slick-back hair and neat city jeans was half a pace in front of the other two, a stumpy little knife in one hand.

Reve stopped beside Mi and touched her shoulder. 'What you been doin, Hevez? Why don' you back off before someone get killed here? You hear me!'

Hevez glanced at Reve but gave absolutely no reaction to what he had said. All his attention was on Mi. 'Say all you want, witch-girl,' he said, his voice trying to sneer but trembling a little with nerves and excitement. There was nothing bold or brave about Hevez. Then he held out his left hand and Reve saw he had a whole twist of Mi's hair in his fist. 'We goin see if this is real or if you go putting paint in it, make yourself a Babbylong whore like my uncle call you.'

Sali, the youngest of the three, sniggered. With his narrow, sloping shoulders and the fluffy shadow of a moustache on his upper lip, Sali wasn't a threat to anyone; he was a sheep, nothing on his own. Ramon, the other one, was a different matter; he was grit-hard and sour, like he had a grudge against the world. He was always ready for a fight. He lived up by the highway, no parents, but he had a younger brother that he looked out for.

Reve didn't care about either of them. It was Hevez he wanted to break. He felt the blood pounding in his head.

'Your uncle Calde . . .' said Mi, her voice oddly matter-of-fact now, as if she had drained out her pool of curses, 'your uncle goin pick up the phone one time, you hearin me, an' he goin hear death talking to him. An' on that day . . . You,' she said slowly and deliberately, 'Goin. Be. Nothin. Nothin. Nothin . . .' Her voice turning harsh and strange as she kept chanting the one word over and over again.

That really spooked Hevez, spooked them all, but it was Hevez who shouted and swore and tried to drown out what she was saying. But he couldn't. He shook his knife at her, threatened to cut off the rest of her hair, and when she still didn't stop he took a step forward.

Tomas always said to pick your time; if you got to fight, make it one-on-one and watch for the snake who carries a blade, but Reve wasn't thinking about Tomas. He threw himself head first at Hevez and hit him hard in the chest, sent him tumbling sideways. Hevez hit the ground with a thud and a startled shriek. Reve was right on top of him, grabbing at his arm, trying to get at his knife hand, and everyone was shouting and yelling. It sounded more like a riot than a scuffle.

Hevez was howling so loudly Reve thought he'd fallen on the blade, and Mi was shrieking but it seemed to be at Reve, not at Hevez, telling him to get out of there, which didn't make any sense; and Sultan was dancing about in a barking frenzy.

Reve twisted sideways, his elbow against Hevez's chin, and managed to grip his wrist. One of the boys darted in and aimed a savage kick, which caught Reve in the ribs and made him gasp. Then Ramon had him round his neck. Reve smelt the sharp tang of the other boy's sweat and felt the air pinched out of his throat before he was yanked backwards and found himself winded, half blinded by sun and grits of sand and with Sultan's sticky-hot, fish-breath on his face.

He pushed Sultan away and struggled to his feet. There was blood on his hands and for a second he thought he had got cut, but then he saw, as Sali and Ramon were helping Hevez up, that Hevez had dropped the knife and was clutching his left arm. His fingers were red and blood was dropping on to the sand. He grimaced and with a whimper pulled a long nail from his arm. That must have been what he fell on, thought Reve. Unlucky for him – apart from the bits of stone and glass with which she decorated her sand garden, Mi kept her place clear of all rubbish.

'You come by here another time,' hissed Mi, still kneeling, still with the jagged bottle neck in her hand, 'and you find you get something come tearing at you worse than that old cut.'

Hevez was breathing hard, his nose pinched and his face tight with rage and embarrassment. 'You got more trouble comin than you dream of,' he said. 'An' I got this! Yeah! See it! I got your hair, you witch.' Ramon and Sali were on either side of him, helping him to his feet, and then the three of them started to back away.

15

'People goin hear what you done, Hevez,' said Reve. 'They not goin to care too much who your uncle; they goin burn you down for this.'

'Burn,' he sneered. 'I show you burn. You nothin but Tomas run-aroun', and she the Babbylong whore.' He shrugged himself away from his friends, all his attention back on Mi. 'An' you,' he said to her, 'you so good telling what goin happen, maybe you see the fool who goin to marry you! You see that man? Cos no one else do! No one in their good mind goin to come near you and your stupid car and your stones!' He kicked at the sand so that it sprayed back at them. Then Ramon put his arm around Hevez's shoulder and said something in his ear and the two of them laughed, and Sali laughed too. And they sauntered off like they had been in some gunfight, all swagger and loud voices.

CHAPTER THREE

They watched them go, not speaking. Reve's rib hurt but it was Mi he was concerned about. She'd dropped the bottle neck and was hugging herself with her left arm; her right hand was threading through her hair, trying to find where he had hacked off a clump. 'A'most down to my head,' she said more to herself than to Reve. She bit her lip and Reve saw a tear roll down her cheek. She smudged it away with her forearm and sniffed crossly.

'He was the one who got hurt,' said Reve, thinking to comfort her. 'A nail! How come you got one nail in the sand there and he the fool go fallin on it?'

She took a deep breath and then stood up. 'Sewn it with nail and glass,' she said. 'Don't you go steppin on it, Reve. Them flower are for that boy and his friends. I knowed they'd come botherin . . .'

'I did step on it, Mi. Nothin happen to me.'

She shrugged, no longer interested. 'You just lucky, Reve; nothin touch you.'

He followed her around to the front of the rusty old Beetle, wondering if she really had done what she had said and made some sort of a trap in the sand. It was just as possible that she only thought she had, or had started and then got bored and given up. It was hard to tell with Mi. One thing for sure though, Hevez was hurting; that old nail could make him sick if he didn't go and clean it quick, not that Reve cared what happened to him.

17

'I don't think they'll come botherin' you again, Mi.'
He said it, but he didn't really believe it. He wanted to
comfort her but he didn't know how. A fright like she'd
had could have pushed her over the edge, started up her
juddering and eye rolling, the fits that took her right
out of this world, that left her sick, bruised, dizzy and
sometimes with her tongue bleeding. 'Reckon you taught
them a lesson.'

Mi didn't respond. She wiped her hands on her faded
blue skirt and then knelt down and began to tend her
garden. She shifted a blood-coloured stone one way, then
her hand, which he saw was trembling slightly, hesitated
over a delicate, eggshell-thin bird's skull, but almost
instantly snatched it back as if the fragile skull might
have burned her. Then she carefully put a shell on top of
a half-buried plastic Coke bottle, dusted her hands and
wiped her eyes again.

He squatted down beside her. He ought to go, but he
didn't want to leave her. And he wanted to tell her about
the woman he'd seen down in the water. He chewed his
lip. Maybe tomorrow, he thought.

'Go on then,' said Mi.

'What?'

'Ask that question you got.'

'How you know I got question?'

She moved a stick, laid another on top of it to make a
cross. 'Cos you carry one big askin face, tha's why.'

So he told her as accurately as he could what it was
that he had seen: a young woman, with floating red hair,
down near the ocean floor, maybe six or seven metres

down. The water had been clear and clean, like the glass in a rich man's car, and it had been like that, like looking through a window, except she'd been way below him, the light shining on her, her hair red, like the red you get when a fire is dying low.

'She look a bit like you,' he said simply when he had finished telling her everything, how he had dived down and there'd been nothing there. 'And she look living not drowned. She look pretty. And she look sad. Made me hurry back and find you.'

Mi pulled a face when he said that, but she didn't look at him, kept shifting things one way or another, concentrating on her little garden.

'Six, seven metre down and she don't look drowned? You goin tell me she swim up and start talkin to you? What you playin at, Reve?'

'Just tellin you what I seen. You think it got meaning? Like things you see sometime. Things you say you hear. You think it like that?'

She turned and looked sharply at him when he said this. 'You not the same as me, Reve. You don't got thing happening inside you all the time.'

'I know,' he said, trying to calm her. 'I know all this you're sayin but I just had to tell you what I seen. Tha's all, Mi.'

'Maybe you tellin' me stories, Reve. Maybe you think you got dreamin power, Reve. Maybe you come in my business—'

'Mi, you just buzzin!' He laughed but uncertainly, worried that her mind was racing away with itself and she would get wound up and start juddering.

She sat back and hugged her knees. She looked miserable. She often looked distracted, or wild, or cross but not this, not like someone was grinding his heel down on her spirit. 'I believe you dream this woman,' she said.

'I don' know. Maybe.'

'Maybe you dream it for me,' she said slowly.

He didn't follow that so he said nothing, sat watching her move her little bits of plastic and stone about.

'Who you think look like me?' she asked after a moment.

'No one. No one in this place.'

'Think.'

He shook his head. 'You different from most everybody I ever seen.'

'Except the woman who birthed me.' She straightened up and looked at him.

'She dead.'

'You said she didn't look dead.'

'I said the woman I seen didn't look drowned. Not the same thing, Mi.'

She gripped his wrist. 'You the one came to tell me these things,' she said. 'Now, I'm tellin you, Reve, I see the meanin. Tha's what I do. An' I see this. She alive and she callin me . . .' Her mood had completely changed. There was something almost desperate in her expression and in her voice too. Sunlight and storm, she could slip from one to the other in a heartbeart.

'She? Alive? Our mother? No, Mi, listen. You the one dreamin now.' He stroked her forearm. She was still gripping his wrist tightly. 'She gone a long time, Mi. Eight years. The police took her away. We know this. She get swallow up in the Castle. Uncle Theon told us all this. Told us no one come out of that prison once they go in. She's dead to us. Hey, if some miracle happen an' she's living free, why she don' come knocking on our door before this time? I don't even know how she look any more, Mi. You didn't see what I seen; you don't know how she look.'

'You tol' me. It's her! Who else? She somewhere and I got to go find her.' She shook his wrist. 'This is what it all mean.'

He'd never had the same dreams about their mother that Mi had; she talked about her sometimes, tried to make Reve remember her, but she was never more than hazy when he tried calling her up: a smile, a smoky laughing voice, but what he remembered most was her absence. When they buried their father she wasn't there. She was a gone-away mother, that's all she was; and now to leave Tomas, leave his fishing, his uncle Theon, leave LoJo, leave Sultan? Leave his whole life behind him and just up and go? The thought startled him.

'Maybe she goin to come find us,' he said. 'If she need us, she know where we are.'

'No!' She let go of his wrist. 'You don' understand.' She snatched up a Coke bottle half filled with sand and started poking little stones into it. Sultan lifted his head and growled.

'Maybe I don't, Mi.' He paused, waiting for an explanation. But she stayed silent, lips pursed, busy with her stones and the bottle. 'So, how 'bout you tellin me all these thing you so sure of,' he said at length. 'Sometimes talkin to you like teasin a crab from its shell.'

It was as if she didn't hear him. 'There's storm comin here. I feel it. Too much comin in aroun' me. Too much. I feel it comin.'

Reve glanced up at the sky over the ocean: blue and clear not a whisper of cloud; and the sea was calm, nudging gently against the beach. The fishing fleet were on their way back. All was as it should be, but not for Mi. 'You tired bein on your own, Mi? You got more trouble from Hevez than I seen today? Somethin happenin you not told me about?'

He reached out to take her arm but just as he did so, she started to tremble, gently at first and then more violently, shaking jerkily, her eyes rolled so far back all you could see was the yellowy whites. She gasped. 'They comin! They comin like a storm. Bringin money and sickness.' She gasped again, gulping air into her lungs. 'I hearin thunder . . .' Her voice was horrible, old and raspy, like an old woman's all of a sudden. She'd done something like this at a meeting once. It had scared him then; scared him now. He didn't know if it was her sickness or some spirit tearing to get out of her.

Sultan lifted his head and howled once and then edged close to Reve. Reve touched his nose and the dog quietened. Reve put his arm tightly round Mi's shoulder and gradually the trembling died away. Her head tilted over, rested on his shoulder. 'You all right now,' he said softly. 'It's gone now.'

After a second she looked up at him, no expression on her face. Her forehead gleamed with sweat. 'Got to leave,' she said. 'Got to leave this place here.'

He stepped over to the back of the VW and took out the water bottle she kept there and handed it to her. She drank greedily and spat the last mouthful on to the sand.

'You never talk 'bout leavin Rinconda before, Mi. You sure 'bout leavin? We got a life here. Maybe Tomas, the Boxer or Uncle Theon stop Hevez bothering, or maybe you talk to Ciele.' LoJo's mother always had time for Mi.

She shook her head. 'I don't like Tomas come near me,' she said.

Tomas and Mi, the two most important people in his life, and there was never an easy word between them.

Then she puffed out her cheeks and exhaled slowly. 'Don't think I want anyone near me, Reve. Too much people askin and wantin me to tell them what goin happen in their lives, when they goin catch fish, pay their bills, have their babies and I don' know what to tell them, 'cept sometimes a shouting voice come burnin up inside me, and it make me sick.'

'Like now?'

She nodded. 'But when I find her, Reve, everythin be different then.' She bowed her head. 'I got thing I got to know, and only she can tell me. I'm grown, Reve. I got woman-time comin on me. Maybe different for you. Tomas tell you all you need.' She looked at him. 'I swear that woman you dream mean only one thing. It mean she ready for me to come looking for her; and this the right time cos I got to leave this place.'

23

'All right.' He stood up. 'But don' you go leaving me. Hey. We talk 'bout this. You don' know where she is, or if she's living.'

'She is.'

'OK. OK. But you got any idea where you start lookin? Even if she livin, she could be anywhere.' She frowned and he let that thought sink in. He knew what it was with her, she thought she could just get up and go and that would be the end of it. Tomas always said wishing never made a thing happen.

'You lookin to stop me goin?'

'No, Mi. That's not it . . . but I don't want you goin off some place an' you get lost, an' I don't know where you gone. Let me do some thinkin, Mi. Let me figure out a plan. I can do that.' He hesitated and then made up his mind. 'An' if you go anywhere, you let me come with you.'

'All right.' She wiped her wrist across her forehead and rolled her head round, easing tension from her neck, then looked at her hands, stretching her fingers out. 'Look how they tremblin, Reve. Always a sign when they go tremblin.'

'You think we got a storm comin? You think maybe I gotta haul the skiff up high?'

'I say that?' She looked at her trembling fingers again, her expression puzzled. 'I feel something like storm in my bones.' Then she clenched her hands into tight fists. 'What else did I say?'

'"They comin," you said. You said you could hear thunder.' He gave a smile. 'It don't sound too good.'

'How long since the Night Men come in the village?'

He pulled a face. 'Maybe six months.'

'You stay quiet these nights, Reve. Tuck you head down.' She turned back to her garden and started moving the different pieces around again.

'See you tomorrow.' She didn't answer. This was just the way she was: half tell you something, leave you wondering. She could drive you crazy, drive him crazy anyhow.

He whistled up Sultan and headed off down the beach. He hoped his jackfish hadn't spoilt. Tomas hated it when a fisherman wasted his catch. That would be storm enough to deal with.

CHAPTER FOUR

Reve walked quickly to the skiff, but before lifting out the red fish box he stood for a moment looking out to sea.

'What you thinkin 'bout this, Sultan?'

Sultan had busily trotted round to the stern, but at the sound of Reve's voice he stopped and looked back up at him. He was a smart dog, smarter than the skinny mutts that nosed the back of the shacks, but not smart enough to answer any of the questions Reve had buzzing in his mind. Sultan cocked his head, waiting, but when Reve didn't say anything else he put his paws up on the stern, sniffed the air and barked. He could smell the fish Reve had bundled under the stern thwart, and he knew they had to be taken up to the cold store.

Reve wasn't thinking about the fish. It was Mi; she was harder to read than the sea. That's what he was thinking. The breeze was just strong enough to put a light ruffle on the sea and keep the heavy air moving. It would die away and then it would be a still night. Nothing heavy, no yellow in the sky: a perfect time for the Night Man to make a run across the border. If they came, it would be a good chance to earn a dollar; there was no way he was going to tuck his head down if there was money to be made.

Then he grimaced. But if there was a spit chance of a storm blowing up out of nowhere, he couldn't risk losing the skiff. Lose the skiff and that would be the end of everything. Maybe he would get LoJo to help him bring it high up above the tideline, just in case.

He lifted out the catch and checked it. The fish smelt all right though the skin had started to dry up a little bit, but everyone said that if you catch and ice a fish on the same day it's going to last fine till market. So that's what he would do; take them straight to the fish store, ice five and keep two for the stove.

He cut up to the right behind the first line of shacks and yards, avoiding the start of the main track which would have taken him by Tomas the Boxer, who would be sitting or lying outside his shack, just staring at the ocean. That was the most thing he did now that Reve was skilled enough to take the skiff out on his own. His shack was at the end of the track, the nearest to the harbour wall and the furthest from the highway. Anyone leaving Rinconda took that road; it was the road he and Mi would have to take if they went off looking like Mi wanted.

After fifty metres he left the path that led behind the village, crossed a wire and skirted a mess of rubbish where pigs were rooting. Then he slipped through a narrow gap between two wooden buildings and came out right by LoJo's place, and on to the main track again.

LoJo's mother, Ciele, was sitting up on the porch of her home, her baby girl on her knee. He stopped and asked her to tell LoJo he wanted help with the skiff.

'When you goin get some muscle in your arm, Reve?' She was easy and liked to tease the boys. Reve always felt this was a different family because of her, different to most families in Rinconda. 'When you goin to get like Tomas the Boxer? He could carry that boat up from the shore on his own back. That's what my Pelo say.'

Mostly people grew old quickly in Rinconda, but Reve thought Ciele looked young, pretty too. Pelo was a lucky man to catch her, Tomas said. Like most people in Rinconda though, they struggled to get by; the shack was storm-battered, the porch warped and in need of replacing. Pelo wasn't the luckiest fisherman, and word was that he struggled to pay his debts to Calde.

'I can lift most anything,' said Reve, 'but I savin my strength for hauling fish.'

She laughed. 'That right? How many you got today?'

'Seven.'

'Seven's good. '

'You tell Lo my message.'

'I'll tell him.' He was just about to move on when she said, 'I saw Hevez pass. He been giving your sister trouble?'

Reve nodded. 'Some.'

'He looked hurt.' Reve didn't answer. The baby girl, Mayash, wriggled out of her arms and Ciele let her down on to the ground. The baby straight away crawled along to the end of the porch where Reve was standing. 'You watch yourself, Reve,' said Ciele, 'and you get Mi move in from that place she got out there; she's not safe.'

'Have you tried telling my sister what to do?' He touched Mayash's nose.

Ciele smiled. 'I got trouble minding my own family

without minding yours, Reve. You tell her. She hears more than she pretends to hear, if you know what I'm saying.'

He saw Ramon and Sali hanging around outside his uncle Theon's cantina when he went to drop the fish off at the cold store. Sali slapped his arm like a tough guy, made a fist at Reve then spat. He wouldn't have dared do that if he'd been on his own. Ramon just looked at him, said nothing.

Reve ignored them both. He shooed a sleeping dog away from the door so that he could get inside and then tagged five of the fish and shovelled ice over them. The truck would collect them in the morning, and money from the sales would be distributed at the end of the week. The system was fair, though there was little enough money out of it; all the fisherman grumbled that they had to pay Calde too much for the transport. But that was the way it was in Rinconda.

He gutted and cleaned the two jackfish he was keeping and put them back in the box, scooping a little ice over them. He glanced out of the door; the boys were still there. Ramon called out something to Theon, who came out and handed him a pack of cigarettes. The boys sauntered off towards Calde's place.

The villagers called him Clever Theon because he wore glasses and read books. He had helped set up the cooperative that built the cold store. He helped manage it too. He had a truck and did a little business up in the city. He was younger than Tomas the Boxer, though one time it was Theon who really ran the village, along with Tomas and Calde. Theon didn't look like a hard man but he must have been. He knew how things worked, but that was all a long time back, about the time Reve and Mi's father was killed and their mother, Theon's younger sister, disappeared. A smuggling deal with the Night Men went bad. Reve didn't know exactly what happened; Tomas wouldn't ever talk about it, but it was after that that Calde took over most of everything in Rinconda.

Reve asked Theon once why he had let Calde take over. 'In business,' Theon said to him, 'things happen, sometimes good, because you make a careful plan, but always there is risk and then things can go bad. Very bad. And people can go bad too. Tomas will tell you the same.'

Reve was ten when Theon told him that. He thought that 'people gone bad' just referred to Calde, but since then he had wondered if Theon had also been thinking about his sister, Reve and Mi's mother, because the police had taken her away. Theon never talked about his sister's arrest. 'That's over,' was all he said and Reve knew better than to pester him, but Theon's relationship with Calde wasn't quite over. Reve had seen Calde and Theon talking, and Calde often drank in the cantina, ordered Theon to bring him this, bring him that. It was hard to imagine that it had once been the other way round. When he mentioned this to Tomas the Boxer, Tomas just said, 'Theon, he like to keep his options open.'

Reve felt his uncle really was smart, a lot more clever than Calde anyway, and he liked his uncle and Theon gave him work: cleaning up in the cantina, paying him a few cents for the bottles that Reve collected from the shoreline.

Theon saw Reve coming out of the cold store and raised his hand in greeting. 'You do good?'

'All right.'

'Your sister was in the village today.'

'I know.'

He took off his little round glasses and polished them on his loose shirt tail. 'She's looking more like her mother every day,' he said. 'About time she gave up all that crazy business, living in a car.'

'Everyone sayin that to me,' said Reve.

'Maybe everyone got a point.'

'She sayin our mother's alive. Wants to go lookin for her.'

He gave a dismissive grunt. 'She do better lookin for a husband. She say anythin else.'

'Said there was a storm comin.'

That made him smile. 'Not tonight, I reckon. Come by tomorrow, Reve. You can help me clean up the place.'

31

CHAPTER FIVE

Reve crossed the main track and climbed the path up to the top of the hill, found the spot where Tomas the Boxer had buried their father. He put down the fish box and sat on it. There were eight white stones on the grave. Tomas had laid the first one, scratched an X on it so that they could find the place again; the hill had graves all over it, most unmarked. Reve had been five. Every year, he had come back, first with Mi and then on his own, to place another stone.

Eight years.

After the burying, Tomas the Boxer had taken Reve and Mi to live with him. He had tried to be a father, but he just wasn't very good at it, wasn't patient with children, didn't know how to talk to them. He was strict; told them life was hard, that you had to fight for what you wanted and he was a hard man himself. People left him alone, even Calde stepped around him, but unlike some parents in the village he never raised a fist against the children, and he'd listen to what they said, though he didn't answer every question they asked, especially when they kept wanting to know when their mother was coming home, which they did all the time in those first weeks they lived with him.

Reve settled well enough. He followed Tomas around like a dog, was happy to copy him when he did his chores, fixed the skiff, mended the net, but Tomas never learned how to handle Mi. She was always strange, collecting bits of plastic and glass and making little sand gardens wherever the fancy took her. And she wandered, day and night. She wouldn't be disciplined, not by Tomas, nor by the occasional woman Tomas brought back into the shack, not that any of them ever stayed long. Mi would stick her chin out and glare at them, unsettle them, and then they'd leave. She hardly talked to anyone other than Reve, and he didn't always understand what she was saying with such intensity, but he would nod as if he did understand because he liked her talking to him.

When she was nine, a year after Tomas had taken them in, she declared to Reve in a whisper that Tomas had a bit of the devil caught up inside him. She said she had seen it peering out of Tomas's eye. Reve looked at Tomas differently after this. He never could see any sign of the devil though. Even so, he started to have bad dreams and found he felt safer sleeping in the little space under the shack.

Her wandering made Reve anxious. He spent half his time looking for her. He usually found her hunkered down some place, mostly Uncle Theon's cement-block pig house or up on the hill, by their father's grave. Once she told Reve that she heard a voice calling her and that was why she went off wandering. He never quite knew how much to believe Mi because she said such strange things, mainly about what she saw in people, like seeing the devil creature in Tomas.

It was about this time that Mi admitted to Reve that sometimes she couldn't remember where she'd been. At first he didn't believe her, but then he understood that those blank periods frightened her. She called it walking in darkness. They were, he now realized, her first fits, little ones. The first serious one didn't happen until she was eleven. Reve remembered it well: just before she got that attack of juddering she accused Tomas the Boxer of killing their father. Just like that, out of nowhere, hard and cold; he remembered how her eyelids had flickered and her voice hadn't sounded like her at all. Tomas had looked like he'd been struck by lightning. He'd lifted a hand to slap her – and then she was gone, twisting and falling and kicking her legs like she had electricity running up and down her spine.

She was sick for a whole day after that attack, and bruised too. When she was recovered she said she wouldn't sleep in Tomas's any more. She said that Tomas looked at her all the time. This divided her and Reve for a while; he didn't believe she meant that about him killing their father. He thought she was just stirring trouble. But she'd said there were things he didn't know; he was too young, and that if he wanted to be Tomas's runaround, that was his choice.

As for Tomas looking at her, the truth was everybody looked at her; they couldn't help it. She was so different: red hair, long legs, sleepy eyes and her strange ways. She didn't care what she wore, sometimes an old threadbare woman's dress that hung from her shoulders and trailed down to her bare feet, sometimes a man's T-shirt knotted round her waist to make a skirt. As she grew older, she became more striking and the way she dressed became more provocative. Ciele took to making patched up skirts and shirts and insisted she wear them; Mi took them, but would only wear clothes with blue in them.

Theon offered to let her stay up at the cantina, do a little work for him. That's when she told him that he had a little devil tucked away in him; 'a devil crab in its hole' was what she said. Theon didn't get angry – he never did, Theon – but he never made that offer again.

She took to walking the shore, going further and further and spending more and more time down on the beach where the old Beetle VW stood on the sand. Reve came in for rough talk too, mainly because of her, and when this turned to throwing punches, Tomas taught him how to box. Hevez and his friends didn't bother him so much after that.

By the time she was thirteen she was living all the time down at the car.

Word about her stretched along the coast and people came from miles to hear the girl who spoke with spirit voices, because that is what she did now, and that's when her meetings started. Now she even had a man who played the drum; the drumming would whip up the crowd, get them excited; maybe it helped them believe in Mi's spirit voices.

Tomas didn't approve of her meetings and wouldn't have anything to do with them. He tried to stop Reve going to them too, but of course he did go, snuck down the beach and crept into the edge of the crowd, always keeping at the back, and then watched how she became this other person, who danced like she was being jerked on strings and who spoke in different voices, harsh and croaky like an old woman, but sometimes the words slipped from her lips like splinters of ice. It frightened him but he still went.

In the mornings he would always go down the beach to see that she was still Mi and hadn't somehow lost herself and become that other person, to see that she was all right.

But she wasn't all right. She wasn't happy. And now, despite all the spirit power people believed she carried around inside her, she wasn't even safe.

Reve brushed the sand from the eight stones so they sat in a line, clear and white, and then he stood up.

He never liked saying goodbye, though it wasn't that which made his heart feel heavy when he hefted up that red box and balanced it on his shoulder. It was looking out over Rinconda and seeing the shacks and the yards, some fires being set for cooking, and knowing that Mi was way out on her own; and that thought brought the dream woman back into his mind, so sharp and real it made the hairs on his neck prickle.

He started down the hill, heading for home. What had it meant really and why did it make him think of Mi and her saying a goodbye to him? He wondered if maybe his mother had looked like that when she'd said goodbye to his father.

Tomas was on the stoop when he got back, rolling a cigarette, the white paper like a slip of nothing in his wide hands. His black hair had dabs of grey round his temples. Other than that he looked as fit and strong as he ever had, even though he had taken to spending the best part of the day lying up in his hammock, holding that Bible on his chest and looking out to sea.

'How many you got, Reve?' The old man's voice was soft, a little whispery, like he got too much salty wind tucked in his throat. But LoJo reckoned it was because Tomas had been in a fight one time and got himself hurt, buckled his voice somehow.

'Seven. Left the best up at the store,' Reve said.

Arella was sitting on a three-legged stool Tomas had put out for her. She stepped across the track most days to pass the time, share Tomas's drink. She was blind as night but sharp, until the rum took a hold, and then it was usually Reve who had to take her back home.

'Seven's a good-luck number, Reve.' She laughed and patted her knee. 'I could have done with catching seven, hey, Tomas? Catch me seven husband. How 'bout that!'

'If you catched seven, maybe one would have turned out good.'

'In this place?' She laughed again. She was always laughing when she was with Tomas.

Tomas reached behind him and tipped a splash of rum in a small coloured glass and leaned forward, folding Arella's hand round the glass. 'Saw you come in little while back,' he said to Reve. 'You go see your sister?'

It seemed as if everyone was asking about Mi. He nodded. 'Hevez was out there. Bein ugly. Him an' another two.'

Tomas lit a match and tipped his roll-up with flame.

'She's spiking folk up like she's always done, tha's wha's happenin.' He shook the match and flipped it on to the ground.

'Why?' Reve said. 'She don't do harm to anyone round here or any place else.'

'He's right,' said Arella. 'When you goin teach Calde's boy a lesson? I hear he nothin but sour fruit, that boy. I hear him drinkin and callin out, him and his friend . . .'

Tomas grunted. 'She get hurt?'

Reve shook his head.

Tomas studied him. 'You make him back away?'

'He left hurt. I just push him a little and he fell.' He shrugged. 'Got hurt that way.'

Tomas face softened into a smile. 'You turning quite the man, Reve. One against three. You keep cool in your head and you can manage trouble like that. Taught you well, eh?'

Reve hadn't kept cool at all, just butted in like an angry hog because Hevez had a knife.

'She give you thanks for steppin in for her?'

Reve didn't answer.

Tomas nodded. 'She's not got the habit of giving thanks to anyone. In my remembrance, that is. She say anythin else your sister? Any prophet talk coming out of her?'

'She think something bad goin happen.'

'Oh?' Tomas let out a stream of smoke. 'Sky goin fall down?'

'She say that a storm comin.'

'Don't look like storm to me.'

'Don't think she mean that kind of storm.' Reve hesitated, then told them the rest of what she had said.

Tomas gave a smoky laugh. 'They comin'? Sound like a day of judgement. Sound like them riders – Rella, what they call them – you got more Bible 'n me – them Calypso riders?'

'They's them.' The two of them chuckled. Reve wished he'd kept his mouth shut.

The sun was sinking low and the breeze had all but died away. Down along the backs of the houses and shacks more fires were being lit, families gathering, figures moving to and fro, a mother calling, a child crying, tinny music.

Tomas topped up the tin mug he used for his rum drinking. 'I hear Calde sniffing in the city, looking for new business. Hear that he . . .' Tomas paused, looking for the word. He liked to find himself fancy words that only someone else like Clever Theon might use. 'Hear that he liaising with a new señor up there. Maybe that we get a visit from the Night Man. Maybe your sister hear something too.'

'She hear voices,' said Reve abruptly, standing up. 'Tha's what she hear. Time you start thinkin about her different. She need help. She don' need your suspicioning.' Sometimes Reve wanted to shake him out of his hammock ways. He turned to Arella. 'Arella, you gonna eat with us? A little fish stew?' It was a formality. Arella always ate with them.

'Jackfish stew'd be fine.' She smiled in Reve's direction.

Round the back was a standpipe with a bucket hooked

over the tap, a brick fire with a black iron grill sitting on the top. Reve set the fire, took down the bag of vegetables Tomas kept hooked up from the ceiling, put on a pail of water to boil and set to work, peeling and cutting. Sultan collapsed beside him, and though he pretended not to be interested, he kept an eye on the fish, in case a piece happened to fall down by his nose.

Reve let the pail with the vegetables simmer a little while and then he chunked up the fish and threw it all in. It would make a good thick stew.

A little later LoJo called by and the two of them went down to the shore and hauled the skiff well above the tideline.

By the time Reve returned, it was full dark and the stew was ready. Both Tomas and Arella were so unsteady from their drinking that they kept tipping one way then the other, almost like they were at sea. One time Tomas had seemed so big to him, but the rum and the days doing nothing had rusted him up a little. Now he made Reve think of one of those old steamers going slowly up the coast, beating against the waves.

Their talk drifted to and fro, sometimes Bible, sometimes remembering old times.

Reve sat the other side of the fire, watching them and thinking. Mi's storm: he didn't feel it in the air but he felt it all the same. It was coming. It wouldn't sweep away boats and roofs, so he and LoJo had wasted their time sweating the skiff up so far, but it was going to come down on her. Poor Mi.

'Did my mother look like Mi?' he asked, cutting in on their talk, startling Arella.

Tomas was trying to roll another cigarette but not managing so well. Reve got up, took the paper and tobacco and made the smoke for him. 'That girl!' Tomas slurred. 'All a time she keep so far away from me. Only see her way down the beach, walking fast. Skinny. Some storm come and it'll blow her away.'

Reve almost flinched because it was so close to what he was thinking and was more true than Tomas in his hazy state realized, but what he said to Tomas was, 'You know what she look like; you just not sayin. Come on, give me straight talk here.'

'All right,' he said after a long pause, 'she look every bit like her mother.' His hoarse voice softened. 'Every bit. Her hair, her eyes, her way of lookin you in the eye . . .'

Then Arella joined in, and as the two of them talked Reve felt his gone-away parents were like ghosts drifting closer in to the edge of the firelight.

'Her people came from up the coast,' Arella said. 'Found her way here when she was 'bout your age. Heart-stealer, eh. Always. I had eyes then and could see you well enough, Tomas, trailing along with boys half your age, and you and Theon lording the village then, with Calde just a runaround for you two. Times a lot different . . . Then she picked your father, Reve. Good-lookin, but weaker 'n a kitten when it came to her. I think she only picked him to give herself some peace. That was how it was: she was queen of the village. And then –' she tipped up her glass and drained the last of her rum – 'queen of nothin.'

'What do you mean?'

'Hey, Rella,' said Tomas, 'he dead. They all gone. Tha's enough.'

'No,' said Reve. 'What did you mean, queen of nothing?'

'All right.' She held out her glass but Tomas didn't refill it. She shrugged. 'It was like this. Your father was not enough for her. I think – you know what I think? – I think she wanted different from this place. You remember how we all call her, Tomas? Call her Santa Fe because she talk 'bout America all the time.' She stopped. 'Your daddy wasn't any good, Reve. That's the truth. And you know, my husband wasn't any good. Men aren't any good. My husband walk out and leave me when my eyes gone dark, and I would have killed him if I could. Isn't that right, Tomas?' Tomas grunted. 'And tha's what I think. I think she killed him because he wasn't smart enough for her. Became queen of nothing, poor girl, eh.'

Tomas roused himself. 'You full of sour wind, Rella. You don't know what she done!'

But it was what the police must have believed, thought Reve, arresting her and taking her away. Was that why Tomas and Uncle Theon both shied away from saying exactly what it was that had happened? They didn't want Reve or Mi to know what a bad thing their mother had done? Funny how the thought didn't shake him, not really. It would stir Mi, though, if she heard people saying that their mother was a murderer. Tip her into a black hole.

'Still soft on her, eh, Tomas,' chided Arella.

'Soft on nothing,' he said, his voice had a sticky rum slur on it.

'An' her hair was red,' said Arella, suddenly speaking up again, 'just like you see in the sky at times, when the sun's going down and a storm's coming, like the red you gonna see in Tomas's eyes tomorrow, hey.' She nodded at Tomas but he gave no response. His head had tipped forward, and whatever colour his eyes would be in the morning, they were closed now. Arella fell silent, though she was awake; her eyes were open and staring towards the heat of the fire.

Reve touched Arella's arm and then helped her to her feet. He walked her back across the track to her shack. 'You want me take you in?'

'No, no. You a good boy, Reve. A good boy.'

'You won't ever say that about my mother to Mi, will you?'

She blinked. 'No. No, I should hold my tongue, eh. Rum slides up your thinkin sometime. Don't you ever touch it, Reve. Now, you go look out for Tomas. He gonna tip an' fall in the fire one time, you don't mind him.' She pulled herself up the two steps to her porch and then went into the darkness of her room, closing the door behind her as Reve turned away. She never let him in the shack. He sometimes wondered if she had some secret hidden away in there.

He crossed the track and, hooking his hands under Tomas's arms, he managed to get him up from the steps and then steered him to his bed.

'Was Arella right in what she was saying?' he asked Tomas.

'No,' he said. 'She had no business sayin that.' He laid

43

his head back on his pillow and closed his eyes.

He wasn't asleep though. Reve knew that because he wasn't snoring. He just wasn't going to say anything else. Reve turned down the lamp and went outside.

It was midnight when Reve crawled to his pallet under the shack. He ached with tiredness, but he still went through his ritual of lighting a candle and then digging up the jar he kept his money in, and counting it out. He put a few cents in every time he sold fish, every time Theon gave him money.

Twelve dollars. It was not very much for all the work he did and all the fish he brought in. How many years would it take for him to earn enough to keep her safe?

He screwed the top back on and laid the jar in its sandy hole. Then he snuffed out the candle, lay back and stared out at a strip of sky that was black and pricked with stars, and thought about Mi, probably sitting up on the roof of the old car, making her plans, her mind fizzing like one of Theon's fruit soda drinks.

Reve turned on his back. Then a moment later rolled on to his side again. Sultan growled in his sleep. As soon as Reve closed his eyes there was the woman drifting in the sea, her face turned up to him, and Mi telling him they had to go looking; and Mi's hands were all shaky; and he didn't want Mi getting so agitated she'd fall into a fit of juddering and never come out of it. He needed to be steady with Mi, all the time, give her no frights.

He put his hand out to touch Sultan.

CHAPTER SIX

Reve woke suddenly, convinced that his mother was a murderer and she was walking down the main track looking for Mi and him so she could kill them both. His heart was banging against his ribs he was so frightened. Then Sultan stirred and it was all right.

It was just a little before dawn. There was no breeze, nothing moving, no sounds, not even the hush of the sea. Everything was still and so warm and heavy he felt he could hardly breathe.

He rolled off his pallet, crawled out into the yard and splashed water on his face. Then tucked his whole head down under the tap and let it run. Stupid. He blamed Arella and the rum she'd drunk.

He pulled on his T-shirt and jeans, and then as the dawn came up he jogged to Theon's cantina, tidied the place, did his chores, put on a kettle to make coffee for his uncle and then went out on the front step to see if an offshore breeze had picked up. It hadn't. There would be no sailing skiffs out this morning.

He didn't like to visit Mi first thing; she could be worse than scrub thorn but he'd go anyway. Everyone saying she should move out of that car, thinking that if she did that she would move back into the village; but she wouldn't ever do that. Instead she would suddenly up and go, that's what she would do; and he wasn't going to let that happen. She wasn't going anywhere without him, no matter how scratchy she got.

Theon came down, talking quietly on his cellphone. He nodded at Reve, said something else into his phone and then ended the call. He fixed coffee and asked Reve to check the hog pen, make sure there was water. Uncle Theon looked after his pigs better than most people. When Reve came back inside, Tomas was at the door talking to Theon. His eyes were red-rimmed and his face stubbled with grey iron filings. It was unusual to see him up in the village at this time of the day.

When Reve asked him what he was doing, Tomas said, 'You wanted me to see Calde. Tha's what I'm doin. Tell him he can put a dog lead on that boy of his.'

'You want me to come with you?'

'I don't need minding.'

'Don't go startin a war,' said Theon.

'Reckon I still know how to handle myself,' he said, setting off again.

'I wonder if he docs,' said Theon, more to himself than to Reve, but when he saw the boy looking at him he added, 'Long time since Tomas worked. One time he could have stood up against anyone in Rinconda . . .' He shook his head.

'You think there'll be trouble.'

'There's always trouble,' said Theon, 'but I wouldn't fret about him. You mind your sister.'

He did. He took the opposite path to Tomas and within a minute LoJo had fallen in beside him.

'What happen you?' said LoJo. 'You hurryin all the

46

time. I seen you go up; I see you go down. Even see
Tomas. See him out of his hammock's a miracle, tha's
what my daddy says.'

Reve didn't answer.

'You goin fishin?'

'No.'

'You take me out in your skiff.'

'Maybe later.'

'You turn a thinkin man all a sudden, Reve. I mean,
you never spin a lot a talk, but you clam tight now.'

'Mi's got troubles, Lo.'

They parted with LoJo promising to check the skiff; if
a breeze picked up he would carry the sail and net down
from the wall.

Mi was sitting up on the roof of the old Beetle, holding
up a green glass bottle, tilting it this way and that to catch
the sun. 'I wait up all the night,' she said, before he could
even greet her, 'but she don't come to me; I don't hear her
voice. You know who I'm talkin 'bout, I'm talkin 'bout
our mother. You understan'? The woman you dream up?
Botherin me all the time now that she only come to you.'
She was cross.

'I don't think she's livin, Mi.'

'Don't matter what a boy think.'

She was wearing a blue T-shirt – it looked new, maybe
a gift – a clean skirt, so faded that the blue in it was just
a memory, and a necklace of shells. He wondered if she
had made it herself; he didn't think it likely.

'You expectin company?' he asked.

'Who tell you that?' she said, giving him a sharp look.

'No one tell me anything, Mi,' he said.

'Cos you don't listen.'

'You dressed up cos you're goin some place?'

He stepped around the side of the car and opened the door. Sure enough she had a jute bag all packed up with her things. 'Are you runnin out, Mi?'

'No.' She hesitated. 'I don't know.' The anger was gone. If anything, she sounded a little distressed.

'You don't go anywhere without me. You promise on that,' he said. He took the green bottle out of her hand and made her look at him.

'All right.' She looked sad. 'Why don' you go do your fishing now? Tha's what you so good at.'

'There's no wind.' But the odd thing was that even as he replied, the acacia tree stirred and a light offshore breeze started. 'I don't know how you do that,' he said.

'Do what?' She had her head tilted back to catch the full warmth of the morning sun. Her eyes were closed.

He left her, met up with LoJo and the two of them launched the skiff.

They fished all day, other skiffs passing them from time to time, and he let LoJo take the tiller and handle the net. He was good, and best of all he talked a little less when he was on board. By the end of the day they had more than a dozen fish slapping and flapping in the belly of the skiff, all of them stacked neat into the red box.

The breeze shifted round, as it always did, and with the mainsail out wide like a one-wing bird, and Sultan, his paws up on the gunwale, barking at any gull drifting close enough to eye their catch, they ran in towards the shore.

Reve could see two figures up by the acacia tree. One of them had to be Mi; he couldn't tell who the other was, not the boys though. They only came in packs.

'She got trouble again?' said LoJo.

'I don' know.'

They beached the skiff, rolled up the sail and set the anchor. LoJo took the fish box up to the cold store, and Reve, his forefinger hooked into the gill of a blue fish, walked over towards Mi's place. He would collect the net later. Sultan, his tail waving like a ragged old sail, trotted ahead.

The second figure was a young man in his mid-twenties, broad-faced with thick shoulders and a short neck, wearing a faded blue baseball hat. He wasn't from the village. Reve wanted to ask what was his business, coming down here to talk to Mi, because he didn't seem like the people who came to her meetings. He seemed too easy in himself. Most people were a little anxious round Mi, had questions. He wasn't like that. There was something different about Mi as well, Reve thought. She sat straighter somehow, held her head differently, looked older. The young man had been before, that was obvious.

The man pushed his cap a little further back on his head. He had tight black curly hair and eyes that studied Reve in a level, unblinking way. He smiled. 'You know how to handle that skiff you got.'

49

'Learn from Tomas the Boxer. Been sailin' almost since I could walk. You know Tomas?'

The man nodded. 'Know most everyone who takes a boat out on this strip of sea.'

'Then you must know a lot of people,' said Reve. He turned to his sister. 'Hey, Mi. I brought you this.' He handed her the fish. He always brought her something. Sometimes she cleaned, cooked and ate them; sometimes she left them out on the sand and the birds picked them clean. This one she gutted and cleaned straight away, put it in a tub of fresh, cool seawater. Then she set a fire and pulled out her grilling tray. Was she going to go cooking for this man? Reve wondered. Was she going to lay out a cloth and find him a box to sit on? What was this man to her?

'Always share the catch?' said the man.

Reve nodded.

'I like to see family sharing what they got.' The man's voice came out soft and light, not as you'd expect from someone so solid-looking. Reve noticed how his eyes followed Mi all the time.

'I'm out here most times,' said Reve. Mi came and sat down by them under the tree. 'Someone got to look out for my sister, livin out here in this old car she got. You tell this man 'bout the boys?'

The man smiled. 'I reckon no one mess with this girl – she getting a name. People sayin she see what comin. That right, Mi?'

She tipped her head down like she was bein shy, but Reve saw the way she looked up at this man, liking him. She looked so pretty. He frowned and looked away towards her car with its strange little garden she had made: long shadows stretched across the sand from the different sticks and scraps she had planted there. Somehow it made the garden look as if it was moving, pointing inland towards the setting sun.

'She's not always right,' said Reve. 'Yesterday she was talking 'bout a storm coming down.'

Mi scowled at him.

The man said, 'Well, if she said that, I'd keep my eye on the sky. Weather can change quick enough, and no man wants to lose a boat.'

Mi shrugged. 'I feel it in my bones. Don't mind what Reve say; he don't see nothin till it smack him in the face.'

The man laughed and then Mi and him talked a little longer while Reve sat silent, just listening and thinking. A couple of times Mi gave Reve a look which said plain as a black cloud in a blue sky that she wanted him out of there, but he pretended not to notice. Then the man stood up and took his leave. 'I got to head back, but I would like to come to one of your meetings. Maybe you'd think of holding one in San Jerro.'

When he said that Reve realized who he was: 'You the one they call Two-Boat?'

'Some call me that still,' the man admitted.

He'd been the first fisherman on their strip of coast to buy a fleet of skiffs, and now near owned San Jerro, his village. He was like Calde, thought Reve, but, he had to admit, without being like him at all; none of his swagger, none of his threat. Two-Boat pulled his cap forward a little. 'I bring my truck next time and maybe you and your sister come over to my village, meet my family.'

Then he was gone, walking out across the scrub field behind the dunes, heading up the coast. It was a good walk to his village, five miles easy. He had made that walk just to see her. Reve said as much as soon as he was out of earshot.

'You got no understandin,' she said.

'You talk 'bout leavin, Mi. I see where you goin. You thinkin of marryin? That what you thinkin?' He knew he should feel good, but he didn't. 'He got money, that man. Rich, I hear—'

'Enough o' that, Reve!' She hugged herself and started rocking backwards and forwards. 'Anyhow, he ask me nothing yet. An' I don' know what I want. I'm not safe here, Reve. I got that Hevez pushin more than you know, talkin things at me. '

Reve reached over and took her arm. 'I know,' he said. There was no reason to be hard with Mi. 'Don' fret you'self. Hey. We figure something.'

'Everythin pressin on me, Reve; tha's why I want her.'

'You could talk to Ciele.'

Mi puffed out her cheeks and stopped her rocking. 'Ciele someone else's mother.'

'You won't go runnin without me,' he said.

'Got nowhere to run, Reve.' She hesitated and he wondered if she was thinking about Two-Boat. Then she said, ''Less we find where our mother livin.'

'Told you, she not livin any place.'

The two of them were turning in circles, smaller and

tighter, going nowhere, like when current, wind and tide all pull the water around and make a whirlpool. Suck a boat down so it never come up. Tomas told him that.

Out on the ocean, if there was a storm coming, all you could do was run in front of it, try to find shelter.

What kind of shelter could he find for Mi?

CHAPTER SEVEN

Money. Money – that was the only thing you could be sure about. Dollars wrapped in a tight wad, wedged in a jar, buried here, under his arm.

Reve was awake again.

There was something grumbling far off. Thunder maybe. Storm back inland somewhere. Mi's storm?

Mi.

Hevez sneering one way, Two-Boat smiling the other, and Mi somewhere in the middle.

Tomas had seen Calde. All he'd said to Reve afterwards was, 'That man don' have listenin ears. I got no threat on him.'

Now, as Reve lay on his pallet under the shack, hearing the sound of Tomas snoring above him, he thought, Tha's cos you got no weight, Tomas: you live in a hammock, drink rum, got hardly no money.

Reve, though, would get dollars. That's what he would do. Be a rich man like Two-Boat. That way you get respect. People mind what you say if you carry dollar in your pocket.

With a dollar in his pocket he could find proper shelter for Mi.

His eyes were wide open now and the dark was solid around him, but he kept expecting to see the sky crackle with lightning because of that thunder that had woken him.

Then there was a flicker of light, and the rumbling was louder.

But it wasn't a storm beating up the sky on the far side of the highway, and that light sweeping across their porch was never lightning, and the voices calling out weren't shouting because some storm was tearing boats from their moorings or ripping plastic from the shacks. That was a truck and cars, maybe two, three, easing down the bumpy track, heading for the wall.

He heard more voices, the bang of a shack door snapping shut.

Sultan stirred, lifted himself, came and sniffed Reve's face, turned round three times and then lay down again. There were sticks of torchlight now, people hurrying after the cars and the truck. He thought of the way gulls drifted in the air above the boats when the nets were being hauled in. There were always plenty who were hungry for the Night Man's dollar.

Reve was one of many.

He shoved Sultan out of the way and rolled off his pallet, pulled on his jeans and scrabbled out from the end of the shack. He checked to see whether Tomas's lamp had come on. Maybe he would sleep through it all: hear nothing, see nothing. Reve hoped so. But whether he woke or not, whether he found out and raged and shook his Bible, it would just be spit in the wind, Reve was going to earn the Night Man's dollar, and that was that.

He slipped through the makeshift gate, picked his way over the stony part of the track and then ran straight down to where the truck and the cars were humped like landed whales on the deck of the pier, men and boys shoaling round, waiting for the boats to come in and the work to start.

This was Mi's storm, wasn't it?

Money and sickness.

Money. That was the Night Man, the smuggling man.

Sickness. That could be him too.

Do the Night Man's work right and keep your mouth shut and you'd be all right, but talk out of turn and then bad things happened. Everybody knew about that: hammer and club and a person turns into a meal for crabs.

Only a fool ended up feeding himself to the crabs, Reve reckoned.

He joined the edge of a group of men gathered in a loose circle round the first car, where a señor stood, a cigar lighting up his face with an orange glow. He wondered if he'd see LoJo. Calde was there, of course, up beside that señor, half in the light of the truck's headlight, his stubbled face turned to the señor, telling him this, telling him that, nodding to one in the crowd, picking out another, to go down to where the boats would come in, be ready to take the line, to hold them steady while everyone else lined up to carry whatever load the boats brought in. Calde was this señor's man, anyone who hadn't known this before knew it now.

He saw the señor talking into his cellphone, his men in suits leaning up against the side of the car, smoking, guns slung over their shoulders, so relaxed, like this was a thing they did most every day. Reve didn't know how you could lean like that, look so easy. Funny thing was, these men weren't so different from the police when they came into the village: stood the same, carried the same sort of gun, looked at Rinconda people the same way, right through them, like they were hardly there.

Reve didn't care about that one way or another so long as he got a chance to do their work. His chest felt tight as a drum; his eyes strained to see into the darkness beyond the pier.

The night was still. The sea was slick and flat like the highway, and there was just enough moonlight for the men driving the black-hulled boats to read the coastline. He itched for the boats to come in, to carry whatever he had to carry, to scurry with all the men round him and earn as much as he could. He could almost feel the wad of notes they would pay him.

Someone lit a cigarette; another murmured to the shadowy figure next to him.

'Hey.' LoJo slipped up beside him, shoulders hunched, like he didn't know whether to try to be bigger than he was or smaller so no one would see him there and tell his father.

'Hey.'

'What you thinkin, Reve? You think we get our share of work when the boats come in?'

Reve nodded.

They waited and talked, and glanced at who was around them. They saw Hevez along with Sali. There was Ramon and a younger boy, his little brother; and then there was something almost like a sigh as the boats appeared.

Reve heard the high whine of their powerful outboard engines moments before he saw the slash of white arrowing in towards the pier. Four boats, five, no, more, six, seven . . . ten! There had never been an operation this big.

One after the other the black-hulled speedboats curved into the pier, their engines suddenly stilled so that just for a second, before anyone moved, all you could hear was the slap of the wash against the stone and the creak of the hulls moving against rubber fenders slung down from the pier's side.

Only a moment though, because then the work started. It looked like chaos but it wasn't. The group Reve had been standing with dissolved as they ran, marking the boat they intended to help unload. Then sacks wrapped tight in black plastic, heavy as a fish box, were hurried to the truck, where two of the señor's men stood, directing where the cartons were to be put. It was smooth as grease.

Reve ran with LoJo, the two of them panting, the night clammy on their faces, sweat running down their arms, making the plastic slippy in their hands.

'You!' Calde called out. 'Move you'self. Do nothing, get nothing. You want to see a beach rat get more than you?' For half a moment, Reve thought he was yelling at him and LoJo, but it was Hevez.

Hevez didn't know much about work, only knew how to swagger and push his weight. He was standing back by the truck, smoking, but when his uncle called him, he ran down to the edge of the pier and took his turn to ferry one of the sacks. Reve nudged LoJo when Hevez staggered under the weight, almost losing his footing.

'Nobody grieve if he fall in and drown,' Reve muttered, running past LoJo to the truck.

''Cept his mother maybe.'

'Who knows about her. She look like she suck on lime all day.'

Reve had just thrown his tenth sack into the truck and was about to run back for his next load when he heard a ratcheting noise that seemed to come from the highway, but higher up, in the air; and growing louder and louder until it sounded heavy as thunder. Helicopter! Everyone froze, thirty-odd figures caught in the moonlight, heads all tilted up at the sky. Now the thunder was sweeping towards them. The air thrummed and shook as if it were being pounded with a jackhammer and Reve found himself pressing his hands to his ears.

Brilliant stabbing columns of white light swept over the frail shacks of Rinconda, slashing big zigzags towards the pier, picking out the smugglers' boats, pinning the group on the edge of the pier unloading the cargo. Then it slowed and hovered above them.

'This is a coastguard warning!' The voice sounded like metal and filled the air it was so loud, louder than the hammering roar of the helicopter itself. 'Move away from the boats. Move away from the truck . . .'

There was the flat crack of first one gunshot and then

instantly another and another and the helicopter bucked and lifted, twisted about and then like a wild giant black hornet jinked first one way and then another while the señor's men's automatic rifles spattered up at it, and then the chopper swept down low along the length of the pier.

And suddenly everyone was running and yelling and scattering back towards the shore, trying to get away from the pier as the chopper howled just overhead, its guns sending out a stream of red dots that stitched lines across the darkness, hissing into the water, rippling and spitting off the stone. Reve grabbed LoJo and spun him hard across into the shelter of the wall that ran like a lip along the seaward side of the pier. He dived after him, scuffing his hands and knees but feeling nothing. There was only noise and fear. He pressed himself into the stone, wishing he could push himself right inside it, wishing he had listened to Mi and stayed at home.

Almost in front of them was the truck. Reve could see two men struggling to pull something heavy from the back, big and awkward – some kind of gun or rocket launcher, he thought. The señor was there beside them, his cigar still glowing, snapping instructions but standing straight, not bothering to scuttle and stoop like everyone else. Calde and two of the señor's men were over on the far side of the pier, crouched down by a bollard, following the helicopter, turning as it turned, guns up and ready to take another shot.

'It comin again!' someone shouted. Two or three people burst from the shelter of a stack of empty fish boxes and pelted up the pier. It was Hevez and Ramon and two others Reve couldn't see so clearly. They ran straight to the side the boats were on and hurled themselves into the water.

There was the whine of the helicopter, the stutter of guns and the brilliant white stalks of light, cutting one way and another, and catching a small figure running as hard as he could. It was Ramon's little brother. What was he doing down here! He was too small to do any of the lifting and carrying so all he could do was get in the way, get shouted at and now, Reve realized, get killed.

The boy's face was suddenly visible in a flashing sweep of the helicopter's spotlight. He looked as if he had a race to win, but he was too late to follow his brother into the water. He ran past the truck and Reve saw the señor glance at him and then turn back to what he was doing.

The chopper wheeled again, the spotlight slipped off Ramon's little brother and before Reve even knew what he was doing, he sprang away from the slight safety of the wall and grabbed the boy, who was running so fast he spun round Reve and made the two of them fall hard. Ramon's brother cried out as he struck the ground, and his fist caught Reve under the eye, but Reve held him tight to stop him scrabbling up and start running again; then, just before the spatter of bullets hissed and whipped across the stone, Reve hauled him back to where LoJo, his eyes white and staring, reached out to grab the boy and pull him into their little bit of shelter.

There was more noise, more gunfire, a sudden loud crump so close Reve felt the air bang his face and his eyes jerked open. A great ball of flame burst up into the darkness from one of the boats. They would all be burned, all those boats and then the houses in the village, they would burn too.

There were rapid pinpricks of light stippling the dark, a blustering crackle of gunfire from the armed men that seemed nothing against the frightening wheeling and banking monster of the air. Then there was a shout from the truck, whatever gun it was the señor had assembled was ready. There was an angry barking cough, once, twice, three times in rapid succession: *Thok! Thok! Thok!*

Then, as abruptly and as terrifyingly as it had all begun, it was over: the stabbing lights were gone and the helicopter itself was scudding along the shoreline, jinking left and right like a big dirt fly, skimming low over the sand, rearing up and over Mi's car. Maybe Mi cast a spell on it, scare it right away. A plume of flame poured out from the chopper's tail, trailing fire like a comet across the sky. It flew straight for a few heartbeats then lurched wildly to the right. A moment later there was a loud *whoomph* and it jerked straight up into the air, hung for a second and then piled down into the ground, erupting in a sheet of dazzling orange and white flame, so bright that Reve had to shield his eyes against the burst of light, even though it must have been at least half a mile away.

There was silence apart from the sea slopping against the pier, the hiss of fire and water. Then Reve heard someone moaning, someone else calling and the pattering of running feet, engines starting up. Some of the motorboats must have cast off and headed into the dark rather than sit there, easy targets, and now they were nosing back to the pier.

He touched LoJo's shoulder. 'You OK?' he said.

'Yes.'

Ramon's brother was hunched against the wall, his arms wrapped over his head, his body quivering still. 'You want to go look for your brother?' Reve said. 'I think he's all right, you know. Maybe a little wet.'

The boy clambered to his feet. Looked down at his torn-up knee raw from the fall. He poked it with his finger and winced. 'You nearly broke my leg,' he said.

'He saved your life,' said LoJo.

'Yeah?' He shrugged. But he peered at Reve and after half a second said, 'I know you. Hevez don't like you much.' Then he grinned. 'Don't like me much either.' Then he ran off, or tried to – his hurt knee made him hobble.

At that moment the truck's headlights flicked on, and in the sudden glare Reve saw men hurrying down towards where the boats had been moored. There was fuel burning on the water and the boats that had cast off as soon as the helicopter attacked were now drifting a few lengths away from the pier, outside the ring of fire. Like hungry dogs, Reve thought, ready to come in again but not too sure if it was safe.

The señor had Calde and his men gathered round him. A moment later bulky Calde was running back to the edge of the pier, gesturing for the boats to come in.

'How many we lost?' shouted the señor.

'One only,' Calde called back.

'One only,' mimicked the señor to his men. 'How that

country pig Calde like to walk round with only one *cojon*, hey?' His men laughed and then peeled away as he gave more orders, to dismantle the gun, strap down the load.

The señor took a couple of steps from the truck towards where Reve and LoJo were watching from the deep shadow of the wall. He flipped open his cellphone. 'It's me, Moro . . .' His voice was low and ugly. 'I want to know who gave a call to these dirt-fly coast-guards . . . Yes. You're the lawyer. You find out.' The señor was silent, listening for a moment and then said, 'Fix it.' He snapped the cell shut.

The señor was now standing so close that Reve could smell him: something sweet and musky, not the village smell of salt, fish and sweat. He noticed now that, though the señor wore a suit like his men, there was something shabby about him too. He wore a stringy vest under his dark jacket, an old pair of trainers on his feet. The señor scratched the back of his neck, looked at the phone in his hand and then made another call. 'Captain,' he said, his voice low, polite this time, 'I have a problem here . . .' and then he turned his back and Reve couldn't hear what else he said. The señor ended the call, took one last draw on the butt of his cigar and tossed it away towards where Reve and LoJo were standing and then walked swiftly back to where the boats were docking.

LoJo let out his breath. 'You think he saw us?'

Reve shook his head, but he reckoned if the señor knew he'd been overheard he would not be happy. 'You heard nothing, hey.'

LoJo shook his head. 'I heard him say—'

64

'No.' Reve was firm. 'You heard nothing.'

'OK. OK. I gotta go, Reve. My family goin to come lookin for me, 'spect me to be dead cos all that shooting . . .'

'And the money you earn?'

'You collect it for me – you know how much I done. OK?'

Reve smiled. 'You don't think I just put your money in my pocket?'

'Why you put my money in your pocket? Your pocket nothing but holes!' With a wave he was gone, running down the pier.

The work had started in earnest again. Reve took his place in the line and sweated another load, and then another, to and fro between the truck and the boats, till his legs felt like jelly, and he stopped to catch his breath.

'So how long we got?' someone shouted.

'No time!' snapped the señor. 'You got no time, so you work double quick. You want to still be here in the morning when the policeman come? You want that? Take your breakfast in the Castle? Then move yourself!'

The señor took another cigar from the inside of his jacket, bowed his head as he circled the match round the tip and then sucked so the flame pulled into the cigar. 'I want those boats gone before they send another helicopter. You think the coastguards got another helicopter, Secondo?'

The man beside him shrugged. 'Maybe they borrow one from the army.'

Moro nodded. 'Just one boat sunk?'

'Yes, señor.'

'Get the engine off it.' He called Calde over. 'Is it deep off this pier?'

'Not so deep.'

'Fix it then. Those engines cost more than a man's life.'

Calde strode over to where the men were gathered, and after some discussion a couple of them stripped off and dived in.

Moro took the cigar from his mouth. 'We lost any of the skippers?' he said to his second in command.

'One. Another got hit, his boat's maybe OK, but he won't be driving it. '

'Calde!' shouted Moro.

Calde came running back; Reve had never seen the heavy man run before. He had a cluster of his men on his heels, and Hevez and Ramon too.

'I want another skipper. Who you got?'

Reve didn't wait to hear who Calde was going to name; instead he ran back to the water's edge for another load. He wanted to be there right to the end, hauling the sacks, sweating hard so they could see how he worked, so they would pay him their dollar.

Down along the pier, a gang of men was hand-hauling a rope that must have been attached to the sunken motor boat. They were sweating it up towards the sand. Reve hefted the last plastic sack up on to his shoulder and trotted back to the truck. As he passed by, the señor saw him and jerked his head, beckoning him over.

Panting, Reve stood, the sack awkward on his shoulder.

'What do you think, Calde?' The señor took out

his cigar and studied its glowing tip. 'You think the coastguards got lucky or you reckon some pig squealed?' Reve's heart pinched inside his chest. They couldn't think it was him. He knew nothing! Unless Mi had been saying more things . . .

Calde looked at Reve. 'If we got a squeal-pig,' he said to the señor, 'it get its tongue cut out. You thinkin this one?' Calde's hand went to the long blade he had hanging from his belt.

Moro grunted what might have been a laugh. 'No. Maybe. I don't know, Calde. Finding the squeal-pig's your business.' To Reve he said, 'Put that sack down.' Reve slid it from his aching shoulder and let it drop at his feet. 'You know how much dollar you carrying there?'

Reve shook his head. He reckoned that whatever this man told him, the sack weighed too heavy to be packed with paper money.

'A lot of dollar. Steal a bag like this from me and a man don't have to work for a long time. What you think about that, hey?'

Reve kept his face blank. If this was a test or something, it was stupid. Nobody was fool enough to steal from these men.

The señor nodded. 'Do I know you? Who're your people?'

Reve shook his head. 'I got a sister is all.'

'Well,' the señor said, 'I seen what you did, hey. With that boy. Pulled him from the bullets. You got *cojones*. A little bull.' He said this over his shoulder to one of his men, who laughed and nodded. 'Maybe little *cojones*.'

He studied Reve, half closing his eyes, as if to get his full measure. Reve kept still. He didn't know what this man wanted, whether he was pleased with him or just toying with him, ready to make fun of him. He didn't care, so long as the man paid him his money. 'You look for work some time, you ask for me, señor Moro. I can always do with someone who got muscle, quick mind, and a bit of courage.' He turned away, the meeting over.

'We get dollar from you?' blurted Reve.

The señor turned back. 'You askin me for money?'

'Yes.'

The señor looked at Secondo and pulled a face. 'Who got money here? You got money, Secondo.'

Secondo patted his jacket and pulled a face too. 'Me, no. I carry no money, señor.'

The señor laughed. A crowd of villagers had gathered around behind them; they too were waiting for money. They stood silent though, watching this pantomime. If these men wanted to make a fool of a boy for speaking out of turn, that was nothing to do with them.

'Calde, pay him.' Calde looked startled. 'Pay him, now. How much we pay these people, Secondo.'

'Ten dollars.'

'So much! OK. Give him twenty, Calde.'

At the sight of money being pulled, the crowd started calling out for their wages too. The señor's men hustled them back, forcing them into a line.

Calde peeled a note from a roll he had in his pocket and held it out to Reve.

Reve kept still. 'Forty,' he said.

Calde growled at him: 'Take this or you get nothing, stupid boy.'

The señor's eyes narrowed, letting the smoke stream up from his mouth.

'Forty. I collect for LoJo. He work alongside me.'

Calde hesitated, then the señor nodded and he peeled another note and handed it over. Reve took the two bills and folded them tight into his hand. Mi would be proud of him.

Reve slipped past the scrummage of men at the back of the truck holding out their hands for money, and then jogged to the edge of the pier just above the tideline, where he could jump down on to the sand. Reve wanted to go show Mi the money he had in his fist. If LoJo would lend him his money, with what he already had saved up it was maybe enough. He needed to ask Uncle Theon about that. Fifty dollars. You could live for half a year in Rinconda on that, if you didn't spend it all on rum.

He was just about to jump when he heard more raised voices. Two bundles of men were surging and swaying like they were struggling to hold down one, maybe two, wild dogs. As they came into the light of the headlights, he saw what was going on.

Two men had LoJo's father, Pelo, one by each arm, and they were dragging him along, ignoring Ciele, who was following on their heels, slapping at them and yelling to let her husband go, and LoJo was there too, beside her, trying to restrain her. In the other group there was Hevez and two of Calde's men: Cesar and Escal, brothers, and another two behind them. And they had Tomas the Boxer. As Reve watched he saw Tomas straighten himself like a giant and swing Cesar one way and Escal the other, but he couldn't shake them free and the man behind him suddenly cracked something down on Tomas's head so that he slumped to his knees. Then the men dragged him, his legs splayed out behind him, up to the truck where Calde and the señor were waiting.

CHAPTER EIGHT

For the second time that day, maybe the second time in his life, Reve acted without thinking. The money still tight in his fist, he ran back across the pier, shoved past Hevez, till he was beside Tomas. 'What you do to him?' he shouted to Cesar and his stupid brother. 'Hey? What he done to you?'

Reve looked around at all the faces, and his anger turned cold in his stomach. He wiped his face with the back of his hand, realizing he was just a boy standing in the middle of these men, getting in the way of their business. He took a breath and readied himself, his legs a little apart. He saw Pelo looking at him, Ciele and LoJo too. Ciele's lips were moving but he didn't know if she was trying to tell him something. He saw the sneer on Hevez's face

The man behind Tomas tapped his stumpy club into the palm of his left hand, and Cesar, still gripping Tomas with his left hand, let his right hand snake to the knife on his hip, but his eyes were on Calde. He wouldn't do anything unless he was told. And Escal was expressionless, waiting for his brother's lead, his hands tight round Tomas's arm.

Reve turned to face Señor Moro; he was the man in charge. It was his word they were waiting for. He didn't like to leave his back to anyone, especially not Cesar, but he was in the circle now so he might as well dance. That's what Arella said every time she stood up after a bellyful of rum to walk back to her hut: 'If you step in the circle, Reve, you got to know the steps of the dance. So you watch me now.'

He lifted his chin and, realizing he still had this man's money in his hand, he shoved it into his pocket. 'Why you got Tomas here? If you got something you want him to do, I can do it instead.' He glanced at Calde. It wasn't the señor who had asked for this; it was Calde. Maybe Tomas had tough-talked him that morning, got under his skin, and this was payback.

'So,' said Señor Moro, as if he hadn't heard Reve's offer, 'we got the little big man again.' He dipped his head towards Calde and murmured something Reve couldn't hear. He feared it wouldn't be good, but Calde just nodded at the brothers and they let Tomas go. Tomas stumbled, almost fell and then regained his footing and shook himself. 'What is this man to you?' Señor Moro said to Reve.

'I sail his boat. He . . .' he hesitated. 'He look out for me . . .'

Calde said, 'His mother the one run with off with the policeman.' He turned his face and spat.

There was a stir from the circle of onlookers. They hadn't known this. Señor Moro, though, grunted as if he had heard the story before.

Reve felt his throat tighten up so bad it was hard to speak. 'Who tell you that!' he managed. 'That never happen!' Reve looked at Tomas, but the big man just stared straight ahead as if he hadn't heard. 'She get arrested.' Reve felt his face flush and burn. People get arrested. No shame in that because it happens; the law is there to stop you getting ahead. That's what Theon said to him one time. Helping the Night Man load his trucks – that would get anyone hard time if the policeman came down. But to run off with a policeman, no one would ever do that . . . and not, their mother – run out on them as if they were nothing. There was so much shame in that it could fill the ocean. 'He just make up that dirt talk!' Reve said, but his words had no bite.

Señor Moro grunted again and then with a sudden edge, he said, 'All right, I got no time for this.' He made a slight gesture with his left hand and Reve was pulled to one side, hardly aware of the firm hand clamped on the back of his neck.

'You,' Señor Moro was saying to Tomas. 'You, Tomas the Boxer – you don't look in so good shape to me.'

Tomas gingerly touched the back of his grizzled head and grimaced.

'You do this kind of work one time, Tomas the Boxer?'

'One time. I work for no one now.'

'You can drive a boat?'

'If you want someone drive a boat, you don't hit him on the head first, hey.' He rolled his shoulders, easing the hurt, and then grunted again. 'But it don't make a difference. I done all the business I ever gonna do, and you got no call on me.'

'One last job. Give you drinking money, Tomas. That's what I hear you do now: kissing the bottle. A boxer and a kissing man, that's how I hear it.'

'Hear it any way you like. I don't need one thing from

73

you, or you,' said Tomas, turning and challenging Calde. 'That time's all gone for me, you understand? You find some other man for your business.'

'Well –' Señor Moro nodded at the man holding Reve, and Reve found himself pushed forward into the circle again – 'how about this boy? He make offer take your place. He good enough to run a boat to Paraloca without getting stung by the patrol?'

Tomas looked at Reve but said nothing.

'If he lose my boat,' continued Señor Moro, 'I come looking for you, Tomas, and I take what little you got.'

'This boy's too young to do your business,' said Tomas.

His shoulders were straight and his eyes unblinking. No sign of the rum shakes. He looked strong. Then he looked at Calde: thick shoulder, pig-eyed. The señor's dog in Rinconda. Had Tomas and Theon been like that when they ran Rinconda? Reve wondered. Is that what Mi had seen in them both. No, Calde was the one with the devil in his belly. He was the enemy.

'I understand,' said Señor Moro. He flicked the tip of his cigar. 'But I got business that need doing. Maybe this man can help me out.' He nodded towards LoJo's father, Pelo. 'Calde, can this man help me out?' He glanced at his watch. 'We don't have so much time.' He sounded as if he had all the time in the world.

Calde nodded and Pelo was jostled forward. He was a small man with a narrow face and a sharp chin and he wore a moustache that drooped round the edge of his mouth and made him look sad. He wasn't sad though; he worked hard, but he liked to joke too, called Reve

74

'Captain Clean-up' because of the way Reve gathered bottles from the seashore. Tomas liked him. Liked his wife too. Reve looked over at Ciele. She was gripping LoJo's shoulders, holding him tight. She caught Reve's eye and Reve looked away; she could lose her man.

'I'll go,' said Pelo, his voice even. 'How much you payin? Paraloca take me a week maybe. I got fishing to do.'

'In one of my fishing boats?' said Calde.

Pelo shrugged. 'I pay you all the time.'

'Maybe this help you pay off the debt, eh.'

'Sure.' Pelo looked at Señor Moro.

'OK,' said Señor Moro, 'let's see.' But as he was pulling out a roll of dollars from his pocket – more money than Reve could imagine having – Reve saw the way Calde looked at Ciele and he could tell that Calde was happy for Pelo to be away for a week.

'Here.' Señor Moro held out a couple of bills.

Pelo hesitated, looked at Tomas, then put out his hand and without looking at how much the señor was giving him, he passed it to Ciele.

'Don' worry, Pelo,' said Calde, all smooth as if he'd dipped his voice in pig fat. 'I'll see Ciele's all right. She need anything, she just ask me. No problem.'

Pelo ignored Calde's offer and turned to Tomas. 'Tomas, you mind Ciele, the boy can fish with Reve.'

Tomas nodded. 'I'll see this pig don't come near her . . .'

Escal, Cesar's heavy-jawed and simple-minded brother, lunged at Tomas, fists bunched, but Tomas stepped to one side, neat as a dancer. You wouldn't think someone so big and carrying so many years could move as easy as that. 'You want trouble off me, Calde, you know where you find me.'

Señor Moro laughed. 'Do your business another time, Calde. Come.'

He beckoned to Pelo and they went together over to the pier's edge, the other men and then Ciele and LoJo following. LoJo was saying something quietly to his mother, reassuring her maybe.

Reve was left alone with Tomas. 'What Calde say, is that true? My mother cheat and run off, didn't care nothin 'bout us?'

'Not now.'

'When you goin tell me? You and Theon, how much you keep from us? Everyone else know but we two? You tellin me that?'

'No.'

'Everyone think that 'bout her now. Think we got a mother who run with a policeman. Everyone goin say we got that streak. Things bad enough for Mi. What you think this kind of talk goin do now? Hey. What you think, Tomas. People still goin believe in what she say? People goin give me respect—'

'Tha's enough! We don' talk here. You come back out of here.' He didn't wait for Reve to answer but turned and headed back towards the village. Reve watched him go. He wasn't a dog to trot after him, get a tidbit of knowing when it suited Tomas to throw it his way. He joined Ciele and LoJo.

Down below them, the skippers were back in their boats, though Pelo's craft seemed way lower in the water than the others. The sunken powerboat had been dragged up on to the sand and three men were manhandling the huge outboard engine on to a handcart.

Pelo called out, 'What you sellin me, Calde? This boat half full of water.'

A flashlight played along the boat's hull and then on to Pelo again; his face looked bloodless and grey in the harsh beam.

'Bail her out.' A tin sailed down into the boat. 'She'll ride high on the way back if you give her speed.'

'I got a choice?'

The man Moro called Secondo laughed. 'Everybody got a choice till they stop breathing. You want to stop breathing?'

Pelo muttered something and then busied himself scooping water from the bilge. He pulled off his shirt and tore it into strips, and used the strips to plug holes in the hull.

Secondo called out, 'Time to go.'

Pelo started the engine; it gave a throaty roar and he raised his hand. One by one the others started up, lines were thrown back on board and the black-hulled boats swung away from the pier in a wide, creaming curve and headed out to sea, the engines peaking to a howl as the throttles were pushed full down. One boat lagged a little behind the others. Pelo taking it easy, Reve reckoned, but even his craft quickly disappeared into the dark, leaving phosphorescent lines scratched on the black surface of the sea for a few seconds.

Señor Moro and his men were already heading for their cars. The rest of the crowd followed. All but Pelo's wife, and LoJo, who stood by her side.

Ciele looked like a widow standing on the wall with her son, everyone else gone from her.

It is a too easy thing, Reve thought, for a family to be pulled apart.

He thought of Mi down on the beach. She'd be curled up in the car, head covered, not wanting to hear all that thunder, not wanting to see the flames; and Tomas would be up in the shack, a tin cup of rum in his hand; and then somewhere in the city this shadow person, his mother, living with her policeman who she'd run away with. The taste in his mouth was sour, but when he tried to spit there was nothing there, just the taste. Shame. That was still there, but his anger had gone.

CHAPTER NINE

The night was still and the sea hardly moving, as if it was exhausted by all that had happened. The moon was a thin crescent, but the stars were bright and the damp sand stretched ahead of Reve like a ghostly road into the distance. Sultan trotted along beside him.

When he had walked back along the wall after everyone else and jumped down on to the beach Sultan had come running from the shack and greeted him like he hadn't seen him for a week. Reve knew he would have been hiding all the time there was yelling and noise, and guns going off. He was too smart to be brave – that's what he told LoJo when he asked how come Sultan never got in fights like all the other dogs in the village. Reve knew that he too had to be smart, not just run smack into things. He needed to think.

He stooped and picked up a plastic bottle, added it to the string of bottles he had trailed over his shoulder and walked on. Mi's storm was over, but there would be more. The police would come tomorrow, maybe even tonight; there would be a hunt to find out who had told the coastguards. The truth, he now realized, was that nothing was ever finished. It was like the beach, it stretched on forever. No end to the rubbish beading the sand either. Plastic. Always plastic. Sacks of it. Bottles mainly, but Reve never knew what else he'd find. He picked up a small plastic lion one time. Didn't know it was a lion till he showed it to Uncle Theon and Theon told him how lions marked their territory by roaring loud as thunder. King of all the animals. Reve had put the plastic lion on a post to the side of their shack, but it didn't look so fierce and he and LoJo used it as a target to throw stones at and then it went.

He'd gather another string of plastic bottles before going back again. Theon gave him a cent for every ten he brought to him. Tomas said no one ever got money for nothing, but to Reve's way of thinking an empty bottle was next to nothing so he was doing all right. He liked walking the beach in the night-time, picking up the plastic, making something better, getting something done.

He made up his mind. If Tomas confirmed Calde's story was true, then he and Mi would go to the city and find her. This policeman would have a name. And there'd be a trail they could follow. It was what Mi wanted. It would get her away from Hevez, maybe give her time to think about this Two-Boat. Maybe their mother would think different, seeing them now. Maybe they would be able to think differently about her running off with a policeman – gone whoring, people would say now, dirt-talk. They would have to live with that, and if they did, maybe they could be a family.

Because even if Tomas said Calde was lying, the talk would still be the same. A girl whose mother had gone whoring, living on her own, no one was goin to care about her any more, no one was going to listen to her talk, and Hevez or some other man would come one night . . .

This was it. They were either going for the city or he would take the skiff and Mi and sail down the coast, find a place in San Jerro, maybe work for Two-Boat. They were leaving.

He walked back to the shack but stopped at the gate a moment, standing in the darkness looking across at Tomas, who was sitting inside, the oil lamp on, the Bible on his lap, a quart of rum by his hand. Sometimes, Reve realized, you live close to someone for a long time and you only see part of what they are.

When their father's body had been found in the middle of the village, right outside Uncle Theon's cantina, no one would touch it, but Tomas walked right up to where it lay in the middle of the track, and with all the villagers watching but saying nothing, he had cut away the net and then wrapped up the body in a piece of sailcloth. He had hoisted it on to a barrow and wheeled it up the sandy track to the graveyard on the hill. When Reve had looked back over his shoulder he had seen that all those people who had been silently watching had just turned away as if nothing had happened. The people of Rinconda were like that; kept things tight. Someone with a loose mouth got it sewn up quick enough, like a tear in a sail.

Reve pushed the gate and Tomas looked up. 'That you, Reve?'

'It's me.'

He threw the strings of plastic bottles into the shed. Then he squared his shoulders and stepped up on to the porch. This was it. No hiding and twisting things away –

Tomas would have to tell everything.

'Is it true?' he asked. 'The thing Calde tell that señor, and everyone listenin.'

Tomas closed the Bible.

Tomas told him only three people had known what Felice, Reve's mother, had gone and done: Uncle Theon, because he was the one who ran the village back then, Tomas, his strong arm, and Calde, their runaround. The policeman was young; he'd come into Rinconda to sniff around their business and then had fallen for Felice. He wasn't the first and neither Tomas nor Theon thought she had any feeling for him. Theon thought this was an opportunity: the policeman was going to be putty; they could use him. Good to have a policeman on your side when you are running boats up from the border, doing business with a señor, the old señor, not this young one who Calde worked with now.

But it turned out that the policeman and Felice wanted to do more than cheat on her husband; they had plans to make a lot of money. She had always wanted money. Arella had been right; they did call her Santa Fe, after the gold-rush town up in the rich north. The plan was simple. Reve's father skippered one of Theon's smuggling boats. She persuaded him to bring the boat up the coast; she would arrange a truck, she said; they would steal the contraband and start a new life somewhere else. Reve's father was good with a boat, but he was not a smart man and Theon used him only out of kindness; Felice was always at him to give Reve's father work.

Felice, though, was very smart; that shipment had

been worth a lot of dollars. It would set them up for life. It would have done the same for Theon and Tomas. They could have been rich men living in some ranchera up the coast.

When the boat didn't come in on time, Theon and Tomas had become suspicious and Tomas had set off to search. When he eventually found it, in a cove a little way up the coast, all the cargo had gone; he also found Reve's father, with a bullet in him. The policeman had shot him like a dog. That's how it was.

Theon raged. They looked like fools, he said, country dummies. Men from the city would walk all over them. So they decided to cover up the story, have it that Felice had been taken for questioning and that the dead body of Reve's father left in the village was a warning that nobody could steal from their business. Theon had dumped the body there.

But the truth was their business was finished. Losing that shipment ruined them. Calde went behind their backs and made a deal with the old señor, and that was it. He took over.

When Tomas was finished, Reve had only two questions. 'What name that policeman carry?'

'Dolucca.'

'OK,' said Reve, and then asked his second question: 'Why you keep all this tuck away from us? Maybe Mi would've turn out different if she'd know'd what happen; wouldn' always've gone wanderin, boilin herself up . . .'

'No,' Tomas said. 'You don't remember, but your sister always gone her own way, act strange. She put worry

83

on Felice.' He nodded, remembering. 'Felice didn't know how to put a rein on her any more than me, eh. Your sister was always goin to be the way she is. And at that time I thought it better you didn' know your mother was runnin free.' He looked up at Reve, who was standing by the doorway. 'I didn't want you and her growin up and goin off to the city to go lookin for her. But tha's where you headin now, eh?'

'Yes.'

'You know, I hoped she would come back, find that I'd taken you both in. Acted right for her.'

'That's why you gave us a home?'

Tomas didn't answer.

'That Bible you got – that the only thing make you different from Calde or the Night Man?'

Tomas shook his head. 'It's what you do make you different.' He sounded weary.

Reve closed the door on him. They had the name. He would go see LoJo, ask him if he could borrow his twenty, tell Mi what he'd found out and then in the morning he would see Theon; Theon would give them a ride up to the city in his truck, or get them on the fish truck; he could do that.

He found LoJo still up. He was outside his place, sitting on the step of their shack. When Reve asked if he could borrow LoJo's twenty LoJo shrugged. They had enough with what Moro had paid to keep going till his father got back, he said. In fact he didn't seem to care about the money at all, and when Reve told him the reason he just said, 'So you goin off to the city, yeah?'

'You look after the skiff while I'm gone?' LoJo nodded. 'My dog too?'

'That dog make up his own mind. If he stop with me, I'll feed him.'

'What happen you?' Reve asked. 'You got some trouble? Pelo make that trip easy.'

LoJo shrugged again. 'Calde,' he said bitterly. 'He come to our place. He sayin thing to my mother. Offer her work in his place, promising good money. Tell her that Pelo could make good money too after helping out the señor. But only if Calde put in a word for him. Asked my mother if she'd like that, him putting in a word.'

'That man more slippy than a ball of grease,' said Reve. 'He just a piece of pig-eyed hog fat, and he stink like a dog; stink worse than my dog.'

That raised half a smile and LoJo bent down and touched Sultan on the nose. 'You don' mind someone hear you call him that? This place got ears all a time.'

All the shacks around them were dark; only Theon's had lights burning.

Reve dropped his voice a little. 'Tomas made promise to your father, Lo.'

'Sure, Reve. I just wish my daddy hadn't gone on that boat.'

'Looked like he didn't have so much choice.'

'My mother say a body always got choice . . . Calde say somethin else to my mother when he come by; it made my mother so angry the baby started cryin. Calde walk away then.'

'On his fat legs.'

'Fat cos he eat up half the village.'

'Look like Ciele don't need Tomas's help.'

'Everybody need help sometime.'

He'd left LoJo then and walked quickly out to see if Mi was at the car and awake.

When he got there, she was sitting cross-legged up on the bonnet of the Beetle. She had her bundle packed up and ready.

He slumped down by the front wheel and stuck his legs out into her sand garden, and Sultan coiled himself down beside him. He told her they were going. He told her Tomas's story.

The edge of the ocean gleamed white where it broke on the sand.

'Knew she was livin,' she said. 'Right 'bout that. Right 'bout most things, Reve.'

'Oh yeah? And if I'd stayed all tucked away when the Night Man come into the village, like you tol' me to do, we wouldn' know a thing.'

She didn't respond to that. Just said: 'It all goin to fall out easy, Reve. You dream her and that mean you find her. That the way these things happen.'

On the way back along the shore he stopped to look at the beached powerboat. It was long and thin, built for speed, and tipped on its back it looked like a skinny whale. He wondered if his father had skippered a boat like this. Jagged holes ran along the length of its hull, silvery against the black. He tapped it. Metal, not wood. A boat like that would cost more than Reve would ever earn in a lifetime fishing, and yet there it was, another piece of rubbish on the beach. Maybe money wasn't the only thing. Sultan sniffed it, growled and backed away. Then he trotted up to the prow, lifted his leg and without waiting for Reve crossed the sand to the shack.

CHAPTER TEN

It was pitch black and so quiet he could hear an animal rooting over on the far side of the track, pig most likely; most people, apart from Uncle Theon, let their pigs root any place. Reve lay there for a moment, eyes wide but seeing nothing, just thinking about what he had to do, the practical things.

He put out his hand and touched Sultan. The dog sighed but didn't move. LoJo would mind Sultan; Tomas would forget to feed him; Tomas would most likely forget to feed himself. He stopped himself thinking about that and carefully swept his hand round to the right, found the jar with the candle, struck a light, then pulled on his jeans and rolled off the pallet.

If Theon didn't know how to track this Dolucca policeman, he would know how to find Señor Moro. A man like that would know where to find a policeman who got a story in his life that could be used against him. The señor would help them, Reve thought. He'd said to come see him. They would. It would be the smart thing to do. Señor Moro was the key.

Reve tried to imagine what this Dolucca looked like, but all he could picture was something like a giant pucker fish, all needle teeth and the rest of his body wrapped in uniform. He stuck his head under the standpipe and let the water wash away his stupid thinking. That was the way Mi would picture things in her stories about people she didn't like, their bellies stuffed with devils. This man was maybe caring for their mother; they would have to be polite. What would Mi do? He hoped she wouldn't start juddering and hearing voices. The policeman might want to lock her up. And what would this woman, their mother, want? If she saw Mi acting strange, would she turn away from them again? She hadn't liked that in Mi when Mi was just a little girl, and now Mi was almost grown maybe their mother wouldn't like having her near, or him too, a fishing boy out of the village she'd run from . . .

He took a deep breath of ocean air. They would find out. That was all there was to it.

He crawled back under the hut and put the coins and the two twenty-dollar notes into his one spare T-shirt, tied it up so that none of the money would fall out, snuffed the candle and then, grabbing the T-shirt he intended to wear, crawled out from under the hut, Sultan following him.

There was just the beginning of grey out over the ocean; sun-up wasn't so far off. He then put the shirt, money, a bit of bread and a twist of bean paste into a canvas bag, slung it over his bare shoulder, gathered up the strings of empty plastic bottles and headed up the track, letting the air dry him before putting on his T-shirt.

The village shacks he passed seemed like a straggle of giant black-backed crabs, the plastic sheets on the roofs pulsing slightly in the faint breeze. Nothing else was stirring.

By the time he was up at Uncle Theon's it was fully

light. It always seemed to him that it was like the sun just took a breath out of that last bit of darkness and then threw itself up into the sky; that's how quickly dawn broke.

Reve dropped the bottles into the bin at the back of the cantina and then went into the kitchen, waiting for Theon to wake up. He unwrapped the T-shirt and counted the money, again, putting it in neat piles. He wanted Theon to change it all for small notes.

After that he did what he always did; he began to clean the place. He gathered up bottles and glasses, swept the floor, wiped the tables and had even started washing up when Theon came down the stone stairs that led up to the roof. He always slept up there, said the sea air kept him cool and he could catch any thief trying to steal his beer.

Theon, barefooted and half dressed, was on his cellphone as he came down the stairs. The second time in two days. Of course he did business on his phone, but not this early, not usually.

When Theon saw Reve he frowned and turned away. He sounded impatient with whoever he was talking to. 'Yes, of course I know that. You think I was born yesterday . . . Yes.' He snapped the phone shut and scratched his cheek, thinking. When Reve started to talk to him he held up his hand. 'Not now!' After a moment he walked over to the front of the building and looked up towards the highway, then came back past Reve into the kitchen and made himself a coffee, which he sipped slowly. All the time Reve just stood and waited.

Eventually Theon seemed to make up his mind and turned back to face Reve. He studied him for a moment. Then, noticing the piles of coins, he swept them into his hand, and without Reve even asking he poured the lot into his cash drawer and pulled out twelve dollars, which he handed to Reve.

'Goin some place, eh?' he said.

'Yes. Goin to the city. With Mi.'

'People skin you in the city.' Theon sounded still irritable. 'Easy like they skin a dog.'

This wasn't going the way Reve wanted. Theon was OK. Didn't talk all the time, would listen, talk sense. But this morning he seemed like he had a wire fence tangled up round him. 'Theon,' said Reve, 'can you give us a ride in your truck?'

Theon barely let him finish his question. 'What you been doin? You been catchin some of them asking-fish, cos all they do is leave a body hungry. What happen to Tomas, if you go?'

Reve didn't bother to answer that. Tomas wasn't sick; he could get out of his hammock and feed himself, that's what could happen. Instead he spoke to his uncle in a way that he never had before. 'Time you listen to me, Uncle Theon. You and Tomas wrap up what happen when our mother ran off with the policeman, wrap it up so tight you reckon no one ever know you get cheated, and me and my sister just stay not knowin for all time. We got a right to find her if we can. We not stayin in this place – not safe for Mi, and I'm done sweepin floors and bein a runaround . . .'

Theon looked at him, clearly surprised, then splashed more coffee into his cup and sat down. 'Sit,' he said. 'What did you hear, Reve?'

Reve described what happened down on the harbour wall. What Calde had said, what Tomas had then told him. Theon listened and nodded, but he also pressed Reve to tell him everything about the action: the unloading, the helicopter coming, boats getting hit . . . all that. He was particularly interested when Reve repeated what Señor Moro had said when he was phoning. 'First his lawyer and then a captain . . . I wonder which captain he has in his pocket . . .' He let Reve finish, and at the end, he said, 'Tomas told you just how it was. I don't know any more. My sister, your mother, she may be living with her policeman. I don't know. She dead to me. If you find her, you can tell her that yourself.' He made a dismissive gesture with his hand. 'I hope your sister treat you better than Felice treated me.'

'But you'll help us.'

'All right, I will, but if you wan' my help, you finish sortin this place for me. I got business comin here.'

'Who?'

'Police,' he grunted. 'Who you think? One thing to run a few boats cross the border; something else to slap down a coastguard helicopter. The "man" is goin to be ragin when he come here, he goin to burn down everythin' 'less I or Calde can give him reason not to.'

'You pay him?'

'Of course I pay. How you think I keep this business. This is the way it is.'

'They won't burn down the village!' Reve said, suddenly worried. 'That señor, he spoke to a captain—'

'The captain he got in his pocket maybe keep Señor Moro safe and clean, but he not goin to worry 'bout what happen here—'

'But Señor Moro is the one! We didn't do anythin, just unload the boats . . .'

Theon gave a humorless laugh and then his attention was caught by a flicker of movement up on the highway. He sounded more resigned than irritable now. 'Here they come.'

Reve could see them now too, coming down from the highway, snaking and bumping down the track, past the first straggle of huts, then past Calde's stone house and his workshops. Three Jeeps. They didn't look like they were in a hurry.

Theon moved to the door. 'If police don't mess with what we got, I fix you ride on the truck tomorrow, early start. Tell your sister – that truck don' wait around while she makes a sand garden.'

'OK.'

'I'll give you a place I know where you can stay, an' I'll tell you how to find that man you want to see, but you be careful – he'll skin you 'less you got something to give him. Let me think 'bout it. But right now, you finish up in here, then you stay out the back. If you hear a name get given by Calde to the police, you slip out and run to that man's place, and you tell his family that the police comin for him. Give them time to get out the way. Maybe save something.'

'You think this what Calde gonna do?'

'Maybe.'

Reve wondered where a man could run to in Rinconda. Then he thought, who would Calde give up to the police to save his own skin? He'd pick someone he didn't like, someone who didn't give him respect. 'What if Tomas get named?'

Theon took off his wire glasses and wiped them on his shirt tail. 'Tomas take his chance . . . Don't look at me like that, Reve. I don't know what goin happen here. I just do what I can.'

Three jeeps. Twelve policemen. Black uniforms, black helmets, black glasses, expressionless faces. A black-back hog was rooting round the cement-block shack opposite, pulling at a loose end of the plastic the family had used to roof their place.

Theon went out on to his front porch. Reve noticed the way he rubbed his hands down the legs of his cotton trousers as if he was nervous but his voice was easy, as if the policeman was an old customer. 'Lieutenant,' he said, 'you have a long drive from the city. Can I give you coffee, something to eat?'

A young woman's face appeared in the doorway of the shack opposite and then pulled back quickly. The hog grunted, tore off a strip of the plastic and trotted off trailing it behind him.

The lieutenant nodded. 'Coffee, Theon.'

Theon clicked his fingers and Reve stepped back into the kitchen and put water on the stove. He took the notes Theon had given him and added them to the money he had in the canvas bag. He put the bag up on a shelf by the back door, where he could collect it later. He moved back to the kitchen doorway so he could see and listen.

'Calde here already?' the officer asked.

'On his way.'

'We have business.'

'Of course.'

The officer stepped down from the Jeep and then addressed the rest of his squad. 'You know what you have to do,' he said. His driver nodded and raised his hand, signalling the others to roll on after him, and then the Jeeps slowly moved off down towards the pier.

The officer slapped the dust from his uniform and came up into the cantina and took off his peaked police cap.

Reve took a step back and the policeman noticing him, said, 'You, make the coffee strong and sweet. This boy work for you, Theon?' He unbuttoned his jacket and sat down. 'You are making good money, then, eh.'

'Nothing change so much, lieutenant. You see for yourself. This is a poor place.'

'But you still have business.'

'An' you get paid.'

The lieutenant gave a short laugh. 'Not enough to pay for a helicopter! You know how much one of them thing cost? More than you're worth, more than this village, hundred village like this. What happen last night is on TV news already. You see that?' Theon shook his head. 'Big mess. And someone has to pay. Minister telephone the captain, captain telephone me, and here I am.'

Reve placed the coffee in front of him.

The lieutenant's hair, like his uniform, his glasses and his boots, was shiny black. It was a little curly and oiled tight to his head. It smelt of something sweet and sickly. Reve could see the bevelled line in his hair where his police cap had pinched. He was not so old, this lieutenant, but how old do you have to be to become an important man, like an officer in the police? Reve didn't know.

The lieutenant leaned forward and sipped the sweetened coffee. 'You have something for me?' he asked Theon.

'Of course.' Theon gestured to Reve, and Reve slipped into the back kitchen, but he left the door slightly ajar.

He saw Theon pull an envelope from his back pocket and put it on the table and the lieutenant touching it with his forefinger, raising the flap enough to see the notes inside. He didn't bother to count them, but he leaned forward and began to talk to Theon in a low voice and Theon listened closely, nodding from time to time.

At that moment there was a sudden burst of shouting in the distance, down by the pier and then the flat crack of a pistol shot. Reve felt a thump in his chest: LoJo wouldn't do something stupid. No. Nor Tomas, not with policemen. Not this early in the day, not without a bellyful of rum.

The lieutenant didn't even look up. 'The round-up, hey,' he said. 'Always someone needs a little persuasion.' Theon nodded, but Reve saw the signal he made, held out behind him, the palm flattened, telling him clearly not to go anywhere, not yet.

Then Calde walked into the cantina, in a clean blue button shirt and white cotton canvas trousers, looking like he was dressed for a wedding, except for the long panga knife he had hanging from his waist. He always carried that. Always liked to have something he could threaten with.

Reve was surprised to see the lieutenant stand to shake Calde's hand. Maybe Calde did more business with him than Theon. Even so, when Calde pulled a grubby envelope from his trouser pocket, the officer checked just as he had with Theon's payment.

'You think we pay you enough?' Calde said bluntly, sitting down beside the lieutenant.

The lieutenant shrugged. 'We leave this place alone, unless you bring attention to yourself. What happened last night that was "calling attention".'

'Coastguard never fly this way. Never at night. Why they do that all of a sudden? You tell me that, lieutenant.'

The lieutenant shook his head. 'Maybe you got someone here who's looking to spike your business. Someone who telephoned, gave information. I don't know.'

Calde looked at Theon. 'You hear anything?'

'No.'

'A'right,' said Calde. 'Maybe we got an informer, a squeal-pig. We can root him out. But what goin happen now?'

The lieutenant tapped his finger on the table. 'We rough the place up a little and we pull in some of the village, four or five will do. Take them up to the Castle.'

He shrugged. 'This is for the newspaper and for TV, so everyone can watch it all on the news. It doesn't matter who they are. We hold them for a while and then, when the fuss has died down, we can let them go. I want one name, one man who we can say is the one who shot down the chopper. A head on a plate. The one who take the rap for it all. You got someone you can give me?'

Calde looked at Theon and then back at the lieutenant. 'And you don't touch my business, or Theon's here?'

Theon said, 'What if we got no one to give?'

'Of course,' continued the lieutenant, 'if you got no one to give me, I can take down the whole village. You want me to do that? My men all ready. Make good headlines, Theon: ELITE POLICE SQUAD BURNS DRUG VILLAGE. Good pictures . . .'

Reve imagined the shacks burning, Arella blindly stumbling down on to the track, Ciele and her baby. Where would they all go? And the boats, would they burn them too?

Calde leaned forward. 'All right, we'll do business, but if we do, you must give us the name of the informer we got in this place.'

'If we hear, we'll tell you.'

'All right,' Calde said again. 'We got someone you can have. How about a beer, Theon?'

Theon poured two beers. 'Who you givin?' he asked.

Calde leaned back. 'The Boxer pushin his luck last night.'

Reve, watching from the doorway, kept very still.

'You got the run of this place, but you leave Tomas

out of your reckonin,' said Theon.

Calde shrugged. 'All right, but you keep him in line, eh.' He sipped his beer and then wiped his lips. 'How about Pelo?'

'You sure 'bout that?' Theon's face was a mask.

'Why not? He take one of the boats back down to Paraloca.' He turned towards the policeman. 'You can pick him up when he come across the border. Easy. You want to make a show here, you mess his place. You want to make an arrest, arrest his woman. No, do me a favour . . .' He leaned forward and lowered his voice. Reve couldn't hear what he said, but the lieutenant laughed and he knew the laugh was bad, bad for Pelo, and for Ciele and for LoJo and the little baby girl, Mayash. It was all bad.

'You're a dog, Calde. What do you think, Theon? You think this man's a dog.'

'He's a dog,' Theon said.

Reve knew he should run, right now, and tell Ciele, but he didn't move. Theon would say something to stop this. He was sure he would.

The policeman laughed again and Calde laughed too. It was the ugliest sound Reve had ever heard. Only one thing uglier – and that was Theon not saying anything. Calde rapped on the table for another beer and Theon pushed his chair back and then seeing Reve, he abruptly signalled him to bring over the jug.

When Calde saw Reve carrying the beer his little pig eyes fixed on him and he said, 'What's Tomas's runaround doing here, Theon?'

'Working,' Theon said. He nodded to Reve and Reve put the jug on the table, but as he did so Calde grabbed his wrist and pulled Reve towards him.

'You one of these sneak rats?' he said. His breath smelt of onion and Theon's beer. 'My nephew complain about you, you and your sister. What you say, runaround? You got a tongue in your head?'

'Leave him, Calde. What you playin? He nothing to you.'

Calde ignored Theon. Calde was the power in the village; Calde would do what he liked even with this policeman sitting here. 'You open your mouth 'bout what you hear,' he said to Reve, his pig eyes staring straight into Reve's, 'and I'll cut your tongue!' He let go Reve's wrist and gave him a push.

Reve staggered back a couple of steps but he didn't scuttle off back to the kitchen as perhaps Calde expected. Instead, breathing heavily, he glared at Calde. Calde, however, leaned back in his chair. 'Why you bother with this boy, Theon?' he said. 'Even his mother didn't want him.'

Reve didn't mean to say anything. He really didn't, but this man made him so angry: 'Pelo done you nothin but favour!' he blurted. 'And you do this! Pig. Everyone think you're the pig—'

Before Calde could react Theon was up and out of his chair and had Reve's T-shirt knotted in his fist. 'You mind what you say in my place, hey! I tell you stay in the back and do your work, tha's what you do!'

He smacked Reve hard round the face and shovelled

100

him through the door into the kitchen and then out into the backyard, kicking the outer door shut behind him with his heel and pushing Reve so hard he sprawled down on to his knees. 'What you think you playin at?' shouted Theon. 'Hey!'

Reve was more startled and angry than hurt. Theon had never raised a hand to him, never raised his voice.

He pushed himself upright and took a breath before turning round to face this Theon he didn't know.

To his surprise, though, there was no more shouting. Theon had his finger up, warning him to stay silent. 'Go tell Ciele to get out of her place,' he whispered, 'before the police get there. Go!'

'And Pelo?'

'I get him word.'

CHAPTER ELEVEN

Reve sprinted down the side of the cantina. Theon had hit him so hard his teeth buzzed and his eyes were all watered up. He should have kept his mouth shut. He shouldn't have spoken.

He turned right, threading his way fast through the tight cluster of shacks and sheds that sprawled back from the main track. The cracks and slips between the huts were tight and dark, like a slice of night had got tangled up there; the wider spaces were splashed with white sunlight. It was hot already.

Theon's was only three hundred metres from Pelo's place, but it was hard not to get caught in wire or trip on rubbish. But he moved fast all the same, twisting this way and that, ignoring dogs and pigs, pushing himself, fretting that he would be too late, that the lieutenant had already called his men up from the pier. Frightened that Calde himself would come down looking for him, wanting to cut out his tongue. Why had he shouted at Calde? He never shouted, not ever – not at Tomas, not at Hevez, not in all his life.

He was a fool. He tried not to be, but he was.

Pelo's hut was much the same as Tomas's. A little bigger maybe, raised up from the sandy ground and patched together with planks of salty wood, scraps of tin and black plastic. Pelo had made a little porch at the front, facing the track, and also one at the back. That's where Ciele was sitting, her baby on her lap. And Tomas was standing beside her, head bent talking. He looked serious. There was no sign of LoJo. He'd be down at the skiff most likely.

'Hey!' Reve called. 'Ciele, you got to come out o' here.' She looked up, surprised, startled by his voice coming out of the darkness. 'Get what thing you can. Tomas we got hardly no time. This place not safe . . .'

'Reve,' she said, 'what you doin?' She looked like some queen to Reve, like Mi tried to look sometimes. Just sitting there, holding her baby. But Reve could hear the strain in her voice. 'This my place. Nothin stirring me.'

Tomas put his hand on her shoulder. Tomas didn't hardly talk to anyone other than Arella, and here he was like Ciele was almost family to him. Ciele didn't seem to be minding.

'What you know, Reve?' Tomas said. 'Thought you gone fishing when I rose up. LoJo gone looking for you. We got police stampin down on the wall, herding people up.'

'I been at Theon's.' Hurriedly Reve told them what Calde had said; how he'd sold out Pelo. 'You got to leave,' he said to Ciele. 'Theon said to tell you. Calde given up Pelo's name. They comin to wreck this place. Hurt you too, Ciele, if they find you here.'

'Cos I turned him down flat, called him a pig,' she said bitterly. 'Told him find some other woman.' She stood up. 'I don't got any place to go, Tomas.'

She held the baby tight to her breast.

They heard the roar of a Jeep's engine gunning down the track; the screech of brakes, the shouted command and then a gun butt hammering on the door.

'Ciele! Move quick. Give the baby to Reve and get down there with him. Reve take them out to your sister. You'll be out of the way there,' Tomas said to her. 'I'll save what I can.'

Reve held out his hands. Ciele hesitated and then passed over the baby, little Mayash. She mewled once and then settled against Reve's shoulder. She felt so tiny. Like a bird.

Tomas hustled Ciele down from the porch and then stepped back into the shack as the front door crashed open. 'Hey,' Reve heard him saying. 'This the home of Pelo the fisherman. You got business here I can help you with?' He sounded calm and steady, as though having police beating on your door was no thing to get strange about. He was just doing what any fisherman does, finding his way through the storm.

'I got to see what's happenin!' said Ciele.

From inside they could hear raised voices and the smash of things being broken.

Ciele made to go back up into the shack, but Reve tugged at her arm with his free hand. 'Come. Come with me.' He stepped back into the shadow and pulled her after him. 'They got nothin on him.' He tucked the baby close to him, sniffing her forehead as he threaded his way through the dark maze of this back end of the village, wrapping his arms round her little body, trying to protect her as he pushed his way through bits of wire and fencing. At the edge of the field he stopped. 'We cut across here. You want to take Mayash now? You OK, running with her? I'll carry her if you like.'

Ciele held out her arms.

They ran through dry maize, heading at an angle away from the village and down to the shore.

They found Mi standing up on the roof of her Beetle, staring towards the village. 'Ciele!' she said, swivelling round when she heard them coming in from the field behind. 'Ciele, you got Mayash. Reve! What happen there? I see fire an' smoke in the village . . .'

Trickly black smoke, plastic and wood. Somebody's place turning to ash.

'Police,' he said keeping his voice calm, telling her to come down, prompting her to give water to Ciele and the baby, to get them something to sit on, and as she did those things he told her all he had heard at Theon's. 'All right,' he said to Ciele, 'I'm goin back find Tomas and I got to find LoJo. Mi, tomorrow – we're leaving tomorrow, you remember. OK? OK? Up by the drain. Our meeting place.'

They were both looking at him.

'I got to find Lo, I got to see Tomas. I think maybe . . . I don't know.' Tomas could be hurt, could be dead . . .

Ciele was holding the baby tight to her chest. 'Yes,' she said. 'Yes, you find them, Reve.'

'OK,' he said.

'No!' said Mi. 'Not OK. What you thinking, Reve?

You stay here. You can't go back into that place; it's burnin . . .'

Reve shook his head, backed away. 'One big storm, eh, Mi. All comin like you say.'

And then before she could say anything he was running through soft sand towards the shore. 'Don't forget, we take the truck in the morning,' he called back. 'Early time. Before sun-up. You got to be there up by the road.'

'What you telling me?' she shouted. 'Who you reckon you are, Reve? You can't stop all thing happenin. When you goin to know that? Come back.'

He didn't know what he could stop. Nothing maybe. When the storm comes, you reef the sail and ride the waves as best you can.

LoJo wasn't down on the beach or up on the wall. Reve stood for a moment catching his breath and rubbing the sweat off his face, his back to an oily-calm sea. If the police hadn't snatched LoJo, he'd have gone back to check on his mother and the baby, and run smack into the uniforms busting up his place.

He started to run as fast as he could back up through the village. A thin scatter of ash drifted in the air and he could smell and taste burned wood and plastic. He passed people hurrying to the shore with tubs and buckets. It did look like a storm had torn through: doors kicked in, shutters swinging off their hinges, a dead dog crumpled at the corner of one shack – not Sultan. He called for him as he ran but there was no answering bark.

He saw Arella gripping the edge of her door frame,

staring with her filmy grey eyes, seeing nothing. 'It's Reve,' he said. 'I'll come back, Rella. Go inside.' He couldn't stop.

'You find Tomas,' she called. 'See he's all right.'

'Yes, Rella.'

He saw two shacks burned down to the sand, people dousing the remains. He could hear the hiss as water hit the hot wood and he saw the family picking through the bits that had been salvaged before the fire took hold.

He saw where a Jeep had driven through a fence, pulled it right down, hit the shack too and smacked away the little porch. If you got a uniform, you can do what damage you like.

A fisherman from the back of the village, a man called Tarak, came hurrying towards him, heading for the wall, his eye swollen up.

Reve stopped him. 'Police gone?' he asked.

'They gone.' Tarak said and spat on to the side of the track.

Reve let out his breath. 'They threw some muscle at you.'

'They can throw what they like, so long as they don't touch my boat.'

'Pelo's place?'

'Still standin.'

Tarak walked on and Reve broke into a run again.

CHAPTER TWELVE

Reve found LoJo tending Tomas. The big man was sitting on a fish crate by the busted front door, and LoJo was cleaning a cut on his brow. Tomas was bruised up, his vest torn, but he was all right. He took the wet rag from LoJo and gave his face a brisk rub, then stood up. 'Bring Ciele home,' he said, 'I'll go check Rella and then come back here.'

As soon as Tomas was gone, the two boys set off back to Mi's car and LoJo told his story, bouncing up and down on his toes, shining up the details, his hands flying this way and that as he described how he had come running back almost at exactly the time Reve had been leading Ciele and the baby away from all the trouble. Tomas was down, he said, looked like a dead man all stretched out on the track, face up. One of the uniform grabbed a can of kerosene from the Jeep, and sloshed some down on Tomas. They'd been set to burn him, burn him and the house too.

At this point LoJo stopped dead in his tracks and grabbed Reve's arm to tell him exactly what Tomas had done next. He'd just been pretending, didn't even move a stitch when the man poured petrol on him, and then more sudden than a twitch-back snake he snapped right up and kicked the can out of the policeman's hands. Sent it flying. LoJo spun his hands round and made a whistling sound as he acted out the whole scene of the flying petrol can and how it come slap down into the Jeep, and those two police standing there like they didn't know which way to turn, because they didn't expect anyone in this place to do anything except kiss dirt for them. But Tomas moved so fast they could hardly see him, like a blur, like Tom and Jerry, like nothing Reve could ever imagine. And Tomas catched up one of the uniform and swung him up high, right over his head, and he looked all set to throw that police way into the ocean.

Reve smiled; LoJo loved to tell a story. In a week's time Tomas would have grown to the size of a mountain. 'All right,' he said, putting his hand on LoJo's mouth. 'All right, but just tell me how come he done all this miracle thing and he just sitting here when I come back? Those uniform got guns and they been burnin up shacks—'

'Just what I'm tryin to tell you, Reve! You don't give a body time to say half of anythin . . . The officer step up, while Tomas got that uniform high up in the air, and the uniform threatening him with his gun, going to put a bullet right in the big man. BAM. 'Cept he didn' because the officer stop him. He say, "You, the one they call Tomas the Boxer" and Tomas say, still with that police up in the air, "I'm Tomas." And the officer say, "You can put my man down and you can go back in this place." And Tomas say, "Tha's all right by me," and he put down the uniform. And the uniform got to be carried and put in the Jeep and the officer say? "You got a good friend in that Theon," and then they gone, leavin nothing but dirt and hurt.'

'Theon guess Tomas get in trouble or he come

down and see what happenin.'

'Theon just clever, I guess,' said LoJo. 'Must have knowed.'

When they got to Mi's, the first thing Ciele asked was whether Tomas was all right and LoJo told his story all over again. Ciele was so happy she said she would cook for them all. A feast. She laughed and kissed Mayash and Mi smiled too, but even though Ciele pressed her Mi wouldn't come with them; she would stay, she had things to get ready. Reve knew there was no point in trying to persuade her and he reckoned now, with the police gone, there wouldn't be any more trouble that night. Everyone would be trying to pull things back together, just grateful that the police hadn't hauled them off to the Castle. Even Hevez would keep his head down, and then tomorrow he and Mi would be gone. He reminded her once again of their meeting place and then followed Ciele and LoJo, who had already set off back to the village.

They ate well that night. Ciele killed a chicken and Reve fetched Arella and they sat round the front of the shack and LoJo told the story at least one more time about how Tomas beat the police and how they wouldn't dare strut down Rinconda unless they brought an army with them, because now they had fear in them for what a Rinconda man might do. Tomas smiled, and that was a first for Reve, the big man never smiled, and he said that LoJo had so much talk in him he could puff up a meatball and make it sound like a feast.

It was as if the storm had blown right through and

they were all all right. Now, sitting around together, Reve thought they could almost be family. Except Pelo was gone, and Mi hadn't come back with them. Probably as well, Reve thought; she and Tomas would have made the air scratchy and sour. He wondered if there would ever be a time when they could be easy with each other. The trouble was that even when he had told her the story of their mother and this man Dolucca, Mi had just dismissed it, saying that's just Tomas's word.

The occasional person had drifted past, mostly heading up to Theon's for a drink. LoJo nudged Reve as Hevez, Ramon and Sali sloped down the track to the sea, Hevez holding the neck of a bottle loosely in his hand. The boys glanced their way, and to Reve's surprise Ramon gave him a nod of recognition as they passed by.

Reve stood up and followed them down to the bend in the track, just to check where they were going. When he saw them settling down he came back to the fire. He would check Mi later, see if she was all right.

A moment later he thought he saw Calde a couple of shacks up the way standing by another family's cooking fire. It was his shape; he looked like a squat ball of grease in the firelight and was maybe looking their way, but Reve couldn't see properly. A moment later the figure was gone. A couple of fishermen who were friendly with Pelo came up to see if Ciele had heard anything from her husband. They had a little more information about what else had happened during the police raid, who'd got hit, who'd had their shack turned over, pulled apart, who had been dragged off. At the end of it all there had been two

111

men from up the village hauled into one of the Jeeps, cuffed and driven away.

Reve didn't know the men who'd been taken, but he couldn't help wondering if it could turn out to be a good thing. 'What you think, Tomas? That lieutenant just say he got to have a head on a plate bring his captain, and he got two now, so maybe nothing happen 'bout Pelo.'

Ciele shrugged and cradled her baby. 'We still got Calde in this place.'

And then almost as if by using his name she had conjured him out of the darkness, there was Calde, smelling of sweet oil, all dressed up in white cotton, his long blade hanging by his side. Sultan lifted his head and growled.

'This a nice picture,' he said.

'No one invite you to this place, Calde,' Tomas said.

Calde ignored him. 'You a pretty lucky woman, Ciele, but I think you should take advice, these shacks here burn down real easy; all this ash and cinder floating, come down in the night, burn your place.' He looked concerned. 'Your baby get choke up easy on the smoke.'

Tomas stood up. 'You got fat grease in your ear, Calde? You don't hear what I'm sayin?'

'No one need to listen to you, Tomas. You're as good as finish in this place and you just 'bout the only person who don't know it.' He smiled. 'Enjoy your meal,' he said to Ciele and Arella. 'I'll come back and talk to you again when this old man stop bothering you, Ciele. I don' think your Pelo meant for him to be moving in on you like this. Maybe I should get him word.' He turned and headed up the main track, walking deliberately slowly, it looked to Reve, with just that bit of swagger so that blade swung out and back enough to make a body notice it, until the dark swallowed him up.

It put a stop on their evening. Tomas fell silent, eventually pushing upright. 'I need to have a word with Theon,' he said.

'Don't you go drinkin in there, Tomas,' said Arella. 'And don't go pushin that man . . .'

'Don't tell me what I should be doin, Arella. Tha's not your place.' That was the first time Reve had ever heard him speak to his old friend like that. It upset Arella, that was clear; she looked down and her mouth worked like she was wanting to say something but no words were coming out.

Tomas thanked Ciele for her meal and said she could call on him anytime she had worry. He nodded at Reve, and then as he passsed by Arella, he touched her shoulder, said her name: 'Arella.' It wasn't a question, just her name, and then he walked up the dark track to Theon's.

It was Ciele who broke the silence: 'That man done me big favour, Reve,' she said. 'And you did too. You and Tomas welcome to eat here so long as we got food to share.'

They tidied up then and Ciele put the baby into her cot and took her inside. Reve, unconsciously just like Tomas had, touched Arella's shoulder. 'Arella,' he said, 'I'll walk you home.'

'That'd be kind,' Arella said and levered herself upright.

Reve let her take his arm. Sultan got up and stretched, but Reve told him to stay. 'He's a good watchdog; bark like crazy if anyone come by your place in the night.' Then he wished he'd kept his mouth shut; there was only one man set to bother Ciele's household and he wouldn't be put off by an old dog whose only tactic had ever been to bark and run.

LoJo scratched the dog's head. 'Sure, he can stay. You coming by again?'

'Later.'

Arella didn't say anything to him on that short walk back to her place, but as he was handing her up the step to her door she gripped his arm. 'Never hear Tomas talk like he done tonight.' Nor had Reve. 'I think he got something he plan on doin.'

'Up at Theon's?'

'Yes. He goin to try teach Calde a lesson.'

'Calde got too many men! He can't go fighting in there,' Reve exclaimed, pulling away from her. 'They'll kill him.'

CHAPTER THIRTEEN

When LoJo saw Reve come back and running hard, he fell in beside him. 'What happen?'

Reve told him.

'But what can you do?'

The lights were burning in Theon's and music was jiggering out of his old monkey jukebox. They paused at the side door, one on each side, leaning with their backs to the wall.

'Don' know. Go in. Tell Theon.' Reve took a breath. 'He'll think of something. Not gonna do nothing.' He eased the door open and checked out the inside.

The place was busy, men lining the bar, drinking beer from bottles, talking quietly; standing head and shoulders taller than them all was Tomas, his vest was torn and the cut on his forehead looked raw, but he was a match for any man in there. He looked steady, even dignified, not hurrying his drink. Reve relaxed a little.

Tomas was down at the end and Theon was across the bar from him, leaning forward, telling him something.

The tables at the far side were filled with old men clacking dominoes and, through the open door at the bar's entrance, Reve could see another group at the table out on the porch, where the lieutenant had sat just that morning. Reve could see the backs of heads, and a stone jug being passed back and forth. He recognized Cesar, because he glanced back over his shoulder into the bar, and if he was there then Escal would be too, and if they were there, chances are the man paying for that jug of beer was Calde himself. Perhaps that was what Theon was saying to Tomas.

One of the old domino players called across to Tomas to join them, but there was an edge to the invitation that Reve didn't quite understand, something veiled. Tomas ignored him, and the old men laughed, cawing like scraggy birds. One or two of the men at the bar turned and smiled. Somebody mentioned Pelo and someone else mentioned his wife. LoJo muttered a curse, but it was bar talk, no harm in it.

Tomas stood there, leaning with his back to the bar, not drinking. He didn't smile; he just looked easy, the talk swilling around him like water around the pier. Then he said something to Theon. Theon shrugged and moved away and Tomas half turned and smacked his hand down on the counter so hard it sounded like a pistol shot. Everyone fell silent. 'Calde!' Tomas said loudly across that silence. 'I got business with you in here.'

If Calde was outside he didn't come running, that was for sure.

One of the old-timers leaned back on his stool. 'Hey, Tomas! Calde don't wear a skirt. What business you got with him?'

His friends laughed and another one chimed in: 'You gone call on Pelo wife yet?'

'She like the way you threw the uniform in the air? Pretty strong for an old man.'

And there was more laughter. But appreciative this

time. Tomas shook his head slightly, but he wasn't distracted by the banter; his eyes remained fixed on the doorway out to the porch.

Reve made up his mind. This was the time to go in, persuade him out of there. He took a step towards the side entrance but LoJo held him back. 'What's he doing here?' he hissed.

'Who?'

'Hevez.'

He was there at the main door. His slick hair a little mussed like he had been in a scuffle, or taken a fall. There was no sign of the other two, just Hevez on his own with Cesar a little behind him, looking into the bar, his eyes narrow, focusing on one man. Hevez turned round as if receiving an instruction from someone, Calde most likely. When he swaggered up to the bar, a couple of men moved aside. He called for a rum and held up a dollar bill. Theon shrugged and served him.

At that moment Escal slipped into the bar. Then Calde's driver, a small man with a thick moustache and a blue tattoo etched all the way up his right arm, came in behind them. Three. All looking at Tomas, and Tomas not moving but watching them as they moved over to the bar together, a little way along from Hevez.

It was like the moves in a dance, Reve thought, or when the fishing boats worked together, rounding up tuna, taking their station, waiting their time, getting ready to throw the nets.

Reve could see it was too late for him to go in now. It would make Tomas look soft and that wouldn't be good, not in front of these men.

Hevez picked up his glass and moved along till he was right beside Tomas. 'I seen you with Pelo's wife, eating her stew. Pelo know you moving in with his wife?' His voice was thin but loud and aggressive. The room fell quiet once more. Tomas glanced at the boy in front of him but didn't reply, his eyes lifted to the doorway, now filled by the bulky figure of Calde. The old men clacking their dominoes stopped their play. 'She give you anything more than her stew?'

Calde's men laughed, as did one or two more drinkers at the counter. The atmosphere felt suddenly sour and heavy with bad feeling.

'What's the matter? You need a drink of rum before you tell people what they come to hear?'

Tomas frowned as if only now hearing Hevez speak. 'What they come to hear, boy?'

It was Calde who answered this. 'Why the policeman didn't arrest you for what you done? You got some special arrangement?'

There was the beginning of angry muttering at this. Reve heard the words 'informer' and 'squeal-pig'. It was all make-believe, Reve knew that. He looked towards Theon, expecting him to say something. The only ones with a special arrangement with the police were Calde and Theon; Tomas didn't have anything to do with anyone. Theon stayed quiet, like Reve, watching.

Tomas said, 'Come here, Calde, and stop yo' play-acting – you fooling no one. You send Pelo off. You give his name to the police. Now you the one bothering his wife.'

Hevez decided this was his moment to speak out again. 'You're the one who give Pelo's name to the police, Tomas!' he said, his voice a little shrill. 'Maybe you want to tuck him out of the way, get him slapped into prison so you can chase Ciele's skirt.'

Almost lazily Tomas batted Hevez with the back of his hand so the boy and the drink went skidding across the floor. 'You should teach your nephew manners, Calde.' Hevez had twisted around and was getting to his feet, his expression pure malice. He saw Reve at the door and drew a finger under his throat, miming a knife cut.

LoJo pulled at Reve but Reve shook him off. He couldn't leave. He tried catching Theon's eye, but Theon didn't see him or didn't want to. Invisible. That's how he always had been. Theon was invisible too. Maybe that was the real reason people called him Clever Theon; he knew better than to mess with someone else's business. Reve felt sick in his stomach.

'Manners?' said Calde, taking the cigar butt out of his mouth. 'You the one with some reputation when it come to manners. Your manners make people disappear, that's what I hear, Tomas. Your manners call the police in. That where you get all your rum money from, eh, talking to the policeman? Is that your business?' He wedged the cigar butt back into the corner of his mouth; his dark bristly face was expressionless.

'No,' Tomas said. 'You're my business, Calde.' He took three quick strides across the room, so he was up close, looking down on Calde, who, a little startled by this, took half a step backwards. But Tomas grabbed him, his hand moving so quick it was a blur and then there it was, tight around Calde's stubby neck.

Reve had seen a snake do that, grip a rat by the neck, fangs digging in and the rat quivering and then still. Calde wasn't quivering but he wasn't moving either; Tomas had his thumb and the four fingers of his good right hand gripping the fat man's windpipe so tight that Calde's eyes seemed to swell up like watermelon, like they would pop from their sockets.

But Tomas had his back to the whole bar. 'In a fight you turn your back on no one.' Another of his lessons, and one that he was ignoring now.

There was faint *phht* sound, and then another, and Reve saw that Cesar had a knife in his hand and Escal had eased his way to the right and he too held a long thin blade. Hevez was up on his feet, rigid with excitement, just waiting for them to cut Tomas down.

Reve saw someone else heft a bottle, grip it by the neck.

The old men at the dominoes table quickly swept their pieces into a cotton bag and shuffled back out of the way.

'Why don't you stick him?' hissed Hevez. 'Get them all, him and that twisted witch girl on the beach.'

Reve stared at Hevez. He was as bad as his uncle! How come someone turn poison like that?

'Go on,' hissed Hevez, 'stick him!'

That was it!

You see a fight happening and you walk away. Tomas had told him that all the time when he was small. Only when you got no choice, then you do what you got to do and you do it quick. Reve wasn't walking away and

120

letting these rats do their business. He bolted into the room.

'Hey!' he yelled at the top of his voice. 'Tomas!'

The two men, Cesar and Escal, hesitated. Tomas swung round, still gripping Calde with his huge right hand. He saw the brothers moving on him and dropped Calde, who flopped down on his knees, wheezing and cursing.

'Keep out, Reve!' said Tomas, but it was too late, Reve was in the room, in the dance. Tomas grabbed him and swiftly pulled Reve in behind him and then, not waiting for the two men to run at him, he took a step towards Escal. 'You goin cut me, before all these people? You think you goin stick me, you try it now,' he growled. 'You want my back. That what you happier with?'

Escal's stupid face was blank and sweaty. He glanced at his brother, then his eyes narrowed to razor slits; the pink worm of his tongue poked out of the corner of his mouth. He lifted both hands, his left with his fingers outstretched, the right with the blade. He looked like a scorpion.

Calde coughed and hawked up spit. 'Finish him,' he wheezed. 'What you waitin for?'

Theon's voice cut into the silence like acid: 'All right, enough, Calde. This my place. You got business, you take it some place else.'

Calde ignored him. 'What you waiting for?' he said again.

Reve snatched up one of the stools the old men had been using and faced Cesar, who kept edging to the right, trying to circle behind them while Escal made his move:

he feinted to the left, then twisted and lunged. But Tomas was faster than the younger man. He knocked Escal's blade to one side and swung his left hand down like a club against the side of his head, banging him hard on the ear and sending him staggering sideways off to the door, where LoJo was watching wide-eyed.

Cesar moved. He sidestepped Reve's clumsy swipe with the stool and stepped into Tomas. And then, though Tomas turned quickly, his right arm up high, bent at the elbow, fist bunched, he was too slow. Cesar's blade caught him in the side. Tomas grunted and jabbed his fist down, cracking Cesar on the forehead, snapping him backwards, the knife still in his hand, crashing into a table before landing spreadeagled on the floor.

Only then did Tomas take a deep breath in through flattened nostrils, lower his arm and shift his weight so that he stood evenly balanced, his legs slightly apart. Blood darkened his faded blue T-shirt.

There was a half-beat of silence, with just the sound of breathing.

Calde didn't answer; he just roared like a wounded bull and launched himself at Tomas's legs, his big panga blade in his right hand, and suddenly there was mayhem with everyone shouting and cursing and grabbing bottles and chairs. A couple more of Calde's men came pushing in from the front porch, while a whole bunch at the bar sided with Tomas.

Tomas hopped clumsily over the slashing blade, kicked Calde's arm and then staggered, clutching his side. Reve edged closer to him, ducked a flying bottle and whammed the stool at a skinny dogfish of a man sneaking up behind Tomas. The man *oophed* with surprise and pain and fell back into the open doorway. Reve saw Hevez still by the bar, keeping just out of the scrum, but he was yelling and beckoning to someone at the side door where LoJo and Reve had been standing. He glimpsed Ramon and Sali standing there but making no sign of moving. He couldn't see LoJo. The fighting swirled around him and Tomas. It felt as if they were like a couple of stray fish caught in the belly of a net. Somebody whacked him in the ribs – he didn't even see who it was, but he didn't fall. 'Never fall.' Tomas hammered that one into him in every boxing lesson he ever gave. 'A fallen man just there for someone to kick.' Maybe Calde had heard the same lesson because he was on his hands and knees crabbing backwards to safety.

There was a momentary lull. Men, bloodied and wary, stood looking at each other. Fights happened in Rinconda but not here, not like this, and never after the police had spent a day kicking in doors and making threats.

Maybe people just had the need to fight stuck deep in their belly and all it takes is a beer or two and an excuse; maybe they felt that Calde had his thick fist too tight round the village, and if Tomas the Boxer was willing to step up to the plate and make a change then they would join in too.

Reve glanced at Tomas. He looked grey in the face and was swaying on his feet. Reve dropped the stool and grabbed him round the waist. If he could push his way to the door before the fighting started up again, he thought. If he could just do that, maybe he could get him down

123

to his place, clean him up. 'You'll be all right, Tomas. I'll patch you up,' he muttered more to himself than to Tomas, whose breathing was rasping in and out, like it was catching and hurting him all the time.

People watched in silence. Except for Hevez, who sneered, 'You might as well take him up the hill right now.'

Nobody laughed at the jibe.

One step and then another.

LoJo appeared, holding up Tomas on the other side to Reve, and Theon hurried round the counter to help too, making a path for them.

They were almost at the door when Theon stopped. Escal had levered himself up on to his knees and was blocking their way. He shook his head, like a dog bothered by flies, and spat out a bloody tooth. He looked up at Tomas, his face creased up and angry, and reached for his fallen knife. But Theon moved with surprising swiftness. He snatched up the knife and stood over Escal. 'What you want, Calde? You want this rat living or you want to bury him?'

Calde reappeared at the other door. He shrugged and then made a gesture with his hand. Hevez, Cesar, the man with the tattoos and a few of the others slouched over to his side of the room, and after a moment Escal hauled himself upright and staggered over to them too.

Reve didn't wait for an invitation to leave; he and LoJo half guided, half carried Tomas out into the sticky night.

'Whoa!' LoJo exclaimed, once they were out on the track. 'Never seen anything before this time. You two the men set to fight the world.'

'Oh, I done my fightin,' Tomas said, his voice so faint and breathy, they could hardly hear him. He was hunched forward, gripping his side.

'No, you like some giant in there!' LoJo's eyes were wide with admiration. He hadn't seen the knife or the wound. 'You teach me how to put a man down, Tomas? You teach me? What you say?'

'Help me get him home,' said Reve, ''fore Calde forget he got whipped.'

Tomas seemed even heavier now, a deadweight on Reve's shoulder, but somehow they managed to stumble down the track as far as Ciele's. She was standing in the doorway, looking out for LoJo, fretting. When she saw them she clapped her hands to her mouth and came running. 'Jesu Maria!' she said. 'What is it with this place!' The boys didn't say anything and the three of them hauled Tomas up the steps and into the room. They leaned him against the wall, just till they could get a bunk ready, but his legs gave out on him and he slumped down on to the floor, his legs splayed out.

Ciele sent LoJo for water while she carefully peeled up Tomas's sodden T-shirt. 'Goin have to cut this off him,' she said.

Reve turned away. He didn't want to see the wound. He felt a pain in his gut and he was suddenly aching in every bone; and his eyes burned too. They were so dry and itching badly.

He thought Tomas looked like a dead man.

CHAPTER FOURTEEN

Reve tried to ignore the blood leaking from Tomas on to the floor. 'We can't stop in this place,' he said. 'Calde goin come and cause you more trouble if he find him here.'

'Boy's right.' Tomas's voice was barely a whisper.

Ciele grunted, pressed a clean cloth against the wound to soak up the blood and then made Reve take over, keeping up the pressure while she stood up and rummaged in a tin. She came back a second later, a needle in her hand and a reel of thread, the end of which she was running through her mouth. 'That hole he got so big you push him out to sea he gonna sink.' She threaded the needle. 'Take off that cloth, Reve. Lo, I want water. And that sheet from my bed.'

They both did as they were told.

There was a tap on the door and LoJo hissed, 'Who goin come lookin so soon?'

Reve stood and silently moved to the door.

Ciele didn't even look up, just slid the needle into Tomas's skin. He breathed sharply and Ciele's brow furrowed a little. Then she started to stitch. Neither Tomas nor she made a sound. It could have been a sail she was mending.

There was a second tap at the door.

'Open it, Reve. Calde don't bother tapping like a mouse,' said Ciele.

Sultan's ears pricked up and he gave a soft growl.

Reve opened the door a crack.

It was Ramon. His sharp face shadowed, his hands held up, palms out to show he wasn't carrying anything.

Reve clenched his fists. 'You on your own?'

Ramon nodded.

Reve pulled the door back wider. He was telling the truth. 'What you want?'

'You got problem,' Ramon said, speaking quickly, that acid voice of his all washed away. 'Hevez want go burning . . .'

'This place?'

Ramon shook his head. 'He sayin Tomas – but tha's not what he really want. Hevez mostly a lot o' talk, but this time he drinkin with the men. They all tightening themselves up, you know what I mean. He'll get 'em all to run out to your sister, burn up her old car.' He glanced over his shoulder as if Hevez was standing right behind him.

Hevez would do it. And worse maybe. 'Why you sayin this to me?' Reve tried to keep his voice even.

'You done me favour. Save my brother.'

Reve studied him for a second. There was nothing soft about Ramon, but nothing hidden either, he thought. 'You didn't step in that fight?'

'Got no grief with the Boxer.' He took a step back. 'You better move fast. They not goin to be drinking their beer all night.'

Reve nodded. 'OK. How many he got with him?'

'Maybe six, I don't know, but he got that fool Escal. That man's animal; given half a chance he'll do your sister harm.' He took another step back into the darkness and was gone.

LoJo looked at Reve.

Ciele was looking at him too.

Even the dog was looking at him.

Where was safe?

The boat? Then he looked at Tomas, his back propped against the wall, his chin on his chest, eyes closed, hardly seeming to breathe as Ciele wound her makeshift bandage tight round his ribs. They wouldn't even be able to lift him into the skiff.

Reve could think of only one place.

'Pack your things,' he said to Ciele. 'Get your baby and what you need. Anything you got to take got to be light. Lo, you go round the backs and get to Theon. Say he got to have Tomas stay on his roof and you come straight back this place. Then you help your mother take Tomas there, using the back way. You do that, then you get the sail for the skiff and go to the beach. You move real fast, Lo. I'll find you at the skiff.'

LoJo looked at his mother, and when she nodded he slipped cat-like out of the door.

Sultan stretched, padded over to Tomas, sniffed his face and then came back to Reve.

'And us? You think we leave this place?' said Ciele.

'You got no choice,' said Reve. 'You want Calde visit you, you stay here. You want to stay safe, you got to go to Theon. Calde won't go lookin for you all if you stay low in the cantina and he sees the skiff gone. He'll think we made a run up the coast some place.'

'You goin to sail off?'

'No, Lo'll take the boat; I'm goin to run to Mi.'

'When you get so old, Reve?' she said. He didn't know what to say. He was just the way he was.

She wiped her hand on a wet cloth. 'It's OK, don't answer. We do what you say.'

While Ciele quickly wrapped a few things in a shawl, gathered up Mayash and settled her into a sling on her back, Reve eased Tomas upright. 'You goin have to stand, Tomas. Can you do that?'

They were helping Tomas down from the back porch, when LoJo reappeared. He took over from Reve, draping Tomas's arm round his shoulder, murmuring to him. 'Just a little way. One step. You all right?' He was so little compared with Tomas, Reve wondered whether he and his mother would manage. But they did, slowly, one step at a time, into the pitch darkness.

Over to their left he could hear raised voices, and there was that acrid smell in the air again. His stomach tightened. Six of them. What could he do against six?

Aware that Sultan was close to his heels, he stepped over the wire and cut through to the dried maize field, holding his arms up high to keep the hard stalks from scraping his face, praying that Mi was ready to leave. He would go mad if she decided to act stubborn and told him she needed to bring a whole bunch of her crazy things with her.

The maize stretched forever, that's what it felt like, shifting and rustling around him. It was just a breeze, he had to keep telling himself, not Hevez and his drinking pals on his trail.

Ten minutes later he was at the edge. He could hear the sea breaking gently on the shore, and there was the tree and beetle black hump of the car.

He stopped and called softly. 'Mi? You there?' No answer. He called again, louder this time. Silence. 'Don't do this,' he said to himself. 'Don't you do this, Mi. Don't go disappear on me!' He slipped out of the edge of the field and scuttled to the tree. Nothing. From there, he ran the few steps over to the car and tapped on the window. No response. He yanked open the driver door and peered inside. Nothing but dark. He swung round, imagining he heard the shuffle of a footstep in the sand. Sultan flopped down by his feet.

'Mi! You here somewhere?' he called a little louder, his voice cracking. 'Mi, you got to come out . . .'

Had they or someone been already? Had she been dragged off by dumb, ugly Escal . . . No. He'd left Hevez and his crew in the village. No one had come here.

'Mi?'

He was tired and finding it hard to think straight. Nothing would stick in his head, just panic thoughts flipping to and fro.

Had she just forgotten they were leaving tomorrow, that they had to meet up at the road, forgotten and just gone wandering?

No, she wasn't going to forget. Mi wasn't that lost in herself. She wanted to leave more than anything.

Or was she hiding? Something had frightened her. Yes.

She could have got a notion, one of her feelings. Hiding was good. Hiding meant that Hevez wouldn't find her.

There was no way she could have forgotten.

He remembered that she'd said to him, 'You can't mind everyone all the time.' She'd probably been thinking of him and Tomas, and Arella – she wouldn't have put herself in the equation. But this was it. She was right. He couldn't mind them all, not all the time.

And he had to meet LoJo or his plan would dribble away like dry sand through fingers. If Lo didn't take the skiff, Calde would know for sure they were all still in the village and he would root them out, wouldn't stop till he had. Reve'd help Lo get away and then come back to the car just to check . . . just to be sure.

He ran. How many times that day had he run down this beach? It seemed like he never stopped running.

Stop running and they catch you.

CHAPTER FIFTEEN

The sand was hard; every step sent a jolt up his spine. Pain was good, kept the brain from telling him how tired he was.

Up ahead Reve saw what looked like a giant insect with a long, long neck scuttling down from the wall. LoJo carrying the sail. That was also good. It meant Tomas was safe up at Theon's.

They met at the skiff and Reve explained what he wanted LoJo to do.

'You take my skiff up the coast to San Jerro. Can you do that?'

LoJo nodded.

'You find Two-Boat – anyone tell you who he is – and you tell what happen here. He'll help. And Lo, you got to promise this. You stay there till . . . your daddy come home.'

'My mother and Mayash goin be safe?'

Reve could hear Hevez and his gang now, somewhere up in the village, yelling the snatch of a football chant. Sultan growled and pressed himself against Reve's legs.

'Safer if you do this thing.' Reve hoped he was right, but he wondered how long Theon could keep her, her baby and Tomas hidden away up on the roof of the cantina. 'Theon figure something.'

'Yeah,' said LoJo, an edge of relief in his voice, 'Clever Theon always figurin. All right, I do it. And your dog?'

Reve looked down at Sultan and pulled a face. 'Take him,' he said. 'He goin be happier on the skiff than riding the truck up to the city.' He picked up Sultan, held him for a moment and then placed him in the bow of the skiff.

They dragged the boat down the beach, rigged and raised the sail. Waist deep in the water, Reve held the boat steady while LoJo scrambled on board, quickly fixed the tiller. Then Reve hauled the bow out through the low surf until the sea was up to his chest. The wind caught the sail and LoJo just had time to raise his hand before he was sliding fast away on a long reach north and up the coast. Reve thought he saw the tip of Sultan's nose up above the gunwale before they were swallowed by the darkness.

Wearily, Reve pushed his way back ashore. He could see a string of lights at the end of the village track and then a gush of flame where Tomas's hut stood. The air glowed and suddenly he could see figures running this way and that, and Arella on her porch. Sparks were spraying up into the night, and more people running, some with buckets.

It would be Mi's car next.

He could leave it. It didn't matter if it burned; she didn't want to live there any more . . . but what if she went back, just wandered back, maybe she'd had a juddering attack and her thinking was all loosened up . . .

Reve ran back, pushing himself to place one leg in front of the other, trying to ignore the aching tiredness and the sharp pain from his bruises.

Halfway along the strand he stopped to catch his

breath and looked behind him. There was a trail of lights coming this way now. He didn't have more than a three or four-minute lead.

He reached the car. He called again, and again there was no answer.

They were right behind him. He had no time to make it into the maize field.

He backed away from the car towards the acacia tree and then flattened himself on the ground just as the group came running up, torches flaring, the flames leaning backwards, like tails.

He watched them, these shadowy figures circling the car, and for two beats they just stopped, stood, maybe no one wanted to be first. The first one would be cursed; they would believe that. They were right too; Mi had a good line in curses. She could tie up a body so bad his hair would go white and his heart shrivel up like a dried fruit. That's what she said, and what a lot of people believed too.

But rum has a way of washing fear down so it doesn't mean too much. Hevez ran up to the car and banged on the bonnet with the palm of his hand. 'You there, witch!' he yelled. 'You come out. You get out now!' He ripped open the door and stuck his head inside. Then he pulled himself back and straightened up. 'She's not there,' he said, sounding embarrassed. All these men come to do terrible things, and nothing here but an old car. He kicked the door angrily.

'Burn it anyhow!' Escal shouted.

Hevez pulled open the door again and first one and

then another man ran up and tossed their torch into it until the inside of the car smouldered and then began to glow red, all the cracks around the door and windows lit like threads of phosphorous. It looked almost pretty for a moment until one of the men loosened his trousers and pissed against the bonnet.

The men whooped a little, but maybe having burned one shack already, burning an empty and wrecked old car wasn't much to hang around for, especially since they didn't have a witch to burn. He heard Hevez trying to organize them into searching for her, but they weren't interested.

'You wan' her so much, you go look for her. Maybe she in that maize field, hey.'

They drifted off back towards the village, leaving Hevez and two other boys standing back from the car, watching it pop and flame and spew up thick acrid smoke. They smoked a cigarette, sharing it between them, and then they too turned away, but instead of walking back along the shoreline, they cut up to the tree, obviously deciding to follow the edge of the field, keeping inside the low dunes that banked the land side of the beach.

'You reckon someone give her warning,' he overheard Hevez saying.

'How? We didn't even know we would do this until . . . until just, you know, down back there.' That was Sali, fumbling for words. Frightened of Hevez, Reve realized.

'Who goin warn a witch?' said Ramon dismissively.

He was cool that one, thought Reve. He risked a lot coming to Ciele's with his warning.

'Yeah . . . let's go find that old Boxer an' his

runaround. Finish it good time.'

'A'right.'

When they had gone Reve slowly got to his feet. He wondered how many people in the village had any idea what Calde's mob really had in mind when they had gone drinking and whooping down on to the shore. Would they have stayed quiet knowing they wanted to burn Mi right out of the village.

The car glowed, the salt-dry tyres smoked. Mi talked about flames sometimes, about a burning place where bad spirits scream and yell. The car looked like it was goin to that place. The heat was like a wall around the car, burning his face, making his eyes smart. Reve didn't cry. He never did, even when he was small and Mi had gone wandering off and he was on his own.

They weren't tears edging down his cheeks because there was no point to tears or to crying; no point in being soft. A fisherman deals with whatever the sea throws at him. A fisherman is on his own, hours maybe days at a time, but that doesn't bother him because all the time he knows what he has to do.

But standing there, with LoJo gone away in Reve's skiff with Reve's dog, and Tomas laid up on Theon's roof, maybe dying from that stab he got in his side, and now Mi just vanished, Reve felt about as alone as could be.

He raked his hands through his hair and forced himself to think. One thing at a time. One step at a time.

The moon hung like a claw in the black sky. Half the night had gone. It felt as if half his life had gone with it.

CHAPTER SIXTEEN

Reve cut back through the field, moving slow and careful, wriggling through wire, slipping like an eel between silent black shacks until he reached Theon's. He waited for more than five minutes, crouched down by the pig shed, looking for the glow of a cigarette, or a shadow that shifted; Calde could have men with eyes on the cantina. But nothing moved.

A few moments later he was in.

Calde and his men had nosed by, but Theon had talked them away.

Now, up there on the roof of the cantina, it was as if they were on an island, a dark ocean breathing all around them; the humps of black, the straggling reef of shacks; the glitter of torchlight, sharks drifting here and there.

Safe – just for a little while. Then up to the road, to the meeting place. He'd have gone there straight, but there was the money to collect. And there was Tomas . . .

Tomas was flat on his back, lying on a thin cotton mattress. He was stripped to the waist. His eyes were closed. Ciele had cleaned him up again and made a new bandage for him. She was now downstairs fixing a crib for Mayash.

'That was smart, Reve, moving the skiff like that,' Theon said. 'You getting to think quick.'

He didn't feel he was capable of thinking anything at all. His mind was a fog of tiredness.

'That man taught you how to fight too, hey,' continued Theon. 'Another boxer in the village maybe.'

'I don't know.' Reve turned away, uncomfortable with the compliment. He'd stepped into that fight because he couldn't see Tomas cornered like that, like when the pack turns on an old dog.

'You saved his life, Reve. And you just a boy.'

Theon had built a low cement-block wall round the rim of his roof, a little bit of shelter when a strong wind came in off the sea. He was leaning against this, twisting tobacco between his fingers, folding it into a leaf of cigarette paper, and then, when the cigarette was rolled, he cupped his hands to shield the flame, the light glinting off his glasses as he bowed his head. He inhaled and then let the smoke drift out of his mouth. Then he leaned over Tomas. 'Here,' he said. Tomas opened his mouth and Theon put the cigarette between his lips.

Tomas coughed and with a grunt lifted his arm and took out the cigarette. 'One time you said it was rum goin kill me.' His voice was a paper-thin whisper. It hardly had any breath in it. He wiped his mouth and then looked with vague interest at the smear of blood left on the back of his hand. He coughed again and closed his eyes. 'Maybe smoke do it instead.' He replaced the cigarette between his lips.

'Smoke? Calde goin finish you long before this tobacco choke you up!' Theon shook his head. 'One time you had a brain. The boy think more than you do.'

'One time . . .' Without opening his eyes, Tomas said, 'Reve, come here.'

Reve went over close to him, eased Tomas's head up and took the cigarette from his mouth. Smoke trailed upward. Tomas coughed and put his hand on Reve's arm. 'You goin then?'

Reve nodded. There was a spot of blood on the edge of Tomas's mouth.

'You know,' he said, 'I wait all my life for her to come back.' He opened his eyes. They were bloodshot and baggy, his stubble was grey and his skin had lost its sheen, the black almost as grey as his beard. 'I should've done what you're goin do. Should've gone lookin for her.'

Down on the track outside the cantina, Reve could hear the sound of men passing, their voices low – the hunt all boozed up on drink had maybe faded out now. Calde would whip them up again in the morning. Too late then; he'd see the skiff gone.

He touched Tomas's wrist. 'If you'd gone lookin, who'd've taken us in?'

Tomas shifted his head slightly so he was looking directly at Reve. 'You goin come back, Reve? Bring your mother and your sister to this place? That'd be something, Theon. Your sister queenin this place again . . .' He tried to laugh but it turned into a cough. When he had caught his breath, he said: 'But that not goin be the way, hey?'

'No,' said Reve. He waited a moment, then placed the roll-up back between Tomas's dry lips. Smoke trailed up between them. 'I don't think that goin happen. I gotta look out for Mi now.'

Tomas rolled his head back so he was looking straight up into the night sky. 'Yes. You got to do that,' he said softly, almost as if he was speaking to himself. 'Don't let the city swallow her up like it done to your mother. Don' let that happen . . .' His eyes closed.

Theon leaned over and removed the cigarette. 'Easy now,' he said with a gentleness in his voice Reve hadn't heard in him before. 'You try sleeping, eh.'

When the village was dark, and the last flames had died away from Tomas's shack, Reve went down the stairs from the roof and gathered up his bundle from behind the bar. Hiding up by the road wouldn't be comfortable, but there was a risk Calde's men would search the truck on its way out of the village, and it was easier for him to slip away now, while it was stone dark. He took his leave of Ciele. 'Pelo come back to you soon,' he said.

'Yes,' she said, 'I'm hopin.' She smiled a little sadly. 'One time you the boy always running chores,' she said. 'Now you're the one tryin to keep everyone safe. Your sister lucky she got you.'

He didn't feel lucky. He felt like they were running away because there wasn't any choice. He felt Tomas was sick and like to die.

'Here,' she said, and to his surprise, she put her arms round him and held him close for a moment. Then she quickly turned away and stepped up the stairway to the roof.

Theon pulled open the door for him. 'When you see the truck coming, Reve, you get ready; it'll slow down but it's not going to stop. Calde going to have eyes on it even if he see the skiff gone. So you and your sister, if she's there with you, just run low and the door will swing open. OK?'

'OK.' Reve hesitated. 'Why you ever work with a man like Calde?'

'People change.'

'You mean he was all right one time?'

'No, Calde was always more muscle than brain. But Tomas and me could put a rein on him back then.'

'Now?'

'Now maybe Tomas and me are different people. An' I do business where I can.'

'With the policeman?'

'If I have to.'

'An' Calde? An' Moro?'

'You're learnin, Reve.' He nodded at Reve and gently closed the door on him.

Reve found his way up to the drain by the road, but there was no sign of Mi. He forced himself not to worry. She had got herself so well hidden, she would stay put until the morning . . . but what would he do if she didn't appear then? There was no going back into the village – that would be the end of them all – but how could he go on to the city on his own, looking for his mother without Mi?

He threw a handful of dirt and stone into the drain to frighten off anything lurking, then crouched down and crawled in. He sat near the entrance, his back curved against the rough concrete, his knees hunched up. In the city there would be more ways of losing yourself than there ever were at sea.

The night was long and hard. Things scuttled in the back of the drain. Something feathery or furry touched his hand, stones rattled down the slope and he swore he heard a footstep and the grunt of someone pushing themself up the steep track. He kept so still, hardly letting himself breathe, even when a mosquito hummed in by his eyes and pierced the soft skin at the top of his cheek and drank his blood.

Maybe a rooting pig, maybe a dog, or maybe one of Calde's men with a gutting knife . . .

He didn't sleep; his eyes never closed once, not the whole night. He watched the moon as it moved step by step down through the ocean of space, like a hook, or an anchor. He watched until his eyes felt salty and burned out. And then he heard first one and then another cock crowing. Early birds. There was no thread of dawn out there on the horizon, but the cockerel doesn't get it wrong. He eased himself up and out of the drain. A moment later he saw headlights flicking on.

This was it.

'Mi?' he called softly, just in case she was hidden somewhere close by. 'Mi, you're not here somewhere, are you?'

Silence.

He felt drained, tired and like he could give up, just sit back down and not do anything, but he couldn't do that.

He had no choice but to go on his own, get Señor Moro to help him, find their mother and then somehow come back for Mi. Maybe his mother had a smart car, a good house, would know things.

He followed the lights, jinking slowly up and down and to one side and then to the other as the driver eased the truck up the broken track towards the highway. Reve hunkered down at a point where the track curved a little to the left before it pulled up on to the road. He'd be out of sight then when he made his run.

The truck seemed to take forever but then there it was, smelling of diesel and dirt, the axles squealing as it slowly rocked up to where he was. He stood and ran lightly up towards the cab. The door swung open, he caught the rim of the opening and pulled himself up and in.

'Just you then, is it, Reve?'

'Theon!'

His uncle wrenched the wheel and jolted the truck up on to the highway. 'Who else you think I goin to trust with my truck?'

'You let me drive it sometimes.' Reve couldn't help feeling some relief; at least this leg of the journey would be easier. He tried not to think about what he would do when he arrived, being on his own, in that place, and without Mi.

'So she didn't make it,' said Theon, as if reading his mind. 'That's too bad.'

Reve shrugged.

'Does her own thing. Her mother was like that. Not

all the conjuring spirits – that Macumba, Macumba. My sister, she only wanted gold.' He hummed a snatch of a song to himself. 'I kept meaning to go down when Mi was holding one of her meetings. I hear what people say – that she really got the gift. Just not steady in her ways. I'm sorry. I'll do what I can to find her.'

Reve nodded.

'She was always the strange one, your sister . . .' He broke off and stood on the brakes so hard the truck howled and screeched, juddering into the side of the tarmacked road.

Picked out in the beam of the headlights was a figure, pale in the light, skirt and top bleached to white, eyes tightened up in the glare, hair a wild halo the colour of fire.

'Mi!'

CHAPTER SEVENTEEN

Mi didn't move of course, just waited for the truck to ease up to her and for Reve to push open the door.

'I was waiting,' she said. 'Like you said I should, Reve. I remembered.' She tucked herself in beside him and stared straight ahead. 'Why aren't we moving?'

Theon pushed the old truck into gear. 'Where you sprung from, Mi? Reve thinkin you walk away on him.'

'Hiding,' she said. 'Seen that Ramon come runnin down the beach on his own and I know,' she said emphatically, 'he got a spite against me, always kickin at my garden . . .'

'Don' think so, Mi,' said Reve. 'He came an' gave warnin that Hevez mean to give you hurt.' Ramon was an ally; maybe if they had been able to stay, he'd have turned out a friend, like LoJo.

'. . . So I come up to the road an' start walkin, an' then I come back, cos I remember, ' she said, as if she hadn't heard what he had said, or maybe simply chosen not to hear it. She did that sometimes. 'The night's almost done; dark's getting thinner.'

She was right. A few moments later Theon switched off the headlights and the highway stretched ahead, a long black line pointing north and to the city.

'I looked for you down on the beach, Mi, but you'd already gone. It was bad last night. Tomas got burned out.'

'I seen the fires,' she said.

'Your old car got burned too. Hevez come down, jus' like Ramon say he would.'

Mi's expression, when she spoke with Reve, was almost always neutral, like nothing touched her, not really; now her voice seemed to shrink and curl up small. 'Why they hate me, Reve?'

Theon looked across at them, shifted gear and said, 'You're different, is all. An' . . . some people got to break what they can't have. Boys mostly.'

'Not Reve,' she said and then looked out of the window. They rode in silence for a while and then she said, 'Why Ramon give warning? I thought he the one who most give hurt.'

'I did him favour,' said Reve.

To their right, for the first hour of their travelling, was the sandy dry scrubland and low dune-like hills of this stretch of the coast. They passed a string of shabby half-towns, ribboned along the highway, stalls stocked with melon and dusty fruits. There were cafes with, it seemed, never more than one or two men sitting outside, staring at them as they trundled by. There were gas stations, each with its own graveyard of dead trucks, piles of old tyres and beaten tin roof, which, as the sun climbed higher, glinted and flared in the bright light. Everything was makeshift, unfinished and already crumbling. This is the way things were outside Rinconda, Reve thought, hardly different at all. But he liked it that the highway trailed along beside the ocean; it looked so fresh and so blue. 'Hasn't your friend Two-Boat got his place somewhere down there?'

he said to Mi, leaning across her and pointing down to a smudge of houses, white stone, the glitter of glass.

Mi started her quiet one-note hum.

'You don' wan' talk 'bout him?' Reve said, shifting back to how he had been sitting before.

She turned her head to look out of the side window, still humming.

'You different person when Two-Boat visit you.' He let that sink in. Then he said. 'You don' do this hummin. I tell you, Mi, if you go hummin next time he see you, he'll be gone for dust.'

She gave a little grunt and hummed louder. Now she was just doing it to annoy him, and she was succeeding. 'You goin stop that,' he said. 'You send Theon to sleep, and you rattle up my thinking. Why you never got any tune in you humming? You just drone.'

'Like a bee?'

'Not as pretty as a bee.'

'Maybe you sayin I drone like an old cow got sick and is looking for some grass. You think I sound like that?'

It was noisy in the cab, but Theon picked up on what Mi was saying and he laughed.

'Maybe the cow's not so old,' said Reve.

Mi nodded. 'No, not old.'

He could never quite tell with her joking, but she made him smile all the same; no one else talked like her. Seeing her like this, sitting up stiffly in the cab, gazing straight out at the long road, her head tilted a little, and the light shining in through the side window so her hair flamed, the image of the drowned woman rose up in his mind. It was almost as if she were right there in the cab. Then it was just Mi sitting beside him. He'd have to be careful with her up in the city – not to let her go wandering off.

At the next stop Theon bought them drinks and told them how to find their way to Señor Moro, pulling a slip of paper from the top pocket of his shirt. 'This what you look for.' It read: 'Slow Bar, Agua'. 'That's his place,' he said. 'And you give him something from me.' He passed over a card with a long number written on it.

'What's this?' asked Reve.

'Business. Always business, Reve, that's what come first. He'll be happy to get this, cos you goin tell him that all he got to do is come into Rinconda and ring this number, and he'll see the man who called that coastguard chopper down on him.'

'All right.' Reve took the card and the piece of paper and folded them into the back pocket of his jeans.

Theon started up the truck. 'I tell you both something. You watch for thief in this city. Thief everywhere you walk. And something else: Moro say he goin help you, he'll want something back. You be careful what you promise.'

'Not goin promise anything . . .'

Theon held up his hand to stop him. 'I know, I'm just sayin. Thing different in the city.' He hesitated and Mi, who had been sitting there not appearing to be interested in any of this, suddenly broke in.

'This man Moro another one with devil in him. I don' think we need this man, Reve. We find our own way.'

148

Theon shrugged. 'Just sayin: everyone got their own learning to do.'

Eventually the highway peeled away from the coast and the land began to look a little greener. To the west the long bank of hills sharpened, like a wall, thought Reve, like it had to keep the ocean from rolling in and covering everything. He wondered what it would be like to live so far away from water, and so high up too – you'd spend all your time looking down.

The occasional ribbon of shops and shacks along the road started to thicken, as if the city were crowding out to meet them. Deeper and deeper around them the buildings grew. It was like their village piled up tight against another village and another: plastic and tin and wood and wire, patched and tucked together, and faces watching, and people, so many people all in the one place, along the roadside and running, sometimes almost under the wheels of the truck.

Reve flinched and shut his eyes and braced himself for an accident that never came. How would they ever find their way anywhere?

'Where in all this place we goin, Theon?' It was one thing knowing that the city would be big because people told you so, but seeing and feeling all the crush of buildings and people everywhere you turned your head . . . There seemed hardly space to breathe.

'Market,' said Theon. 'This where I come get my supply for the cantina. And that's where you get down and make your own way. I'm back here this day week,

149

so if you want me, you look for me then. In the market. Sud – that's what they call it.'

'I like the city,' said Mi, her eyes gleaming and her head turning all the time as if she could somehow scoop everything into her mind. 'City got life running in it. People like fish in the sea – you ever thought that? – 'cept fish you can see. You can't see nothin when you're in that boat you got. Here, here everything is all around. We goin find her, Reve. We getting closer all the time. Closer an' closer.' She patted her knees and then turned and smiled at him. 'Trust me.'

A whole city all around them! And she thought all they had to do was get down from the truck and there their mother would be. He knew it wouldn't be like that. Whether she liked it or not, they would have to start with Señor Moro.

The truck cut through the centre, all gleaming shops and wide roads, a miracle place with people in suits and swinging skirts, carrying bags and wearing shiny shoes, and then they were in a dustier part of town. It still had high buildings, and shops, but not so smart. They wound this way and that until they came to the market itself: a sprawl of stalls and awnings, and people shovelling and shouting and haggling. Theon found a place to pull up the truck. It was right beside a wall with a poster of a man with slick black hair and longing eyes staring down into the face of the most beautiful girl Reve had ever seen.

'Here,' said Theon. 'This the place – you make sure you remember it, all right?'

A grizzled man in a battered straw hat peered up at the cab. His eyes creased as he recognized Theon and he gestured for him to get down. Theon lifted his hand, signalled five minutes and the man turned away. He looked like a farmer but where were the fields? There was no space for anything in this place, just buildings and people pushing in all around and Reve had to crane his head to see even a slip of sky.

'Reve not going to forget this place,' said Mi. 'Not with that girl on the wall. Look at him, Theon, Reve one minute in the city and he fallin in love with a dream woman! I'm goin to have trouble pulling him away from this place. Reve,' she said with pretend sweetness, 'wake up now! No one look like that in real life. She a painting.'

'No,' said Theon, 'some women can look like that.'

Mi turned away, not believing him.

Reve smiled. Mi hated being told she was wrong about anything. 'Don't worry, Mi. Only one person we go looking for. I know that.'

'All right,' said Theon. 'Remember what I tell you. You keep your money safe, and when you meet the señor, you be more careful than anything. You get nothin for nothin, in this place. He draw you in easy enough, so be watching, Reve.'

Reve nodded. He would be watching all the time.

'And . . .' Theon looked out of the window at the bustling market, like he was chewing over something he didn't know how to say to them.

Mi gave him a sharp look. 'You got something to tell about our mother,' she said abruptly.

'I done things in my time . . .'

Mi wasn't looking at him; she was staring fixedly out of the cab window at the fading poster up on the building. Reve knew she was listening though.

'Felice only ever run with the money. Remember that. She knew what she was doin when she left you.'

Reve looked at him.

Mi started her humming. Reve put his hand on hers, but she didn't stop.

'What you wantin to say, Theon?'

'Don't go expecting too much,' said Theon.

Mi jerked her hand away from Reve, pushed open the cab door, jumped down and was gone, pushing her way through the bustling market. Reve snatched his bundle with their dollars stuffed in it and was slithering across the seat to follow after her, when Theon caught his arm.

'I'm sorry,' he said, 'but you be ready for what you find. And, Reve, remember, you give that number to Moro.'

'OK. OK. Got to find her, Theon.' He didn't think she would run far, but how far did you need to run in this place before you got lost and something happened to you? He jumped down from the cab and scanned the crowd, hoping for a glimpse of her wild flame hair. Nothing.

He hadn't taken one step in the city and this was it: he'd lost her!

'Hey. Scuse me.' He threaded his way as quickly as he could down one of the twisting routes through the market. 'Scuse me. Please . . .'

CHAPTER EIGHTEEN

'Scuse! Scuse!' Right on his heels two half-pint street children in surprisingly clean white vests were grinning and one of them was mimicking him. 'What you got, country?' said the slightly taller of the two. His teeth were white and his eyes were shining, and he was dancing up and down on his toes, bobbing like a boxer ready to duck and weave any which way. The other child was darker-skinned, flat brown, and hair so short Reve couldn't tell if it was a girl or a boy. Girl, he thought, maybe. She stood behind the boy and looked at him out of solemn eyes.

Then, as he watched her, she slipped back into the crowd, leaving the first child slinging all his patter at him. 'Where you from, country? You got some place you gotta go? You lookin lost as city chicken. You lost, country? I show you. I know the way round every place. You ask anyone. I know most thing 'bout any place.'

Reve tried to keep looking for Mi, but the boy was distracting him. 'I don't need nothing,' he said, trying to push him to one side.

'Don't push, country. Don't push me, 'less you want to fight,' and he even put up his little fists bunching them up near his face. 'I could be a fighter. I could be Cashew Clay. You hear of him, country?' and he darted in with one little fly punch. Even though Reve was worried about Mi, he couldn't help smiling, but as he made to step round this half-size street champion something collided into his back and threw him off step. At the same moment his mocking assailant skipped to one side and snatched his bundle from where it was slung over his back, then slipped like a rat between a mountain of grain sacks and carts stacked up with onions and bright yellow peppers.

'Hey!'

Reve dived after him but lost his footing and fell flat on his face. No one paid any notice, just kept stepping by and around him. He scrambled back to his feet and caught a glimpse of the little girl-boy looking solemn-eyed at him, before disappearing again but in the opposite direction to the way the boy had taken. How could he be so stupid, and so clumsy?

And all their money! Everything gone and he hadn't got down from the cab five minutes. How would they get to Moro or survive long enough to track their mother down? Mi was going to rage at him . . .

He scrubbed his head, frantic; should he follow the boy, or go in the direction the girl went?

He started after the girl and then pulled himself up. It was a trick. She had reappeared so that he would do just that, follow her and then, no doubt, he would end up miles from the market and completely lost. They wouldn't want him chasing after them here, because this was their patch. This is where the fast-talking boy would be, already tucked in somewhere, checking what Reve had wrapped in the bundle. Stick around long enough and he would see them both again, he was sure of it. Meanwhile he needed to find Mi.

Reve squeezed past the cart and the grain and, knowing there was no point in running, he walked as swiftly as he was able down an alley of stalls, sidestepping vendors, drunks and lounging young men in jazzy shirts with hair oiled and spiky. He looked left and right, keeping his eyes skinned.

Out of the corner of his eye he saw a brown ankle and a scuffed trainer sliding in under a stall, and quick as lightning, as if he were snatching a slippery jackfish out of the net, Reve grabbed and pulled out a child who immediately yelled and cursed him so violently and loudly that the stallholders came to the child's rescue and Reve had to back rapidly away.

The market was so big. It seemed to stretch on forever, and nothing was in straight lines. He tried to remember particular stalls, but they were all food or grain or coffee and there seemed to be a million faces, dark and sweating, wide-eyed and dark-haired, shouting and jostling and he couldn't even remember where Theon had pulled up the truck, and he couldn't see the wall with the picture of that beautiful woman on it.

Where was Mi?

He was feeling dizzy and it was so hot the air was thick in his lungs. There had to be a tap or fountain maybe or ice . . . He found a fish stall, and when the vendor was busy he scooped out a palmful of ice and ran round a corner and then wiped it across his face and dabbed his neck, and slipped a smooth icy pebble into his mouth, closed his eyes and let it melt down his throat.

He took a deep breath and tried to think straight.

You don't just sit on a boat and expect something to happen; you look for the place where the fish run; you watch the sky and the way the wind moves across the water; anything else is blind sailing, and a blind sailor only ends up one way: drowned. He looked around him. The only way to see anything in this place was to get up on something and look down.

He found a flatbed truck whose driver was unloading sacks. He offered to help and the man, already drenched in sweat, let Reve climb up beside him. He worked there for twenty minutes, scanning each quarter of where they were every time he straightened his back. The last sack was bundled down, and the man said, 'You don't work like a city boy that for sure. Here –' he pushed a dollar into his hand – 'Ask for Cedo any Friday and I'll give you work. Wha's your name?'

'Reve . . .'

At that moment, he heard shouting, a high-pitched whistle, and then, about a hundred metres down to his right, he could see a surge of people and red, he was sure of it, a fuzz of red hair. He leaped down and ran, ducking and weaving, until he got to where the commotion was. He burrowed through a wedge of backs and shoulders and there was Mi, head back, hair sticking right out like she had an electric storm ripping up from her skull. Her eyes were rolled in that way that scared Reve because it meant she was having one bad juddering fit, and sure enough she was, trembling and her arms stretched in front of her and all her fingers out tight.

The man in uniform, the one who had been blowing

the whistle, was trying to take her arm and lead her out of the market, but she was rooted. He would have to carry her if he wanted to move her any place.

'Excuse me,' Reve called. 'Excuse me, sir.' He remembered Tomas saying anyone in a uniform, no matter how low down he was, liked to be called sir, and it didn't cost you anything to say the word. 'She my sister. This happen to her times. I'll take her, sir.'

The uniform looked down at him. 'You prove it? You got papers?'

Papers? He didn't have thing other than the dollar bill he'd just earned, and he wasn't giving that away.

Someone in the crowd came to his rescue. 'Wake up officer, can't you see this boy just in from the country? What paper he goin to be carryin?' The speaker was a large woman and her large arms were folded imposingly across her large bosom.

'I got my job here . . .' the policeman tried to say but she just huffed at him.

'Let the girl go, she sick; got a fit on her is all.' The crowd murmured their agreement.

Reve came up close to Mi and touched her arm. It was rigid, all the muscles locked and trembling. He needed to get her out of the crowd and out of the sun. 'My sister sick, sir, an' she get like this sometime. I need to find her a quiet place. Please.'

The policeman scowled. 'Well, your sister made me lose a thief. I had my hand almost round his neck but then she made all that yowlin and . . .' He threw up his hand angrily. 'Oh, take her out of here! Before

157

I march her straight to the Castle.'

'Why don' you march you'self off cos you don' do no good roun' here!' And the large lady swung herself slowly round and forged her way back through the laughing, crowd, which then dispersed. The policeman turned on his heel and walked off.

Reve stroked Mi's neck and talked to her. 'You all right now, Mi. Nothin happen to bother you now. I got you . . .'

Gradually her arms relaxed and her breathing slowed and her eyes closed. She shuddered once and let Reve move her slowly through to the back of a stall where there was a little shade, and no people milling around them, and there was a box he could sit her down on. 'You all right now, Mi. What happen to make you like this? You give me enough fright to put me in my grave . . .'

'Gave me fright too,' she said. 'Felt myself stuck in that place where there nothin but voices screamin at me.'

This is how she had once described it to him: like being trapped in the middle of a storm of noise and shouting, sometimes voices, sometimes just noise. 'What tip you this time?'

'Him,' she said.

Mi lunged forward, straight past Reve, so fast, like a snake strike, and had the small boy gripped by the arm.

'That's him! He the one who thief all my things!' exclaimed Reve. 'Took all the dollar we got!'

The boy was wriggling like a fish, but Mi had him fast, her mouth set tight and her jaw jutting with determination to keep a hold of him.

'You let me go!' The boy suddenly flopped to the ground, but Mi was ready and dropped down with him.

'He thief from you . . . well, this one owe me favour,' she said, dipping her head to one side and studying her catch. 'That police was goin snatch him but I started shakin and shoutin so this boy could skip free. Didn' like that policeman pickin on a child . . .'

'You put that judderin on! I thought you took bad.'

'It turn real on me,' she said with a shrug. 'Got myself stuck.' She gave a rueful laugh. 'That happen sometimes.' The boy had stopped wriggling and she let him sit up. She still kept a hand on him though. 'Maybe you come back to thank me,' she said to the boy.

'No,' he said glumly. 'She made me come back.'

'Who she?' asked Mi.

Reve saw her, the girl-boy with the shorn head and solemn eyes, peering at them from the corner of the stall.

Mi took her eyes off her catch for a moment to look around at the girl. 'You always do what she tell you?'

'Course not! You goin let me go?' exclaimed the boy angrily.

Mi released him and he dusted himself down, fussy as a church lady.

'You got my dollar and T-shirt and things?'

'She put it safe.'

Reve looked at the girl and she silently held out his bundle. He took it from her and checked. All the money was there. 'How old are you?' She looked about the same as the boy. How could children so young run free and not get lost in this place?

She shrugged.

'Doesn't she talk? Don't you talk?'

'When she want,' said the boy carelessly. They were a team, that much was obvious.

'What's your name?' said Mi.

'Baz.'

'I give her that name.' The boy puffed himself up. 'I can do that. Give name for anything. But I real best at other thing. I just about the quickest pair of hands you ever seen.' He flashed them under Mi's nose, wriggling his fingers, so she almost smiled.

'The uniform still caught you, eh? Even with your magic fingers,' said Reve.

'What you say, country boy? He only caught me cos o' her.' He nodded at Mi.

Mi looked surprised. 'Me? How come I got anything to do with your catchin?'

'Cos you look like someone.' The boy shrugged. 'Tha's why I stop.' He slapped his knee and turned to his partner, the little girl. 'Never stop when you makin a run, Baz, you remember that.' Then he got to his feet and so did Mi.

'I know that already,' said Baz, and she went and stood beside the boy, and the two of them looked at Mi so steadily that Mi half turned her head away.

'Stop your staring.'

'Not just your hair,' said the boy. 'You got the face too.'

'Got my own face,' said Mi. 'Don't belong no one else.'

Baz tugged at Mi's wrist. 'Come with us – we got someone to show you.'

Mi's eyes lit up with sudden interest.

'No!' said Reve.

'Come,' insisted Baz.

Mi frowned.

'We agreed,' Reve said. 'We don't wanna go wanderin', Mi. We do that and we never find her. We got to follow what we agreed . . .' He kept his voice low and gentle. 'I mind you all the time, Mi, you know that. Come on, we do it my way.'

Mi turned her face away from him.

'I the one who seen the woman in the sea. She come to me . . .'

'Where you got to go?' said the boy suddenly. 'I know every place. You wanna go somewhere, I take you there.' He shrugged. 'Only fair after what you done,' he said to Mi.

'What's your name?' said Reve.

'He's Demi,' said the girl. 'That's cos he's half of nothing.'

The little puffed-up boy, Demi, made to kick her but she slipped easily out of range. 'And you a monkey shadow,' he said.

'An' if I'm the shadow, you the monkey.'

Baz's face stayed solemn all the time, though Reve could see this was a game they played, the two of them, all the time, banter and tease. He couldn't talk like that with Mi, she would crack like a bowl, leave nothing but splinters digging in his hand. He almost envied these two children – half his age and yet he got the sense they knew exactly how to deal with the life they'd been given. They didn't seem worried, not by the people they thieved from or by the threat of the man in uniform; just water off a gull's back.

'We looking for a man who own a bar in Agua. You know Agua?'

Demi glanced at Baz. 'Course we know that place. Who the man you got business with?'

'Moro.'

'Yeah,' he said carelessly, 'we know that man.'

Baz's eyes seemed to have grown rounder as she stared at them. 'Why you got to see him?' she said.

'Listen to her! She too full of question. You mind your business, Baz, you know that. Come on – we can take you to Agua. We don't want to do nothing more here.'

Before anyone could disagree with him he set off. Baz skipped to catch up with him and Mi and Reve followed behind.

'You really think this man will help?' asked Mi.

'Said he would. It goin give us a start, Mi, tha's all. Point us to the policeman, Dolucca. Moro goin to know how to find that man. Then we find her.' It sounded easy when he said it like that.

'Won't it be fine when she see us and take us in, Reve?'

He hesitated. 'Yes.'

'We goin to see the Night Man in the daytime. The world all upside down in the city,' she said, and she took his hand – something she had never done before.

CHAPTER NINETEEN

The two children were like fleas, hopping this way and that, skitting between cars, slipping through crowds, leading Reve and Mi away from the market area, down a rumbling throughway steaming with trucks and buses and then on to quieter streets. All the time the girl, Baz, kept looking back at them, checking they were there. Sometimes, Reve noticed, she pulled at Demi, making him slow down and wait for them.

At the corner of a street called Tombre the children shouted at them to run just as a dusty red tram came hissing down beside them. They did, but when Baz and Demi swung up on to the back rail and hung there like a couple of spider monkeys, Reve and Mi fell back. They couldn't do that. How could they, cars and motor scooters going this way and that? It was all too much. They slowed to a walk, catching their breath, and decided all they could do was follow the street in the direction of the tram.

Baz and Demi were waiting for them at the next stop. 'They got no tram where you come from, country?' Demi asked. 'How you get 'bout a place 'less you can hop a tram? You two so slow seem like you walk backwards all the time.'

Baz told him to mind his manners, but he just wiggled his fingers under her nose and said, 'I got magic fingers. I don't need nothing 'bout manners,' and he sped off again.

They did catch a tram, but at a stop this time, and Reve paid the fare for all of them: four to Agua, and they sat and watched the city stream by. It was only a few stops and Demi told them that what they were seeing was the river side of the city. All the smart and shiny shops were up near the city centre, but they weren't allowed up there, he said. They needed to practise their skills more. They had a teacher, he said, and this was the person he wanted to take them to. Their teacher told them where to work. The market was good for them, Demi said, because they were so small. He said this with pride, as if being small was something he had designed himself.

After about ten minutes the tram swung into a huge square. There was a fountain with a big pool round it; the stone was grey but the water splashed and looked like silver in the sunlight. The whole square was drab, with tall narrow houses on one side, with some of the windows boarded up, gaps in the tiles and a thread of tiny alleys leading away into whatever lay behind. There were a few shops, but they didn't seem to sell much that anyone would want, and there was a street market at one corner and a few bars near where the trams and buses pulled up; but the fountain was something special – neither Mi nor Reve had ever seen anything like that, water pouring up into the air in the middle of all this hot, dry, hard stone city.

The children jumped down ahead of them and ran to the fountain and splashed their faces and each other. 'You can drink it,' said Demi. 'It's a'right – don't make you sick or nothing and you don't pay for it. 'Bout the only thing that don't cost.'

They cupped their hands and drank; it tasted of metal but it was cool, and both he and Mi were so tired and hot and hungry that it was good to run that water over their wrists and splash their faces. But Reve was cautious all the time, and he saw that Mi was too. He liked these two children; you couldn't help but like them, but he didn't trust them. Not really. He kept his bundle close and he eyed the end of the square with the bars. That was where they had to go next.

'You sure that man goin see us?' Mi said, brushing down her ruckled skirt and then giving her knee a good scratch. 'I don't think he even goin recall who you are, Reve.'

'Most people not like you, Mi; they got memory for things. Come on. You ready?'

'Wait.' She kicked off her sandals and dipped her feet one at a time into the cool water, then made a business of drying them off with a strip of yellow cotton she unwrapped from round her waist.

'You ready yet?' he asked again.

'A'right,' she said.

The two children had their heads together. 'You still sure you want to go there? We don't like that place too much. He come where we live, give people hard time unless they pay him money.'

'Call it rent,' said Baz. 'They call it rent, Demi. It happen all over.'

'Don't matter what they call it; still him taking money

165

an' . . . other thing too. You got any place you can sleep? We can show you place you can sleep won't cost you much dollar. You got anywhere?'

Reve looked up at the sky; it was well past midday. 'We don't need to think about that yet,' he said. 'We go meet the man now. You don't have to come with us. It's that one there, isn't it?' He pointed to a bar where he could just pick out the sloping letters of the name 'Slow Bar'.

'You got seein eyes, country.'

There were two lizard-like men leaning up against the wall by the entrance. One was chewing on a toothpick and the other's face was a mask behind a pair of dark glasses. They both wore black and the one on the right with the toothpick had a whirling pattern of tattoos etched into his shaven head and down both arms, purple lines against his dark skin.

'We lookin for Señor Moro,' Reve said. He tried to make his voice sound sure and steady, like he would speak to Theon. 'He in there?'

They didn't even look at him.

'What you want, Demi?' said the man with the toothpick, chewing it over to the edge of his mouth before speaking. 'I don't see your Barrio Mama holdin your hand.'

Demi stuck out his chest. 'I here on business; delivering these people.'

'Oh,' drawled toothpick man, 'deliverin, that right? That not your usual business. She do the deliverin most times.'

'Not what you think,' said Demi, a little less confidently this time. 'We just helping. They come see Señor Moro.'

The second man tilted his head a little, the better to study Reve and Mi, though Reve sensed his eyes were just on Mi, in her little patchwork skirt. He didn't like the way these men looked them over like they were meat or something, but he said nothing.

'You takin over business from the old lady?'

'She not old,' said Baz firmly, speaking for the first time.

The second man laughed. 'Hear her speak. Didn't think that little spike had words.'

Reve had had enough. 'You goin let us through?'

Tattoo stood to one side. 'Free country,' he said in his mocking drawl, 'free entry. Maybe cost you to come out, specially your girlfriend, unless she happy to give a little favour here,' and he patted his cheek.

Mi stalked past him and entered the bar and Reve quickly followed. He just heard Demi cheeking the man as he was goin in: 'You think any right mind person want to catch disease from you, you got less brain than you got hair and that not sayin too much.'

Reve glanced over his shoulder before the door swung shut behind him and saw Demi and Baz dancing backwards with the tattoo man making a dash for them but giving up after only a few paces – with legs half the length of his, the children were too quick. Reve wondered if he and Mi were going to have to learn to be as fast as them.

The room was gloomy, the lights gauzed in something

blue that made what light there was seem cool, a little like being underwater. There was a man at the bar leaning on the counter, smoking, eyeing them and two women in skirts so tight Reve didn't see how they would be able to move from the stools they were perched on. Down at the end of the room, in a corner, were two figures; he couldn't make out their faces. Their heads were close together, like they were praying, or planning something too secret for the barman to hear maybe. There was the thumbprint glow of a cigar being sucked on.

Reve felt his chest go tight and he hoped that when he spoke his voice wouldn't shake. It didn't usually even when he got angry, or had to face down Hevez. But this was all different.

Mi moved a little closer to him. 'You talk to the man, Reve,' she whispered. 'You can do that. You know what to say in a place like this.' He couldn't think why she said that; it wasn't as if he'd ever been in any bar in his life, other than Theon's cantina, and that was as different to this as shark to jackfish.

'We don't give nothing to children in this place,' the barman said.

Reve believed him, but he hoped that maybe 'nothing' didn't include a bit of information about the policeman who took their mother. 'Is that Señor Moro down there?'

The barman looked at him a moment. 'It is.'

'He told us call by here,' Reve said, which wasn't strictly true, but he didn't want this man taking it into his head to throw them out before they even got a chance to speak with Moro. Mi was standing so close her shoulder touched his.

'Wait.' The man slapped up the hatch in the counter and walked through and down the room.

The figure with the cigar looked their way and the barman beckoned them down.

'Who this then?' The voice was an ugly growl like he was trying to be some old dog, though Moro didn't seem that old to Reve. His face was smooth and he smelt of sweet soap and cigar smoke and he was dressed just as he had been down on the pier, a shiny expensive-looking suit over a working man's vest. It was as if he wanted to show he had money but he didn't care too much about it. His eyes were keen and he looked at the pair in front of him without saying anything for a moment. Then he smiled. 'You the boy!' he exclaimed and smacked his hand down on the table. 'Zavvy, this boy look a little skinny but he got the *cojones* of a bull, I tell you. What's your name, boy? I forget. And who this you got with you? Come here, girl! Let me see you what you like.' He leaned back and switched on a side light. Mi didn't move.

The man he had been talking to, Zavvy, had a narrow face and oily black hair slicked back into a ponytail that tipped the collar of his jacket. He looked at Mi and Reve but said nothing. He had a fat ring on his left little finger, and Reve wondered why a man would wear a ring. There was something about him that unsettled Reve; he had a strong feeling that this was someone who scuttled in the shadows, not in daylight; you wouldn't see him in normal time, doing ordinary things, like hauling a skiff. Whatever business Moro did with this man, it wasn't anything that Reve wanted to know about.

'My name is Reve,' said Reve, knowing that Mi wouldn't do anything this man said. It was up to him to do the talking and find out what they needed. But somehow, because Zavvy looked so sinister, Reve found himself speaking to Moro with greater confidence. 'You said I could call on you for favour, Señor Moro.'

'Did I?' Moro looked amused. 'And what kind of a favour would a boy from a nowhere fishing village and his pretty girlfriend want? You looking for a job maybe. I could find a job for someone like you, Reve.'

Reve took out Theon's card with the number on it. 'I got to give you this. Theon give it me to pass on. Whoever call up the coastguard the night we got the boats runnin in use this cellphone.'

Moro took the card. 'So,' he said, 'Theon give you this?' He laughed quietly. 'I love these small places. Everybody scratch to make a living, scratch out anyone who step in your way,' he said, more to himself than to Reve. He put the card down on the table in front of him and then looked up at Reve. 'No hurry, Zav, eh. We find Calde's squeal-pig in our time. No one go anywhere from that place, except this little bull and his pretty friend. So why you come here, boy?'

'We come lookin for our mother.' Reve tried to make that sound matter-of-fact not like they were lost or a pair of babies.

Moro exhaled and a heavy pool of cigar smoke hung over the table at which he and his companion were sitting. Moro raised an eyebrow. 'And?'

'She go off with a policeman. Eight year ago.'

Moro leaned back and let a stream of creamy grey smoke filter out of his mouth. 'Yes, I remember Calde telling me 'bout that now. That's a long time, eight years. I don't have all this business eight years ago. Eight years is a long road, almost a lifetime in the city. Maybe in eight years you could be sitting here, boy, in my place!' He laughed. 'You thirsty? She thirsty.' He snapped his fingers and the barman came down to them. 'Beer? Something stronger?'

Mi shook her head.

Reve hesitated. 'Water,' he said. 'Thank you.'

Moro nodded. 'Careful and respectful. I like that. Very good. Now, this lost mother – how you think I can help you with this? Sometimes I make people go missing; I don't go looking for them.'

Zavvy gave an oddly high-pitched laugh and Moro smiled as if he had said something witty.

'And your father? What happen to him?'

Reve hesitated. 'He got killed.'

'Oh? By your mother, maybe?'

It wasn't true, not really; Moro was playing games. Reve didn't respond, but he felt Mi tense up beside him. Zavvy laughed again.

'Or maybe that policeman . . .' Moro pulled a face. 'Bad things happen,' he said. 'I'm sorry.' He didn't sound particularly sincere. 'And losing a mother is a bad thing all right . . . whatever she done. But –' he shrugged – 'one policeman. One woman. Is this all you can tell me?

'The policeman carry the name Dolucca,' said Reve.

171

'Maybe important man now.'

Moro leaned forward, suddenly fully engaged. 'Oh! Captain Dolucca. You are right; he is important. A big man in the city. I make business with him, but . . . he is not a man you can trust. Who can trust a policeman who has power, eh, Zavvy? But if we know that man is carrying secrets, well then maybe we're the ones who can make him dance the way we want.' Moro slapped his hand on the table and laughed – 'Captain Dolucca, well, well. This is good – very good!'

'It would be useful for you,' murmured Zavvy, leaning a little towards Moro, 'to have knowledge about the Captain. Hmm?'

Moro laughed again. 'Of course.' He tipped the ash of his cigar into the palm of his right hand, looked at it for a moment and then dropped it on to the floor. 'And the woman, your mother, she stay with her policeman?'

Reve shook his head. 'Don't know.'

'You goin to tell us her name?'

'Her birth name's Felice.'

Moro pulled a face. 'That don't mean nothing to me. No one get call Felice in this city – that's country name. She ever get call anything else?'

Reve looked at Mi. 'Santa Fe,' he said, remembering what Arella had told him, how she'd always wanted to go north, look for dollars.

Moro gave a grunt, or maybe it was a laugh; Reve couldn't tell. 'Santa Fe, not many saint in the city.' He paused, letting smoke curl up from the corner of his mouth. 'But I know someone carry half that name. She nothing to Dolucca, not now, but maybe there's history there.' He looked at Mi, standing there, her head bowed, staring at her toes. 'Lift your head, girl,' he said. 'Let me see your face.'

Mi looked up at him and then quickly away as if his eyes scorched her.

'Maybe this girl's not your sweetheart, eh?' he said to Reve. 'Maybe she your sister.'

'Yes,' said Reve.

Moro suddenly became more businesslike. He pushed the stub of his cigar into an espresso-sized cup and let it sizzle and die. 'We can do business. This woman with the half-name, maybe she your missing mother. I help you find her and we see!' He patted Zavvy on the shoulder. 'If you stay at the centre, my friend, all things come to you . . . a beautiful woman, a murdered husband, a young policeman . . .' He pushed the cup with the stubbed-out cigar a few inches across the table, then moved a glass up beside it on one side and a coin on the other. 'When you put pieces together like that, you get a picture. And a picture always tell you something.' He laughed and then he said, 'I think I bring all these pieces together.' He nudged the glass against the cup. 'Make a family: the Captain, your lost mother and you. How 'bout that?'

Moro raised an eyebrow when Reve didn't answer. Then he shrugged and turned to his companion. 'Did I tell you, Zavvy, about this boy? When we have that business with the coastguards, he was like a little bull. And then he walk right in my door! Very good. I like that. And,' he said, switching his attention to Mi, 'Reve's sister. You look like this woman, I think. He doesn't, but *you* do. Maybe you are like her. Hmm?'

Mi looked at him. 'Where is she?' she said. Her face was completely without expression.

Moro smiled. 'She is close by. Leave this with me. I will make a meeting.' He pushed the table away and stood up. 'Come, I will show you something Reve-from-the-village-of-Rinconda, and I will show you too,' he said to Mi.

'All right,' said Reve, taking Mi's arm, feeling her initial resistance. Then she allowed him to lead her and they followed Moro out through a door at the back of the bar and up first one and then a second and then a third flight of stairs. This man was not so hard to deal with. Reve could ask about Pelo, find out for Ciele.

Eventually they came out on to a flat roof space. They were high enough to see the city stretched around them. Higher buildings, some of them domino blocks of glittering glass and steel, crowded in behind them, cutting their view of the centre; before them was Agua, with its fountain now diminished, the size of a bottletop in Mi's crazy sand garden, and beyond that the ragged-looking older mansions that faced the eastern side of the square. 'Behind them,' said Moro, 'is the Barrio. You see?'

They saw a tangled patchwork of crumbling buildings cramped around by an unsteady sea of tiny roofs tilting in every direction and little thread veins wriggling into the distance; alleys maybe wide enough for two people to pass by each other, Reve guessed. Not so different to Rinconda, but bigger and with all the air squeezed out of it. At the edge of this sprawl was a wide brown river. It was hard to see if the river was running or whether that colour was from mud. The Barrio looked like a trap, a place you would get lost in.

'All that you see down there don't look so much, eh. What you think?' asked Moro.

Reve didn't know what to say. 'I don't know.'

'That place is my business. Where you got people, you got dollar. That's a lot of people down there; a lot of dollar. And I tell you something else – this woman you looking for is there.'

Their mother, in that place! His heart sank. To live in there you would have to be a crab, scuttling from one hole to the next. She never found her gold, her Santa Fe, that was for sure.

'You know, for me,' Moro said, 'for me the Barrio is like a garden, a business garden.' He paused and stood there silently for a moment, looking down across the tangled ripple of roofs and alleys. 'If you hungry enough I can give you more than anything you goin get in your no-place village.' He placed a large hand on Reve's shoulder. 'I got no family, bull boy . . . What you think? You want to make good money? Easy money? I'm offering you something here.'

Money. Yes. They would need money. If he had a job then perhaps they could find a place, not in the Barrio but some other place, and their mother would come to them . . .

Before Reve could answer, Mi, who had been fidgeting beside him while Moro talked, suddenly erupted. 'No!'

175

Moro ignored her. 'Think what I'm sayin.'

'We got to go!' Mi said, and started to pull Reve towards the doorway. 'Reve, come!'

Reve shook her off angrily. You got to think about offers. Theon always said business should come first. 'I'm sorry, tha's just the way she talk.'

Mi made an exasperated sigh while Moro smiled. The sun was dipping below the tall buildings behind them, throwing long shadows across the roof. 'You have somewhere in the city you can stay?' Moro asked.

Reve shook his head. He never got the address from Theon.

'No? I can give you a room right here.'

Mi gave Reve's arm a pinch that made him suck in his breath. 'We got friends,' she said and started to hum, little staccato bursts, like dots across the air.

Moro laughed. 'Tha's good,' he said. 'All right, you go to your friends. But remember, Reve, you got a friend here. All you got to do is sign on the line . . . that's just a manner of speaking. You make sure you come back. We goin wrap this up – the great Captain Dolucca and your Santa Fe. I can fix all this tomorrow. But don't you go in the Barrio on your own, trust me. Come back tomorrow. Any time. I get someone take you in there, find this woman.'

Reve felt Mi shudder beside him.

'All right, but we got to go,' Reve said apologetically. 'She get unwell. It happen when she go stressin.'

Mi jerked at his arm again.

'But we come back, señor.'

Moments later they were down the stairs, and with

Mi all the time leading the way, still humming and loudly now. She could be so annoying, fuzzed up his thinking; he hadn't asked the señor half what he wanted to. 'I didn't say nothing 'bout LoJo's father. Could have done that, Mi. That man can do thing for us,' he said, clattering down the stairs after her.

'Wha's the matter with her?' said the barman. 'She soundin like a fire alarm.' Zavvy was still at the table, staring at them as they ran down the bar, Mi leading.

They burst out through the door, running past the lounging lizard-like men and into the square. They didn't stop until they had reached the fountain, where they stood breathing heavily. Reve was facing Mi, his hand gripping the sweaty bundle with his money in it; she was looking away from him, hands at her side but clenched into fists.

'You embarrass me,' said Reve. 'You know that? I never been embarrassed before, but I know what it is now! And you done it, Mi.'

The humming was gone, but her eyes kept flicking away from him and back to the entrance to the Slow Bar, as if she were expecting those men to come running right after them. She pulled a face and squeezed her eyes shut, like she was trying to push something out of her mind maybe. Then she puffed out her cheeks and exhaled. 'And you don't know who you been talking to?' she said. 'You telling me you don't know him?'

'Who is he then, Mi?'

'Devil is who.'

CHAPTER TWENTY

A siren wailed, a thin, twisty sound that seemed to come snaking their way.

'Devil?' exclaimed Reve. 'The devil don't help; he get in the way. He strut like Calde, swagger like Hevez. You make no sense!' Then he looked away from her, angry at himself and her. What were they doing? Running from Rinconda, running to this place!

'You think that man, that man in there, just want to do us favour?' she said, still agitated, still looking back across the square to the glinting pale blue light of the Slow Bar, as if she somehow was expecting a long arm to come snaking out of the door and snatch them back.

Two hundred metres away, the two lizard-like men still lounged against the door. Señor Moro had no intention of chasing him and Mi.

'No. I don't know. Maybe.' He twisted the neck of his bundle. 'But even if you right, Mi, 'less we get help, we goin nowhere.'

She turned and looked down towards the opposite side of the square to the tired old houses that fronted the Barrio. 'We goin there.'

The sun was low, the square almost empty; an old lady in black threw breadcrumbs down for pigeons. A couple hurried by, heading for the tram stop, each of them pulling a suitcase on wheels.

'We step in there and all we goin do is get lost. You got to let me do the leading.'

'No! That man playin. He got a devil in him, Reve, I swear. I hear it in his voice. He want to pull us in, like fish on a line, Reve, you know. We keep away from him, and I tell you all we got to do is go looking for our mother in that place. People goin to know her. She got hair like mine, look like me. We can, Reve, we can find her . . .'

He suddenly realized he was exhausted, and hungry, and Mi probably was too . . . and Theon had warned them.

Then the sun was down, and though Agua had a scattering of street lights the darkness suddenly thickened around them. 'All right,' he said, 'we find somewhere for tonight, go looking tomorrow. Can't stay here like a pair of fat pigeon for anyone to knock down.'

'I'm not pigeon,' grumbled Mi but she agreed they couldn't stay there or go wandering in the Barrio, not in the dark, so they bedded down in a doorway of one of the empty buildings, on the Barrio side of the square. Reve used his bundle as a pillow and leaned up against the side of the doorway. Mi sat beside him, her arms clasped round her knees, her back straight, and though Reve couldn't see her face, he knew her eyes were open, like his.

On the far side of the square, the blue lights of the Slow Bar rippled in the darkness and made Reve think of the sea.

There was traffic: trucks and coaches rumbled by, cars too, but not so many. The tram ran till late; all those

179

people, faces staring out and not seeing them, rolling on with their lives.

It must have been late in the night when it fell quiet, as quiet as a city can get. There was always that rumbling in the distance, sometimes a voice shouting out, or a car door slamming. Hardly anything drove by their side of the square, except for a police van which rolled slowly past about every thirty minutes or so, a torch beam playing along the pavement, poking carelessly at windows and doorways. But though the light once woke Reve as it slipped over his face, the van never stopped.

Reve woke, his neck aching and his arm stiff from the weight of Mi leaning on him. However, it wasn't that that made him open his eyes but someone easing his bundle out from where his shoulder was pressing it against the wall. His eyes were gummy with grit and tiredness and blindly he tried to grab at the thief.

The someone skipped back a pace and, as Reve struggled to sit up, shove Mi off him and focus, a small boy grinned at him. Demi!

'Jus' testing you, country,' he said, his eyes wide with pretend seriousness. 'I bet you got something fat an' easy for pickin in here.' He jigged up and down on his toes and shook Reve's bundle by his ear. The girl was there behind him like his shadow. 'They's caterpillars, all wriggled up like that,' he said to her, and his face flashed a grin.

Were they serious? Robbing him and then just standing there to mock!

'What you know about caterpillar? You only know about dippin yo' hand and talking bigger 'n you are,' she said. 'Give it back.' She was very still, so different to him. It was as if he wanted to be noticed while she would prefer to be invisible.

'Give it back, Demi.'

Demi danced off down the pavement and then stood there about fifteen paces away from them, like he was wanting them to give chase.

'What's he playin?' said Mi grumpily. Her hair was squashed all over one side, her legs were scuffed and dirty and her skirt crumpled.

'He can't help it,' said Baz.

'Someone goin teach him, then,' said Reve. He wasn't going to have some half-pint thief steal a whisper from him. Not this second time. No. Reve didn't get cross, not really, but in the city everything seemed set to spike him up.

He didn't reckon he would have too much trouble catching Demi, even if he was fast on his feet.

He was wrong.

The thief gave a yip of delight and sprinted along the edge of the square with Reve after him and gaining, so Reve thought. Then Demi glanced over his shoulder, saw Reve on his tail and he gave another yip and spun like a top, dancing off down a slit of an alley. The change in direction was so swift and sudden that Reve, pelting after him, skidded past the entrance and had to turn back on himself. He saw Mi starting after him, but the girl was holding on to her arm, slowing her down. He couldn't wait and started down the alley, surprised how dark it was, and how narrow, and it twisted too. Run a little crooked, he thought, and he would scrape his elbows against the wall. He couldn't see his thief, but that just spurred him to run faster.

The alley spilt into another, a little wider this time. There was wire mesh overhead and sunlight filtering down through rubbish and plastic caught up on the wire. He blinked, paused to catch his breath and make up his mind which way to go. The light was strange, the way it came through the wire, dappled, flickering in his eyes, like being underwater, and the air was heavy too, and thick in his lungs. He wiped his face and looked right and left and realized he was already inside the Barrio. People lived here all pinched together; there were doors ajar and he glimpsed faces looking out. There was the smell of cooking, and the sick sweet smell of waste.

'You seen a boy runnin?' he asked a skinny stick of a man with his white hair tied back with a bootlace.

'Boy always running,' the man said unhelpfully, his words jerky and strange-sounding to Reve's ears. The man stepped back inside his place and pulled the door tight.

The alley split into three; each way looked the same to Reve.

'Reve!'

He looked back the way he had come and saw Mi and Baz coming after him. Mi was smiling.

'Wait here,' Baz said. 'I tol' you he just playin. Want you to follow, tha's all. You don' need go runnin. I'll get yo' thing back.' She trotted off down the middle alley.

'I got a feelin, Reve! I really got a feeling 'bout this. Feelin we almos' there! This is it!' She squeezed his arm and put her lips up to his ear, as if she was going to tell him a secret. 'You know what that little girl tell me? You know this place they take us to? This someone they want to take us to, the one who teaching them things, you know . . .' she could hardly get the words out straight she was trying to talk so fast. They were tumbling from her mouth. 'This someone . . . I tell her who we lookin for, Reve. I tell her she call Santa Fe, and I remember the devil man say a woman here got half that name. Half that name, that's Fay, and she say, Baz say, tha's who we goin to! Tha's who we goin to! This like when I hear thing and it turn true; like you see the woman in the sea and it all come to meaning this thing that happenin now! You bring us here, Reve, and now we goin home, cos Baz and Demi tol' Fay 'bout us, how they seen me and I got fire-red hair . . . .' She held him tight, her arms holding on to him as if he might disappear at any second. She never did that. Never hugged him. He gently pulled himself away.

He couldn't believe what she was telling him. In all this place! Two little street children who happened to live with their mother . . . 'Mi, you sure 'bout this? That girl could be telling thing that you want to hear. You know, tha' happen when you come to the city. You got to be careful cos people tell you thing—'

'She tell the truth, that little girl. I know she tell the truth. I can tell.'

'Hope you're right, Mi.'

'I'm right! I'm right! I'm always right, Reve.' She laughed excitedly. 'We almost there, almost home, hey. What you think our mother goin say when she see us, when we come walkin in through her door? I think she goin want us more than anythin, hey. I think she goin tell us all 'bout everything. You think she'll cry? People cry when they happy sometime. I seen that. I don' cry. You don' cry. Don' recall you ever cryin, Reve; even when you nothin but small, you got a serious face, most serious face in Rinconda . . .'

She was so happy, but all he could do was shake his head. He leaned against a wall and closed his eyes. This was not home, and it was certainly not a place to get lost in. He wondered how long the children would be before they came back to them.

He opened his eyes, about to ask Mi whether she really trusted these two children when he realized that straight opposite him a sallow face with oil-black hair and a droopy moustache was staring out at him. The man smiled and his teeth were long and yellow.

Two doors further along, a young man stepped into the alley, tight black jeans and pointy white shoes. He flexed his fingers and then buttoned up his shirt. From somewhere behind this man Reve could hear the sound of a woman crying.

The man opposite with his wolf-like smile was still looking at him through his glassless window, and nodding his head. Come on in, he seemed to be suggesting. Come on, country boy, bring your sister with you . . .

Reve pushed himself away from the wall and stood by

184

Mi. A moment later Baz reappeared with his bag in her hand. Behind her was Demi. He grinned and shrugged his shoulders. 'Thought you goin be quicker on yo' feet, country.'

Baz handed him the bag and Mi jumped to her feet. Reve checked the contents and slipped the money into his back pocket. 'A'right. Thank you, but you . . .' he said to Demi, 'you don' touch my things again. You hear me?'

Baz looked at him with her solemn eyes and Reve felt as if he had done something wrong.

Demi laughed. Nothing seemed to bother him.'Come on,' he said. 'Everyone follow me. I take you see Fay.'

The two children led them further into the Barrio.

On a boat you got the coast, or you got the sun. You have something to tell you where you are, but here in this place, where every alley runs around on itself and is tangled up worse than an old net, you have nothing.

They reached a dead-end courtyard with a grey wall on one side, mounded up with rubbish and bones and something wrapped up in a stinking old carpet piled on the top of it. Opposite was the back of a building with a domed roof, bleached white by sun and neglect. Stone steps led up the side of this wall. 'This a good place if you get lost,' said Baz. 'Hey, Demi?'

Demi shrugged like he didn't care what she showed them.

'Me an' Demi come here. That wall's a bad place, but up on the roof is good. No one ever go there.'

They followed her back out of the courtyard and on. East, Reve reckoned, though he wasn't sure. Baz and Demi walked quickly, turning left, ducking right, never hesitating until they suddenly burst into a little group of young men squatted round in a circle, playing dice for dollars.

One of the men looked up. 'Hey, Demi, what's this?' He eyed Mi. The others stood up.

'You bringin in country guests, Demi? You know you always got to pay, if you bringin in guests.' The young man was a good bit taller than Reve, but skinny.

'These two friendly with Señor Moro,' said Demi importantly. 'You got any business, you talk to him.' He sauntered on and the others followed him. Reve tensed and put himself between Mi and the men, expecting the rest of the little crowd to move on him right away. But they didn't; they shrugged, backed off. One of them said mockingly, 'So you got the señor's favour, Demi. You goin be king of the Barrio?'

'Tha's me,' said Demi.

Demi led them on through the maze, ducking through a gap in a wall, up a ladder and across flat crumbling rooftops, down again, and then over a series of dry ditches. 'Your sister goin to do real good in the city. Fay say pretty girl's like gold mine, almost much a gold mine as me. I can conjure thing out o' thin air like a magic man.' Then he blew on his fingertips like they were so hot they had caught fire.

Baz snorted. 'Only thing you conjure is fat-nothin air comin out your mouth.'

Mi seemed nervous but excited too. She didn't seem to mind the way they were getting deeper and deeper into the maze, but she kept a tight grip on Reve's wrist. 'You ever think of getting married, Reve?' she asked him.

'Where that come from, Mi? What you thinkin? No, I never think 'bout marryin.'

They were close to the river now and the land was all bristly, stump grass and baked mud that hummed with flies; it smelt bad too, like something had died and been left to rot in the sun. The river itself was nothing but a thin slide of water over mud.

'That's our place, up at the top.' Baz pointed to a derelict warehouse two storeys tall, perched out over the river.' She'd stopped beside a wide ditch, rank with greasy sludge. A couple of railway sleepers served as a bridge.

Demi ran ahead across the bridge, skipped up some steps that were down at the end of the building and disappeared through a battered galvanized door into the warehouse.

'You think we got problem if we go in this place?' Reve said to Baz.

She looked at him and bit her lip. Her eyes were round and dark; he found it hard to match her quiet gaze, and she was only half his age. 'What problem?'

'Come on, Reve! What you sayin?' Mi flapped her hand, as if he was just another pestering fly. 'We're here! Baz, can we go see her?'

Baz ran across the old rail sleepers, Mi followed, hands out on either side to balance and Reve came behind. Baz pushed open the door. 'Our place is on the top,' she said again.

*

A makeshift ladder led up to the next level, a wide dirty space, concrete dust, rag and plastic littering the floor. It smelt sharp and sour. The air was heavy with it. Reve thought that the smell could just be lifting off the river. The place needed a storm, waves coming in off the ocean, give it a chance to wash clean. Why didn't anyone clean here, pick up the rubbish? There was money in plastic, or Theon wouldn't pay him.

There was another ladder and another floor and then a darker space with no windows, and a door that the little girl knocked on. Three sharp raps and then she pushed it open and went in.

Mi looked at Reve and then she took his hand and they went in, stopping just inside the door. The air was fuggy, and though there were windows, they were so smeared and grubby that the sunlight had trouble cutting through the glass and throwing a dirty square of light into the centre of the room.

CHAPTER TWENTY-ONE

'This them, eh?' The voice was husky, like it had been dipped in smoke and rum, or like maybe it had come out of the back of a dream.

Mi squeezed Reve's hand. The woman was sitting at one end of a table on the far side of the room. Her hair was a stormy tangle, and yes, it burned a little like Mi's. Reve stared at her and wondered if this could possibly be their mother. She wasn't so old, wasn't young either. Her face was pale, not like anyone from the village; she wasn't dressed like a village woman either. She had a white shirt, man's shirt, and creamy stained jacket, the sleeves rolled up just to her elbows, and she was wearing trousers. There was a bottle in front of her, and a saucer, black with butt ends. She was smoking a thin black cigar.

She was like a faded-out memory of the woman he'd seen down in the ocean. That was it. Nothing more than that. Reve felt a moment of disappointment, but more for Mi than for himself. He had never had Mi's conviction that somehow they would find their mother and then everything would be all right. This woman didn't look like she could be anybody's mother.

There were a couple of children over by the window and a little boy, as young as Demi and Baz, sitting down on a mat, watching a streaky black-and-white TV. A girl, about the same age as Mi was tending a pot bubbling over a stove. She didn't look at them. Whatever she was cooking was more important than a couple of stray blow-ins.

'Well, step in. No one goin bite you here. Let me see what my clever children brought, brought in for Fay to take a look at, just like I ask.'

Demi was grinning. He looked so happy, Reve reckoned, that if he'd been a dog he'd have been wagging his tail so hard it would have spun him right round; Baz didn't show anything though. She had slipped over to a corner, as if she wanted to disappear.

Mi tossed back her head and stuck out her chin, like the way she did when she was ready to face a storm or cut words with someone maybe ready to give her trouble. She gave his hand a little tug but Reve held her back. He felt safer by the door, in the shadow. She was trembling, not so you'd notice, but he could feel the tremor in her fingers.

'Why you change your name?' asked Mi.

The woman didn't answer, but her hand paused for a fraction as she was lifting her cigar up to her mouth. She sucked in smoke and then puffed it out sideways, half closing her eyes as she regarded them. 'How long you been in the city?' she said. 'Look like no time to me; you got country writ all over you.'

Demi nodded his head vigorously. 'S'what I said, Fay.'

She ignored him. 'And you got the señor expectin you – tha's what he tell me,' she said. 'Called me up all in a worry you get lost in the Barrio. He didn' want that. Didn't want that at all. Told me to find you an' bring you in.' She exhaled lazily. 'What you say to that man? You got something special, child?' Her attention was all on Mi. 'You got somethin that man want? Maybe you different from the ones he usually got business for.'

What did she mean by that? What business? It was him the señor had wanted to offer a job to, not Mi. Sweat dripped down his neck but he felt suddenly cold. Why was this woman leaning forward and peering at Mi as if she were something that maybe could be bought or sold?

'Come a little closer,' said Fay. 'Step in the light.'

Neither of them moved.

Why had Señor Moro called this woman? Reve remembered the way Moro had looked down from the top of his building out over on the Barrio and now he imagined him throwing out strands of web like a spider, winding a strand round them and dragging them back. Theon had warned them. He had said that if Moro offered anything, he would want something in return. Was it really Mi he had plans for?

Why hadn't Baz or Demi said anything about his call?

Reve felt as if he and Mi had stepped blindly into a trap. He glanced at Mi, but she didn't have eyes for him, just for the woman.

'Why you change your name?' Mi said again. 'Why you don' tell me that?'

Fay tilted her head to one side, like Mi did sometimes, and took another pull on her thin cigar.

'You sayin you don't know who we are? Or why we come lookin?'

The woman gave a short laugh. 'My name Fay, all

the time. You can call me that if you got business with me. And you here cos my Demi bring you in,' she said, patting Demi's arm.

Mi tightened her grip on Reve's hand.

'He lead you by the nose,' continued Fay, 'tha's why you here. The señor got his intentions for you. I don't need to know nothin more 'n that.' She sucked on her cigar. 'Why do we do things, Demi?'

'Business, Fay,' piped Demi.

'Business,' she agreed.

Reve noticed Baz looking at him and Mi, and then at Fay, watching them all, her eyes round and dark and her face still and serious. Those children had brought them here because they had been told to, not for any other reason. Señor Moro told this woman, Fay, and she told her runarounds. That was it.

'You got no memory then?' said Mi stubbornly. 'One time you carry a different name and before you go running up to the city . . . You got no recall of that?'

'Different name? Everyone carry different names in this place.' Fay flipped out a cellphone and checked a message. The phone's light made her face sharp and hungry-looking. 'You boyfriend and girlfriend? Bit young, the boy, eh? I can find you better boyfriend if you want, someone with a little spending money . . .'

Reve couldn't take his eyes from her. Didn't like the way she smoked and looked at them as if they were some funny thing the tide had washed up. He didn't like it that she and Señor Moro seemed tied hook and line. 'Mi,' he said softly, giving her hand a tug, 'she not the one we

192

lookin for, Mi. This not the place. We back up a little, eh?' It wasn't safe.

'No.'

'What you sayin to me?' said Fay, her voice still husky but with the warmth stripped out of it. 'People been tellin you things?' She ground her cigar into the overflowing saucer. That somehow was like a signal because the two children, Baz and Demi, slipped behind Fay; one on the left, one the right. 'Cat got your tongue?' she said. 'You got nothin more to say? Course you got thing to say. So come on, come a little closer now. You half in shadow; come up here to me. Step in the light like I tol' you.'

Mi let go of Reve's hand, smoothed her skirt and took two paces forward into the dirty square of light. 'We come looking for you,' she said; her hand go up to her hair, pushing a strand away from her eye.

Reluctantly Reve moved up to be beside her and for the first time he felt Fay's eyes on him, eyes that widened momentarily as her gazed flickered between him and Mi, and when she spoke there was a sudden note of uncertainty, a slight tremor, like the first ripple of wind on a still sea. 'That right?' Fay said. 'Someone tell you 'bout me?'

Reve saw that little Baz sensed the change too. She looked up at Fay and touched her arm.

'We told that Señor Moro we lookin for someone,' said Mi, 'and he said you might be that person.'

'Did he?' She was staring at Mi and her thin, pale face looked touched with red. 'Why'd he do that?'

Mi was staring right back at her. 'Don't you know who we are?'

'Where you say you come from?'

'Come from a village on the coast,' said Mi, 'and we lookin for a mother we had, a mother who run off on us, years back. Mean somethin to you now?'

Fay sat very still for a long moment. Then she pulled a face and shrugged. 'That place got a name?' she said coldly.

Mi's trembling was clearly visible now. 'Called,' she said. 'A place called . . .'

'Rinconda,' said Reve for her, putting his arm round Mi and holding her tight. She told him one time that when her trembling was this bad it was like a weight, a stone slab pressing down on her, bringing dark into her head and then the voices would start up. 'We didn' mean any harm comin here. Yeah. We make a mistake comin here. Mi, come on.'

With an effort she pushed him away. 'No!'

The woman sat back in her chair. 'What you want with this mother you lookin for? No one come lookin for someone 'less they want something. What you want?'

'You don't know!'

'I got children looking all the time for this person or that. Children no one want. You nothing special here. What you expect? You expect a little free this, eh? A little free that? Where do money grow, Demi?'

'It don't grow on a tree, Fay.'

'It don't. So what you expecting, girl, you and this boy here? And mind you don't go makin thing up. I don't have time for lying children! Tell you that for nothing. Demi, ain't that the truth?'

194

'Truth, Fay,' said the little thief.

'Truth,' she echoed.

Reve took half a step back. He saw that Baz was still watching him; she didn't miss anything. He wished Mi would give up.

'We not the ones tellin lies here,' said Mi.

'Mi,' said Reve, trying to get her attention. 'Come on now.' He pulled gently at her arm.

But Mi didn't come on. She started to judder. Her fingers were stretched out tight and a moaning sound was coming out of her mouth.

'Stop that!' snapped Fay. She looked at Reve, as if he was responsible. 'She crazy, that girl? She sick? What you do bringing a sick one here, Demi!' She stood, pushing her chair so savagely it spun back, clattering to the floor. Both Baz and Demi flinched away from her, as if expecting her to lash out.

'I just done what you asked, Fay,' said Demi. 'S'all I done. You said bring them in. You said the señor was lookin for them and we'd make money, Fay . . .' The words tumbled out of him. Baz remained silent, looking at him.

Mi's moaning was like the sound a person makes when they have all the air sucked out of them after a belly punch.

'She's not sick,' said Reve. 'She just get this way when—'

'I know how she gets!' shouted Fay.

How did she know?

'I know what you both are; and I don't care. You hear

195

me? This is my place! You don't belong here!' Her words rasped like nails across the thick air, and her eyes were wet stone, cold, hard and blind. Like she saw them but not them, not him and Mi but some other children that she didn't want, didn't want at all. 'I am not the person you looking for. She long gone. She don't exist any more. You understand? She walked out of your life and you better off without her!'

Her face was a tight white mask; she looked like some bad-dream woman; nothing, nothing like the woman in the ocean. He wanted to move, but he couldn't. Mi was trembling worse, her legs locked straight, her head tight as a snap-line quivering in a gale. 'I'm giving you one chance, you hear me? You leave this place; you go. You find your way out of here. Go on back to your village. Go!'

'Fay!' said Demi. 'You can't let them go! The man said he wanted them here. He said—'

The back of Fay's hand caught Demi with a hard smack that sent him staggering back, one hand clutching the side of his face, the other out to stop himself falling. Baz's eyes widened but she never said a word. 'Out!' Fay said again, glaring at Mi, as if Mi was the horror. 'I got no place for you here! You hear me?'

Reve could see a vein on her neck thick as a worm. He pulled Mi, pulled her back through the door. 'Come on, Mi, down the stairs. Please. Come on! We got trouble here.' He begged and urged and guided her down the ladder, half expecting this Fay to burst out of the door and come raging after them, or call up people even worse than her, people like he had seen staring at them in the Barrio, young men who would tear into them like dogs.

But there was nobody waiting for them outside and no sound of her gang scrambling down after them.

Reve took a deep breath of Barrio air – anything was better than that sour den. He felt shamed and his eyes were hot. But they were out now and away from this woman, this one-time mother. This runaway mother. This woman bitter as smoke, who'd shouted them away like they were stray dogs. They were wrong to have gone looking for her. He took another breath.

'Are you a'right, Mi?'

She didn't respond so he put his arm round her. He could feel her still trembling badly so, gently, he guided her to the sleepers where they could cross the ditch. The sooner they could put distance between them and this place the better they would both feel. But when he tried to lead her over the little makeshift bridge, she twisted out of his grip and stood facing the old blistered warehouse, her arms tight at her sides, as if to clamp herself together.

'You got nothing!' she screamed up at the building, at the woman she had thought would embrace them, her voice all ripped and raw. 'You got nothing!' Then she began sobbing and her eyes were squeezed shut, but in between the sobs she still shouted: 'I see you! I see you! I see what you are! You devil woman! You tangle up with so much bad thing . . . You got a devil eatin you. An' you try burnin us out of your heart, but all you got now is nothin, nothin . . .' The stream of words became choked by her miserable sobbing, and then she retched into the ditch, gasping and coughing up spit and tears.

Reve put his arms round her again and held her tight until the weeping died away and her eyes were no longer rolled up white and frightening, and the trembling had eased. He held her like that even though he still half expected Fay or her gang to come skidding and sliding down that ladder from her lair. 'You a'right?' he said gently. 'Can you move? We got to go, a'right?'

She was breathing hard, gulping in the sticky air.

'Mi, you a'right now?'

She nodded and he felt a wave of relief. His deepest fear was that one time she'd have such a storm inside her it would take her right away and he would never get her back.

'We goin now,' he said.

'A'right.'

He led her back over the makeshift bridge, trying to remember the way they had come, hoping to find somewhere they could hole up and hide before someone come looking for them. He imagined Fay, calling the señor on her cellphone, shouting at him, shouting at the children in her den.

How had it happened like this? One thing after another: the woman in the sea and then nothing but one storm rolling into another, the one Mi had seen coming.

They ran.

Had he been able to see back in the den, he would have been surprised. The woman, Fay, wasn't shouting and raving; she wasn't on her cellphone. She was sitting right

198

back where she had been when they had gone in, her face pale and drawn, and though her eyes were dry, they were stretched and full of hurt. Baz was beside her, touching her arm. 'You got one of your bad spiky feelings, Fay?' she was saying. 'That what you got?'

Demi was over by the window, sitting up on a ledge, hugging his knees, not looking at anything, just hugging his knees tight.

CHAPTER TWENTY-TWO

They ran.

For more than ten minutes they ran, cutting across the ditches, the patches of scrub, before threading back into the twisted and steaming alleyways of the Barrio. Then when Reve sensed Mi couldn't run any further they took a break, leaning up against a wall.

Where would they go? Reve wondered.

There were people all round them now, eyeing them and passing them by. But Reve reckoned it better to ask no one, not in this place. He tugged Mi's hand and they moved on, turning left, turning right, winding their way back into the heart of the maze.

'You got any feeling which way?' he said to Mi.

She shook her head and looked down at her feet. A moment later she said, 'You the one, Reve, out in the sea. No road signs there an' you manage.'

'An' you the one who pull sign out of the air, tell people what goin happen. You pick the way, Mi.'

He was trying to tease her a little, but she looked utterly beaten. He'd not seen her like this ever before. 'I got nothin right,' she said. 'Didn't know she goin blind us away, pretend not to see who we are. Didn' know that goin happen. I read your dream woman wrong, Reve. That bit you say about her waving her hand? She just waving us away, even though she know who we are.' Her voice was flat.

'A'right,' he said. 'We go this way.'

They came to a corner kitchen with a large fat woman standing in the doorway, her arms folded. They had passed through this place before, he was sure of it. The smell of frying clawed up his belly, telling him he hadn't eaten all day. He stopped and Mi stopped beside him. The woman looked down at them. 'This a payin place,' she said.

Reve rummaged in his pockets and pulled out a few coins. Fifty . . . sixty cents. He didn't want to spend more. He didn't know how long they would have to survive on what little money he had. The woman looked dismissively at what he was offering.

'Where you from? You want a charity kitchen,' said the woman, 'you go find a church.'

'Where that?'

She looked at him as if he was some poor dog with only three legs. Then abruptly she turned and went back into her tiny place; it looked so small as if she would hardly fit inside, she was so big herself.

He turned away, giving Mi a tug, but they had only taken a couple of steps when the woman called them. 'Here.' She held out a corner of bread and piece of cold sausage.

'Thank you,' said Reve.

The woman shook her head. 'Don't come back this way, and you take that girl of yours out of here.'

'Which way we go?'

The woman looked at him with incredulity. 'You want me act like some tour guide! What you think this place is?' She waved her hand, 'You go on out of here. Give my kitchen bad name having beggar children crawling on my step.'

Reve ducked his head. 'A'right,' he said turning away. 'We're goin.'

They set off again. It was a narrow alley, a slip of dark with wire overhead, and it seemed like he had been down it before. They pressed on and then came to the courtyard with the outside stairway, the place that Demi had said was safe. Reve led Mi up to the domed roof with its little flat edge, like the turned-up rim of a priest's hat. From the top they could see lanes and alleys twisting around away from where they were like dark veins running through the body of the Barrio. To the east were the backs of the tall buildings that lined the square where he and Mi had spent the previous night. There was no traffic in the Barrio, and though he could hear people, voices, sometimes shouting, sometimes at their work, it seemed strangely quiet after the constant blur of traffic out on the streets.

They would be safe enough there, could rest a little and eat the bread. He pulled Mi down and then leaned against the dome and he broke the bread in half and gave her her portion. It was dry but not too bad and the sausage was good. He gnawed at it and then realized she wasn't touching hers.

'Come on. You got to eat.'

She turned her head and spat – blood.

'You bite the inside of your mouth again?'

She shrugged. 'We ever goin get out of this place?'

This place.

'It make you want the ocean, Mi. Make you think Rinconda something better 'n this,' he said.

When she didn't answer he turned and saw tears running down her face, streaking through the grime; he didn't know what to say.

'Hey, we make a mistake, got taken in by a couple of slither-back thieves, and that woman nothin to us, Mi. Nothing. I tell you, she not even a dirt shadow of the woman I seen.'

He didn't know what else to say. They were alone in the city. Theon wasn't due back for another six days, and the only place they knew was the Slow Bar. And they had to keep well away from there; away from Moro with his smile and his hand on Reve's shoulder while all the time what he wanted was Mi. Reve was sure of that now. Maybe he wanted to give her to that strip of grease from the bar, the one he called Zavvy.

'We'll find some place safe. Don't you think about her,' he said. 'She never anything to us—'

'No. You wrong, Reve. She the one. That woman birth me, birth you too, and I don' know why but she don't want none of us.'

The way Mi remembered their mother all those times she talked about her, she was like light shining in through a door, a voice laughing and singing. She wasn't that any more; she was hard, cold and dark. That's what Reve felt.

Mi pulled a face. 'Something make her ugly inside.' She sniffed and wiped her forearm across her face. 'Hope it don't happen to us.' Then she looked around. 'I see nothin, now. Nothin. Got no feeling about which way to go . . . no feeling what to do 'bout anything.' She sounded exhausted.

He felt like he had a rope knot tied up in his belly.

'An' the people in the village, comin out more an' more, askin question 'bout this, 'bout that, like I got the answer to everything. I'm runnin dry, Reve. Sometime words come in my head, sometimes the well dry as bone. Tha's what it feel like. An' I got more comin at me . . . the boys in the village. All the time . . .'

She was so slight, skin, bone and air, like a bird, shadow bird. 'Hevez.'

'Him,' she agreed. 'He's a whole streak of nothin. Dog in the dirt.' She frowned at the food Reve had put on her lap and absently started to eat it. Tearing at the sausage, little bits and then hungrily, till it was all gone. 'A girl should have a mother tell her about what comin round the corner; tha's what a mother does.'

'Other people you can ask, tell you thing.'

She didn't respond, just sat hunched up; skinny arms hugging her skinny self, chin resting on her bony knees.

He felt she had turned so small he could almost lift her up, rest her on the palm of his hand. He sat back down beside her. 'We find our way back, Mi. We find a way round these things, nothing so bad we can't find a way round it.'

She leaned her head against his shoulder. 'I feel I taken us a wrong way, Reve. Got a bad feeling . . .'

'Shh,' he said. 'We stay here for a little. We safe here.

Wait for the sun go down. Then we can move, find our way to the market, find a truck goin our way, ask for a ride. We can do that . . . or I find a little work in the market, earn some dollar before we go back . . .'

They slept there on the roof, leaning against each other. When he opened his eyes, the sun was low. Down over that half-dried-out river long shadows were creeping across the Barrio; heavy purple clouds were piling up on the horizon. He frowned. Storm cloud. He wondered if it would just sit out there on the coast or move inland. His neck was stiff, and Mi, light as she was, felt a dead weight on his shoulder. She was muttering in her sleep, frowning.

'We been lookin for you.' Baz was standing at the top of the steps. 'Fay told us we got to find you.'

Reve didn't move for a moment. 'Why?'

'Señor Moro looking for you and your sister. Got his men in the Barrio and out in the streets. Fay want you out the city to where you come from. She don't want you go with Señor Moro. You know she shout sometimes, but she don't mean what she say to be so bad.'

He eased his arm out from behind Mi, wiped her damp forehead with the tip of his T-shirt and then stiffly got to his feet. He leaned over the parapet, looking down into the shadowy courtyard.

'I'm on my own,' the girl said.

'A'right.'

'Where is Demi?'

'Looking for you.'

'But you found us.'

'Yes. I'm good.'

'How old are you?'

She shrugged.

Mi woke and sat up. When she saw Baz she looked puzzled. 'You come to take us back? Fay change her mind, want to give us to the señor?' she said, sounding like she'd chewed on something sour.

Baz shook her head.

'Why that man Moro bother with us?' Mi said. 'We nothing to him.'

'Fay don't tell us thing like that, but . . .' Baz hesitated as if she was about to say something else about Fay, but then this solemn little girl just said, 'I'm goin show you the way out of the city. You coming?'

They followed her down from the roof. Outside the courtyard she put her fingers to her lips and whistled, high and piercing. She stood for a moment, listening. A half-moment later they heard another whistle, answering hers. She made them wait in the shelter of a doorway, and then a couple of minutes later, Demi came running up to them.

CHAPTER TWENTY-THREE

There was a short exchange between the two children. Demi clearly saw himself as the boss and didn't like Baz making the decisions, even when she was right. He blustered and bounced on his toes while she stood quiet. 'Why go that long way?' he said. 'Fay say take 'em out quick; nothing quicker than Agua, skip a tram out to the quarter. Take no time. Your way we goin be duckin and hidin all night. You want that?'

'Safer. Señor got shady men looking a'ready.'

'Baz, you so full of worry you fill a worry bucket. Come on – we go this way.'

He set off, and after a moment's hesitation, first Baz, then Mi and Reve followed him. They wound their way quickly through the alleys.

Ten minutes later they were at the foot of the cut that led up to Agua. 'See?' Demi grinned. 'Nothin hard when you follow Demi. Tram we want is up on the west side; if we run I bet we catch one right now . . .'

'Check no one waiting on us up there, Demi. Go on.'

'Me? I'm not—'

'Go on.'

He pulled a face and went. They watched him run up to the corner, stop, look left and right and then beckon them.

They were on their way home. These two could take them to the edge of the city; then they would catch a bus back along the coast. Theon would figure a way of dealing with Calde. Tomas would be stronger . . . That was it. A day at a time and let the storm blow itself out.

He took Mi's hand. 'You all right?' The air seemed even heavier and stickier, if that was possible, and the brightness had gone out of the day. The light felt yellow and a black cloud that only a little while ago was hanging on the horizon was now sweeping inland.

Mi didn't answer for a moment. Then she said, 'I think we should be runnin, Reve.' They were just up at the corner and she suddenly took off along the edge of the square, moving fast, Demi sprinting to catch up. Reve cursed. Why did she do these things?

And then he saw the car.

It came squealing across to the cut where Baz and Reve were standing and slammed up on to the pavement right in front of Mi and Demi. Three men piled out. One grabbed Mi, and though Demi was fast, spinning around and taking off back down the pavement, the men were fast too. One of them caught his arm and swung him off his feet. Demi skidded across the pavement, managing to break the man's grip, tumbling in a ball. Then he was up again, jinking round the second man and flying past Baz and Reve. 'Go!' he shouted at them. 'They comin on my heel.'

Baz was already running, but Reve was rooted to the spot. He saw Mi tumbled into the back of the car. The man that had started after Demi pulled back. 'Get you next time!' he shouted, and snapped his fingers. His companion laughed and they swung back into the car, which bumped off the pavement, its tyres squealing on the hot tarmac as it accelerated away, screeching around the fountain roundabout, then down the east side of the square, and pulling up with a jolt outside the Slow Bar no more than three hundred metres from where Reve was standing.

Moro had taken her! Reve felt sick in the pit of his stomach. He was stupid. He was an idiot.

He felt a hand on his arm.

It was Baz. She must have just slipped round the corner and out of sight and then sneaked back as soon as the car had pulled away. Demi was right behind her, shuffling his feet, glancing this way and that, looking like he hardly needed to be there; that it was nothing to do with him that Mi had been taken.

'No.' she said to Reve. 'You don't go there. Not now.'

Of course he was going there. He shook her hand off. 'You plan this? Fay plan this?'

'No.' She pulled at him again.

'Leave him be, Baz. Country boy's all cooked in his head.'

'That right?' Something snapped. 'You the one take us this way, Demi. Hey! Maybe you done it on purpose, feed Mi to that man!' He wanted to grab the little boy and shake him like a rat. 'That what you done, eh!' Abruptly he turned away, disgusted with himself. Why blame the boy? He, Reve, he was the one to blame. He should have had his eyes open.

'You want to go 'cross to that place,' Demi said sullenly, 'you go, but we seen kids goin in there, all ages –

209

that right, Baz? Goin in and not comin out. So you go if that what you want to do.'

Baz was standing right beside Demi, his shadow, two or three inches smaller, eyes that would melt a soft woman. 'Seen 'em, Demi.' Her eyes were fixed on Reve, looking up at him. 'Fay say we never go near that place. Never. She rage if we do wrong thing. That man the spider,' she said.

Reve stared across the broad dusty square, half shadowed now, the old buildings cracked and peeling, boarded windows. In the middle the fountain spluttered silently and then died. The tram they had been going to catch swung round the far end and slipped away down an avenue to the right. There was hardly any traffic: a truck, dirty vans pumping oily smoke from their exhausts. The only thing shiny in all that wide space was down the far end of the square, where the buses and the trams stopped, where there was a row of cafes, a corner market and the glinting blue lights of Señor Moro's bar.

Mi would be so frightened.

'Come on, we got to get back, tell Fay,' said Demi. 'She know the señor, don't she, Baz? She can give him talk. Get your sister maybe . . .' He didn't sound convinced.

'Why'd she send you looking for us in the first place!' exclaimed Reve. 'Cos that man over there told her to, tha's why!' They didn't answer. 'Your Fay just his runaround.'

'Fay different to what you sayin,' said the boy defensively. 'An' why Fay so sweet on you an' the girl? You real slow, nothin like me an' Baz. An' we been with her a long time, yeah. Long time. Almos' family. That right, Baz?'

Something warm and wet slapped the top of Reve's forehead. Rainwater trickled into his eye. He blinked.

Baz didn't answer and Reve wasn't listening, not really, but the word 'family' jostled him. 'A'right,' he said bitterly, 'I tell you what you do. You go tell her that if she help us this time, she won't see us never again.'

The rain was slow and lazy, slapping the dusty ground here and then there, like it was testing where it should fall. Demi stared at him for a moment, then he and Baz ran off back into the Barrio.

The blue lights of the Slow Bar flickered at him from the far side of the square.

Cars passed and then he darted across the road and into the wide open space of Agua, jogging down the length of the square, the rain falling around him, running down his neck. He didn't even feel it.

He just kept thinking. How do you walk into the middle of a web and not get caught?

CHAPTER TWENTY-FOUR

A minute or so later Reve was crossing the road on the far side of the square, skipping round behind a tram and then stepping up on to the wide pavement. The market at the corner was closing, the thickening rain hastening the traders to pack away the remains of their vegetables and the few stallholders selling cheap clothes were bundling jeans and shirts in plastic and then tossing them into the back of vans. The pavement was almost empty, just a man standing in the doorway of the Slow Bar, and opposite, parked on its own, a police car.

What did Moro want Mi for? Because she was pretty? She didn't look so special, not after a night in the city . . . What was his plan? A man like that always had a plan. He was clever, like Theon.

The man at the door of the bar was small, whip-thin, his head tilted forward, arms folded, an S-shaped shadow man. Reve straightened his shoulders and walked up to him. 'I got business with Señor Moro.'

'That so?' The man lifted his head: a thin, weathered, familiar face, a heavy black moustache . . . It was LoJo's father!

'Pelo!' Reve couldn't believe it. 'What you doin?'

'Working for the man,' Pelo said drily, 'That what it look like to me.'

Reve shook his head. The last he'd seen of Pelo was in that boat, the spreading white V of his wake into the darkness, his family left standing on the pier. And then Calde giving his name to the police . . . Reve suddenly registered the police car parked right there. 'Pelo, don' you know police lookin for you? Theon said . . .'

'S'all right. Theon got me word. Told me keep low.' He grunted. 'Never been lower 'n this place.'

'But that car!'

Pelo pulled at the end of his moustache. 'No,' he said, that same dry tone in his voice, 'I'm safe enough.'

'But you goin back? You heard what happen?'

'When this man let me drive his boat –' he tilted his head towards the closed door – 'he done me favour,' he said. 'Now I owe him. That's what he say . . . and he got a long reach.'

Yes, thought Reve bitterly, he had – reached right out of the bar and snatched up Mi, easy enough.

As if reading his mind Pelo said, 'I seen your sister gone in not ten minutes ago. You hopin' to get her?' Reve nodded. 'There wasn't anything I could do. You understan'? I just hold the door here.'

The rain had started to hiss against the pavement. Reve stepped closer into the doorway. 'Tha's my plan.' It wasn't a plan at all. Just one of those things you have to do.

A hint of a smile crossed Pelo's face. 'Jus' like that? I hear you took on Calde's men in the cantina – you an' the Boxer.'

'How you hear 'bout that?'

'Word always get back to Señor Moro. You know what I mean? An' you done favour to my family.' He shook his head. 'You something, eh.'

Reve didn't feel he was something.

'You gonna do the same thing here?' he said still in that same dry way he had.

Reve shrugged. The business in the cantina had been different. 'Someone pull a knife on Tomas.'

'I know. Someone always pull a knife. You got to have someone watch your back, Reve, that's what you got to do.' He pushed open the door.

For a moment Reve thought that maybe Pelo would come in with him, stand at his shoulder.

But the door swung behind him and he was on his own.

'Well. Well. Well. The bull boy from the sea. What did I say, Captain? Everyone come to Moro's bar. Everything happen here.' Moro laughed, a rich oily sound from deep in his chest.

It took Reve a couple of seconds to adjust to the bluish gloom of the long room. There was no sign of Mi.

The shirtsleeved barman with the long face was on his left, drying glasses. The counter was gleaming, and bare apart from a tray of tall thin glasses, a jug of iced water and a bottle of red wine. Down the room two tables had been pushed together and covered with a white cloth. Moro was at the head of the table, a big bowl of pasta in front of him from which he was scooping out vast helpings for his guests. Zavvy was on his left and beside him was the shark who'd snatched Mi. Sitting with his back to Reve was a broad-shouldered man in the full rig of a police commander, silvery tabs on his shoulder. A policeman sitting down with the spider. Same all over.

Reve didn't care if they wrapped their arms around each other; they could eat and drink and tear up the city as much as they wanted. It was Mi he was looking for.

The policeman twisted round to look at Reve. 'Since when you interested in street rats, Moro?' he said dismissively, turning back again, accepting the bowl that had been passed to him and immediately spooning the pasta round his fork and funneling it up to his mouth.

'You don't know this one? You surprise me, Captain. You who have the whole city under your thumb.'

'Where is she, señor?' said Reve.

The señor smiled. 'She? She's all right.' He lifted his hand. 'You wait, eh. I done you favour. You'll see.'

A wind must have picked up because the rain was now slapping against the window. Reve was aware of the door behind him opening. 'Just till the rain finish,' said Pelo. 'Is that a'right, señor?'

'Sure,' said Moro expansively.

Reve wondered whether Baz and Demi had really gone and told Fay what had happened. If they had, wouldn't they all just take shelter from this rainstorm? Keep their heads down?

'See, Captain,' continued Moro, clearly enjoying himself, 'it is my job here to please. This boy looking for his sister . . . who I'm giving a little shelter to. An' you looking for promotion, maybe governor of the city. That could be your future, Captain. I can help you with that too.' The señor was spinning another web, this time

215

to snag the Captain. But how could Mi have anything to do with that? Just a girl from the country . . . Maybe he wanted to make her a thief. Was that it? Well, she wouldn't do it, wouldn't do it for him, this big man with all his power, so much power he made Calde look like a rooting pig.

The Captain laughed and raised his glass. 'You can fix all that, eh, Moro? If you do that for me, I think we can do business.'

Reve shifted uneasily. What if it was something worse than being a thief? He felt the skin tighten round his eyes and his heart banged in his chest. He forced himself to breathe, like Tomas had told him. Did they think they could keep him standing there forever, make him be a do-nothing. He needed something to wake them up.

He glanced over at the barman, who was leaning over the counter, talking quietly to Pelo. He saw the water jug, and the bottle of red wine. Pelo was listening to the barman, but his eyes were on Reve.

Outside a tram rattled past and there was a loud blast on a car horn. 'Sounds like my driver getting impatient,' laughed the Captain again. 'He going to find himself on the late shift if he's not careful.'

Reve made up his mind. He twisted back and snatched up the bottle of wine from the counter, spun it so that he was holding it by the neck and, just like he had seen the cantina men do, he smacked it hard down on the edge of the counter, shattering the base, red wine splattering his arm, dripping down his jeans and pooling on the floor. He was left gripping the neck, pointing the splintery glass mouth at Moro's face.

That got their attention.

The shark was on his feet, a stubby gun in his hand, but Moro had a restraining hand on his arm; behind him Reve sensed that the barman was ready to move too. He took a step forward and away from the counter just to put himself out of reach. He couldn't afford to turn his head to see for real; he only had eyes for Moro. This was it, he was in deep water now.

'What you think, boy?' said Moro. 'You goin to do something with that bottle or just stain my floor?'

'You got my sister. I want you bring her out here now. We done nothing 'gainst you . . .'

Moro put up his hand. 'Wait,' he said. 'You better learn some patience, bull boy. I got a thing to play out here, and some thing take time. You,' he said to Pelo, 'fetch the girl. You want to see her, see she all right, you go with him,' he said to Reve. 'And you,' he said to the barman, 'you clear up the floor. My pasta's cold.'

The men at the table laughed and settled back into their places, the shark, Secondo, slipping the gun back into his shoulder holster, and taking his jacket off and hanging it on the back of his chair.

Reve felt a hand on his elbow. 'You give me that. You made your mark,' said Pelo quietly. Reve let him take the jagged remains of the bottle and then Pelo ushered Reve down the room towards the door at the back. It was the door that Reve had been through before when Moro had taken them up to the roof and shown them the city, his city.

As they were passing the table Moro beckoned Reve. 'Here.'

Reve stepped over to him. Moro smiled and patted his cheek. 'Frighten of nothing, this one.' Then, in a move that was so quick Reve had no time to react, Moro had gripped the back of his neck in his right hand, yanked him forward and had his face pressed up against the blade of a small knife he had in his left. Reve could feel the steel against his cheek and could just see the tip up by his eye. He stiffened. Held his breath.

'You think you can manage with one eye? Slow you down a little, maybe make you think a little, eh. That might be a good thing. What do you say?'

Reve reckoned it was better to say nothing.

He felt the blade prick the skin on the underside of his eye; he could smell the garlic on Moro's breath; all he could see were the shiny black hairs on the back of Moro's hands.

'You want me to take him through, señor?' Pelo sounded as if he couldn't have cared less whether or not Reve was sliced up like a salami, but it seemed to distract Moro. He gave a *humph* and then with a flick of his wrist he nicked a line down the side of Reve's face. He smiled and patted Reve's cheek again, but the other side from where he had cut him, and sat back in his chair and Reve straightened up. His face stung a little and he felt something warm running down to his chin. He hoped it wasn't tears. He couldn't be weak, not in front of these men. A little cut was nothing.

'Good. No sound. I like that. Are you not impressed

with this boy, Captain? Does he not even seem familiar to you? Not at all, no?'

'Should he?'

'Oh yes . . .'

Pelo nudged him through the door and then, instead of going upstairs, he turned left down a corridor which had two doors on the left-hand side. Reve pressed his forearm against his cheek; it came away smeared with red. 'You were lucky,' murmured Pelo, unlocking the door and swinging it open.

He didn't feel lucky. But if he had had to pay an eye to get to Mi, then that's what he would have paid.

It was an ugly room with a scabby tiled floor, a sink, a barred and rain-streaked window that looked out on to a closed-in yard with tall metal gates. No way out there, then. Just inside the door was an iron-framed single bed with a thin stained mattress and no bedding. A bare bulb hung from a wire in the middle of the ceiling, casting a sickly orange light over everything. Standing in front of a long mirror over on the far side of the room were two young women.

Even though he was expecting to see Mi, for a split second Reve didn't recognize her. She was standing in front of the mirror wearing a green, backless dress, like dancers on one of those TV shows might wear. The other young woman Reve had certainly never seen. She was wearing skinny jeans and had pins tucked into her mouth. She was twisting Mi's wild red hair into a knot at the back of her head.

'Mi?'

Mi stood unmoving, a statue.

The girl took the pins from her mouth. 'A'right,' she said. 'You look more pretty now than when they drag you in. Who this visiting?'

'Her brother,' said Pelo.

The girl raised her eyebrows, glanced at Pelo and then slipped out of the room.

Mi turned round. She didn't look like like Mi, not the Mi of twenty minutes ago. No. Almost took his breath away, seeing her look so different.

'Knew you'd come and get me,' she said. 'The man said that to me, but I knew it anyhow . . . What happen to your face?' Her own was a mask under the make-up the girl had put on her; her voice was brittle, just under control.

'I'm a'right . . . They hurt you?'

'Done nothing 'cept put me in a dress, pat powder on my face. He say he want to show me someone. I look like a street woman, eh?' Her words started to speed up. Sentences tumbling together. 'They made me drink something, Reve, and it's fuzzing up my mind . . . This the hole, Reve. This the sinkhole goin take me down to the place where bad spirit come . . . You got cut on your face . . .'

'Shh.' He took her hand. She fell silent, her breath coming in little sips. He gently guided her to the bed and made her sit and then looked at Pelo. 'What did they give her?' he said angrily.

Pelo grimaced. 'Just saw her bundled in, but I reckon they just give her something to quiet her down . . .'

'Quiet her down and then pretty her up for the

Captain. That man,' he said to Pelo, 'he the one they call Captain Dolucca?'

Pelo nodded.

There was such a sour taste of bile in his mouth, Reve almost gagged. Moro was going to sell her to that man, the man who'd run with their mother!

'Is there a way out the back, Pelo?'

'No. Place like a fort, Reve. Those gates locked up all the time . . .'

The door behind him pushed open and the barman appeared. 'Señor says bring them in.' Then he saw Mi. 'Phoof! Maria work a miracle or something. Maybe I get her paint me up, give me looks.'

'Need more than a miracle to do that for you, Bo,' said Pelo, pushing him back out of the doorway. 'Don't need you back here. We're coming. '

'All right, fisherman. They come from your village, eh? Don't get cosy – that what the señor tell me to say. Don't get cosy.'

He went back down the corridor. Pelo looked at Reve, his thin, weathered face thoughtful, like he was weighing a catch, seeing what it would bring, whether it would pay off Calde and leave a few dollars over for his family. 'Bring her in, Reve,' he said, and then very quietly murmured, 'If any chance happen, you make a break, all right. I won't stop you. That's maybe all I can do, but if I'm standing at that door, you got a way clear out to the street.'

'And then what?'

Pelo put a hand briefly on his shoulder as Reve guided Mi past him. 'Miracle. Miracle the thing we all need.'

CHAPTER TWENTY-FIVE

'All right, this is it, Captain,' Moro was saying when Reve and Mi came back into the bar, with Reve keeping a firm hold on Mi's arm. 'I need to be sure you don't forget what we agree. I need to be sure none of your dirt-fly helicopters come buzzing the coast, eh, when I got business . . .'

That seemed so long ago: the helicopter, bullets ricocheting off the stone wall, a little boy running, flames . . . There'd been no time to think then.

'You got my word,' said the Captain, leaning back in his chair.

'Yes,' said Moro, 'I know all about words . . .'

At that moment the Captain saw Mi and he froze, the cigarette halfway to his mouth. Moro's Secondo, the shark, twisted round and looked at them. And the greasy Zavvy studied Mi too – it was only Mi they were interested in – before turning back to Moro, raising an eyebrow but saying nothing.

Moro seemed highly pleased with himself. 'I tell you,' he said smiling, 'I always give people what they lookin for. This what you lookin for, Captain. This woman remind you of someone, eh?'

The Captain blinked and puffed at the cigarette, letting the smoke curl up out of his mouth. 'It's nothing,' he shrugged. 'She's like a woman I knew.' He hesitated. 'Very.' He stubbed out his cigarette.

'I know,' said Moro. 'I know.' He emphasized the two words, scoring them heavily as if with a thick pencil. 'Like her mother, eh? Maybe when you first seen her. Long time before you were captain of the city. 'Bout the time you were planning to take a step up the ladder.'

The Captain pushed back his chair and came round to Reve and Mi. He barely saw Reve; it was Mi he was looking at, devouring her almost, like a hungry dog. He had maybe been good-looking once, dark shiny hair swept back from his brow, a long straight nose, but there was something greedy and hard in his eyes.

Mi shivered, even though the air felt thick and clammy. Reve tensed and edged a little closer to her, so their shoulders touched. Should he grab Mi and run, just run through the door and out into the rainstorm? Pelo wouldn't stop them. That's what he said.

Mi shivered again and took a sharp breath. Her eyes were unfocused.

The Captain turned away. It looked to Reve like it was an effort to do so. 'What exactly is it you think you know, Moro?' he said, going back to his chair.

'Maybe some things other ears shouldn't hear.' He leaned across the table to offer the Captain one of his cigars. 'But we're all friends,' he said, smiling. 'Friends. Business partners. This is it, eh? You got my support, Captain –' he nodded at Secondo, who snapped a light for the Captain – 'and I'll help you climb the ladder to mayor, I'm telling you.'

'This girl,' said the Captain 'how did she come here?'

'Came looking for her mother. Tha's what they tell me.'

223

'Here? In this place!' The Captain laughed – it didn't sound genuine to Reve – and then he puffed at his cigar and made a performance of examining the glowing tip. 'I don't think so. Her mother disappeared a long time ago.'

'She not so far away.'

'I think maybe she's dead.'

'Oh no,' said Moro. 'It's the husband, this girl's father, you thinking of, Captain. Eh?' He paused and nodded. 'You remember? He died so you could bring this girl's mother to the city. Now such a story would not sound so good in the newspapers: "POLICEMAN MURDERS MAN AND STEALS HIS WIFE".' He held up his hands as if framing the newspaper headline. 'And she's not the only thing he steals, that's what I hear. A consignment of . . . drugs, eh? A lot of money for you, Captain, a lot of money and a beautiful woman with red hair – just like this one. You would like to read that story in the papers, Captain?'

'No!' The Captain's inital response was abrupt and then he shook his head, as if the idea was almost childish. 'That's not how it was.'

'Oh? This is how I hear it: there is a young man, eh, he don't even make lieutenant yet, but he go to that village many times because he see this is a good place. It got a nice little business comin in on the boats, and maybe he get paid a few dollar not to pay too much attention to this business. This village has something else he likes: a very pretty woman, who is also smart. You remembering this, Captain?'

And he told the story that Reve had learned back in Rinconda.

224

'Funny how people always looking to make run, start a new life, shake away the old. Don't you find that, Captain?' said Moro.

The Captain didn't respond.

'But the old life don't ever get shook away,' continued Moro. 'It just don't happen. Didn't happen for that husband; he never got to run away with his pretty wife.'

The Captain tipped the ash from his cigar on to his plate and leaned back in his chair. He looked at Moro and then he shifted his gaze back to Mi.

Moro nodded as if some kind of agreement had been made between them. 'They say it looked like an accident when that husband got pulled out of the ocean all wrapped up in his fishing net.'

'Maybe he got killed for stealing,' said the Captain. 'This is how these gangs work,' he said, his voice level. 'A businessman like you know that.'

'Of course. But me – this is not what I think happened. You know why? Because this is the time when this handsome young policeman suddenly gets so much money that he buys himself a big house in the city. When they come to the city . . . I don't know what happen then.' Moro lifted his right hand and then let it drop down on the table with a soft smack. 'Now he has this money, maybe he is not so interested in a village woman. Maybe he begins to worry that she knows too much about what he has done, and so maybe she get frightened, hide herself away . . .' Moro let the smoke trickle out of his mouth. He was enjoying this. 'And so this is it. Who care about these things?' He carefully tipped the ash from his cigar

225

on to the table. 'Except maybe all the newspaper in the city. I think they like this story.' He pulled a face of mock concern. 'Maybe the story make TV news . . .'

The Captain ground out his cigar. 'This is nothing Moro,' he said. 'A story. Who's going to listen to this – just words? Words are nothing without proof.'

'Words are always something, Captain. A story like this –' he pulled a face – 'not going to sound so good for someone who got political ambition. Very least it's going to put a block on that man's career even if there was no proof . . . Except we got proof standing right here. These young people. This pretty girl, so like her mother . . . You want to go on TV, Captain?'

The Captain ran a finger round the collar of his shirt. He was sweating badly.

'Are you threatening me, Moro?' he said.

'Captain,' said Moro reasonably, 'this is business.' He reached across the table and poured the Captain a drink. 'But I tell you one thing puzzling me, Captain. How about this boy? This boy mean nothing to you?' He looked at Reve for the first time since he had begun telling his story. The Captain looked at him too, his eyes hooded. 'He don't look so much like his sister,' continued Moro. 'What you think? How long you know the mother, Captain? How long you courting her under the nose of that husband of hers? Four, five years? Maybe she have a child in that time?'

Reve felt as though there were threads of web drifting down around him and Mi and the Captain.

'Maybe there is a different father for this child. That

226

thought ever come to you, Captain? Maybe you get to be a father and she don't tell you. Fay someone who have many secrets, I think. So what do you think, Captain. This is a good boy. A boy any father be proud to have. Little bull. He get that from you, I wonder, Captain? Are you his father maybe?' Moro smiled.

No! Reve felt his face burn. This man his father? No, not ever, not in a million years. Why didn't Mi say something? But when he looked at her he saw that she was lost in herself, staring straight ahead as if at something only she could see.

He felt the Captain's eyes on him. Maybe wondering.

Moro nodded. 'I tell you what we do, Captain.' Reve tightened his grip on Mi's arm. He watched them all. Any chance at all, and he'd move. Better to die than get caught up like this.

'You take the girl.' Moro held up both hands. 'See, I give her to you. Like you are getting her mother again, but all young and pretty and not so messed up, eh? I hear your wife is used to your ways. You can tell your wife something.' He smiled and shrugged.

The Captain grunted.

Moro turned to Mi. 'You the one with all that seeing skill, eh? You seen this coming, did you?'

She didn't respond. She couldn't. She was halfway between this place and somewhere else. Didn't matter how much anyone talked to her, she wouldn't hear them. It didn't bother Moro too much. He flicked the ash off his cigar on to the table. 'And I keep the boy, work for me. I think if anything happen to this girl, the boy will come for you. He has a killing look, eh? You think?'

Moro's Secondo leaned forward to help himself to the bottle of wine, and when he did so he left the shiny leather holster exposed. Good dollar you pay for leather like that.

'But that won't happen, Captain, because we will make good business partners, and no TV journalist ever hear a word of this story, and you, my dear Captain, you keep climbing the ladder till you get to be mayor. We make a good team. What do you say?'

The Captain didn't answer for a moment. He just looked at Mi. Then he nodded. 'Maybe.' He licked his lip and then touched the corner of his moustache with his finger. 'Yes, maybe we do business, Moro, but no more surprises.'

'No.'

Outside that car horn blared again. Longer. And Reve heard, even through the shut door and the slap of rain on the window, the sound of voices. Like a party of children, yelling and running in the rain, having fun. Free.

Outside the web.

The Captain stood up. 'That's my car again. Is something happening out there?'

Pelo opened the door a crack and then shook his head. 'Nothin I can see.'

'OK.' The Captain came over and then stood behind Mi and reached out to take her arm. Reve saw that the Captain's hand was trembling slightly. 'OK, Señor Moro,' he said, 'we got a deal. I'll take the girl; you keep the boy.'

Reve felt rather than heard Mi make a high keening

sound, so high it didn't seem to come from her at all but from somewhere above her head, like a scratching on glass. The Captain's hand closed on her arm.

'Let go of her,' the Captain said to Reve.

Reve shook his head. 'No.'

The Captain blinked as if the answer was just a little bit beyond his understanding and then quite suddenly he slapped Reve, hard enough to make his head jerk back. Reve felt the click of something on his lips, a ring it felt like, and the warm sting of blood in his mouth.

What was it with these people? Reve thought. Tomas, for all his boxing, never hit him, not once. But he didn't let go. If he let go he would sink. He felt as if he was on the lip of a dark hole, Mi's sinkhole.

'Let go!' said the Captain, trying to control his anger.

Before he could lift his hand again, Mi opened her mouth, and the cry she made was so piercing it felt like the thick air in that bar was being shredded. Reve's eyes watered and the Captain stepped back, bumping into the bar. Moro and Zavvy just stared, while Secondo twisted round in his chair, his eyes wide as if he could see something other than Mi, Reve and the Captain standing there. Maybe the others did too. Mi's cry pierced louder and louder and then suddenly snapped into silence and Mi said something in a voice that wasn't hers. Some words that meant nothing but sounded harsh and dark and seemed to come from the pit of her stomach.

The men stared at her, appalled.

It frightened Reve too; this was somehow more 'other' than anything he had heard from Mi before. He kept a tight hold of her wrist, as if by not letting go he could stop this terrible noise.

The darkened window suddenly burst inward, as if the rain had bunched its fist and punched the glass. Shards shivered and sprayed into the room, and then almost like an afterthought a heavy-looking brick skidded across the floor.

Zavvy threw himself sideways; maybe he thought it was a bomb, but no one else moved. They were all staring at Mi, as if she had done this thing.

Through the shattered window Reve glimpsed shadowy figures running in the thick rain, mouths wide, five, ten, more maybe, he couldn't tell. They appeared and disappeared in that grey wash of water, like shoaling fish.

Moro was barking orders into his cellphone. 'I want you all here, down in Agua now!'

Reve pulled at Mi's arm. 'Mi, now!' and he took a step towards the door.

But Mi didn't move. She stood rigid, tight as a wire and then she suddenly screamed, not the weird keening cry but a noise like a splinter. Even Moro flinched.

That instant, another brick sailed into the room and smacked into a table, sent an ashtray, a beer bottle and a couple of glasses flying. And then another one. And Mi was still screaming.

'What are you waiting for!' Moro shouted. 'Get that witch out of here, Captain! You, Pelo, and you –' he shouted to the barman – 'out there! No one goes round bustin my windows. Go!'

For a couple of heartbeats nobody moved. Mi's terrible unearthly keening stopped. Reve's eyes were glued to the revolver poking out of the lieutenant's holster. This was it. There wasn't any other magic going to happen. This was the city. Here the only thing that was going to talk, Reve saw, was a dollar or a gun.

Another stone cracked into the window, more glass. Moro had his cellphone clamped to his ear. 'You come here.' he barked. 'Now! Off your asses!'

Reve let go of Mi, darted forward and snatched the gun; and then it was in his hand, snug and heavy. He swung it round at the Captain, who flinched and stepped back a pace. Then, wildly, Reve swung it back to the men at the table, while with his other hand he tugged Mi to the door.

The rain hissed in through the broken window.

Reve had his arm right out straight. The gun was heavy and wobbled a bit in his hand, but he managed to focus on Moro, squinting up one eye, taking aim. He would do it, if they made him. His finger was on the trigger. 'No one taking us!' he said. 'You hear me, señor. You right about me. I kill anyone try to stop us.' His voice sounded thin against the rain and the thick silence in the bar itself, but he would do it if they made him.

He backed to the door, pulling Mi with him.

'Of course, the little bull,' Moro said. 'Maybe you shoot the Captain here. He give you reason, eh? Taking your mother.' His voice was smooth, tempting, a spider testing the web.

Reve's gun swung to the Captain. His face looked slick

231

with sweat, but his eyes showed nothing. Reve knew he was just waiting for his chance. They all were, ready to jump on him, kick the gun from his hand, use their weight and anger to smash him, a boy who shamed them with a gun.

Behind him, out in the rainstorm, there was a sudden heavy *whoomph* of something bursting into flame. And shouts. A siren somewhere.

He straightened his arm. Mi gave a shuddering deep breath and Reve blinked. 'No,' she said.

He let the gun drop a fraction and the two of them edged another step backwards and another. 'A'right Mi,' he said quietly. 'When I say.'

'Enough,' said Moro. 'Stop them.' Reve turned in time to see the barman pulling a gun from under the counter, but Reve kept his aim on Moro. Any second. Any second. How would it feel, the crack of the gun, the bullet slamming into the back of his neck? He trembled but tried not to. 'Tell him put it down,' he said. 'I can hit you from here. Hit you or one of the others. Maybe I shoot you all . . .'

Moro didn't flinch but his jaw was tight. He wasn't liking this. 'Stop him,' he said, the voice a little strained now. 'Just do this thing for me. Ario! Earn your money.' Secondo didn't have a gun, but maybe he did earn good money because he took a step towards Reve and then faltered as Reve swung the gun a little to the right, pointing straight at him.

'You one stop from dead, boy.' He pulled a blade from his back pocket and flicked it open. 'Drop the gun.'

There wasn't a plan. Nothing. They were done – grilled and ready to burn, like a couple of jackfish over the flame. Secondo took another step. Reve's eyes were glued to the knife, its blade was fat and wicked-looking.

He pulled the trigger.

Nothing. Not even a click.

'Safety catch,' said Moro, grunting with surprise and pleasure, suddenly relaxing. 'You got to learn about these things before you go killing, boy. All right, Ario, take the gun. Pelo, deal with what is going on outside.'

Reve bowed his head.

Secondo stepped forward and pulled the gun from his hand, but before he could do anything else, there was a crack and his face crumpled in shock as he staggered backwards, the gun clattering to the floor, his shirt already reddening before he hit the bar and slumped down on to his bottom.

Pelo had shot him.

'Go!' said Pelo. He had the door kicked open behind him and he leaned back out of the way as they turned and ran, his gun now trained on the men inside the bar. 'I'll follow you, eh. This place not for us, Reve. Go!'

They went, running out into the rainstorm, water streaming down their faces, drenching them in seconds.

CHAPTER TWENTY-SIX

Five paces. The edge of the pavement.

A car burning right in front of them, the rain slashing into the flames and hissing, and the light bright in their eyes, flickering white and orange and blinding them to the darkness beyond the flame. There was another explosion off to the right and more flames and the acrid stink of burning gasolene, and there were children somewhere out there, running and shrieking, ghostly grey shapes in the rain.

Then Mi stopped so abruptly Reve almost ran into her. 'Mi! Run. Don't stop!'

He shoved at her but she didn't move. He glanced back – the Slow Bar's door was closed, but Pelo couldn't keep them in there forever.

'Look!' she said, grabbing his arm, pulling him round. 'There!'

On the other side of the road, curtained by the driving grey rain, was Fay, her flame hair washed down around her pale face. It was almost as if she were underwater, almost like the woman he had seen. He couldn't make out if she was smiling or just staring, but he felt there was hunger in her look.

'What she doin, Reve? She comin after us now?'

It was only a second, them standing there like that, Fay on the one side of the road, them on the other, rain pouring down on them, the gutters rushing, but it felt so much longer. Then Fay made a sharp, almost impatient gesture with her hand. Reve didn't know whether it was to them or to her children, but like a flock of birds all her ragged, rain-sodden little army took off, scattering back across the square towards the Barrio, disappearing into the grey of the storm.

Then Fay turned and hurried after her children and Mi took a shaky breath.

Behind them there was the crack of a gunshot and then another one and then Pelo came running out, doubled down. 'Go!' he shouted. 'Get away from here! Go!'

They took off down the pavement and were just about to pass the Captain's car when the door swung open and a hand beckoned them.

Mi responded more quickly than Reve. She grabbed him and pushed him into the front and then piled into the back.

It was crazy; there was Demi so charged up he was bouncing on the passenger seat. 'Baz got that police so mad he gone running for her! Fool! He catch nothing but rain. You hear me hooting this horn?' He blasted it again. 'I done that!' Demi was gabbling, words tumbling out of him. 'Fay say: stir it up! You know how to drive this thing? I got the keys. You better know how to drive!'

There was another flat crack of a pistol shot and Reve twisted around.

'Don't look back!' yelled Demi. 'Drive!'

But Reve did look; they had to wait for Pelo.

A dark figure stood hunched in the doorway of the bar.

Another shot.

Pelo was spinning round, one arm out straight like a dancer.

Crack! The back window of the car spiderwebbed, a small bullet hole in the centre. They shrank down in their seats.

Mi picked a tiny shard from her arm and frowned at the blood prick.

'What you waiting for, country?' screamed Demi. 'Put you' foot down!'

'Pelo? You see him, Mi?'

Mi craned her neck and saw the dark shadow of a body sprawled on the ground, and the man, the barman, running towards them. He was so close she could see his white teeth. It looked as if he was grinning. Behind him, figures piling out of the bar and into the rain.

'Gear stick! Where the gear stick?'

Another gunshot, and Reve flinched as the side mirror exploded in a silvery burst of glass and metal.

'All you got to do is put yo' foot down! Go!' Demi yanked at Reve's arm. 'It's automatic, country. Go!'

'Reve!' Mi's hand touched his shoulder, and he twisted back to see her door being yanked open – and there was the barman, reaching in to grab Mi.

Reve jammed his foot down and the car leaped forward, screeching against the kerb and then jolting up on to the pavement. Instinctively he jerked the wheel. It probably saved them because there was another shot, but this must have gone wide as they lurched back on to the road and now Reve had the measure of the steering. They

236

accelerated away from the edge of the square, skidding on the wet surface, the tyres spinning, skating in a slow arc and then catching grip again and heading down one of the wide boulevards that funelled into Agua. Rain smeared the windscreen. He could hardly see a thing and he had no idea how to get the wipers going.

'OK! OK! You got it, country boy! Baz say you never manage a car; I say any boy can do a thing like that, come natural to a boy. When I get a little taller I goin drive all over this place . . .'

Reve slammed on the brakes to avoid someone running across the road and the car jigged wildly, throwing Demi hard against the door.

'Whoo!'

Reve felt his neck wound up tight as a wire spring. His eyes flicked to the mirror. Lights. One. Two. 'We got to go back for Pelo.'

'Who's that you talkin 'bout? . . . Right! Right!' shouted Demi.

Reve braked, yanked the wheel down and they slid around into a narrow street.

'Down the end. Pull up.'

Reve braked, jolted them to a stop.

'You think they see us take the turn?' said Mi, peering out of the rear window. Demi was looking back too, half turned round, fingers drumming on the seat.

'Dunno.' Reve sat rigid, staring into the rain-dark alley, his hands gripping the wheel tightly. He didn't want to let go and see that his hands were shaking like old Arella's did sometimes.

A moment later two black cars roared down the road, passing the alley in an eye blink.

'Whoo! Tha's sweet, country. We vanish them!'

Reve looked in the mirror and saw that Mi's eyes were on him. 'We got to go back, Mi.'

Demi made a noise like a puffed-out whale. 'We got to do what?'

Mi quietened him. Then she put her hand on Reve's shoulder. 'We can't do that, Reve. You know we can't go back there. We got to let Pelo go.'

'Who this Pelo man anyhow? I don't see him doin much of nothin helpin you out of Moro place.'

Reve ignored him. Is that what Fay had done? he wondered. Just let them go? Is that what that look on her face had meant? He bowed his head. 'What am I goin tell LoJo?' he said. 'What am I goin tell Ciele?'

'You tell what happen,' said Mi, her voice unexpectedly gentle.

'You goin say nothing to no one 'less you move you'self!' said Demi, scrambling out of the car. 'Come on. We gotta move real quick.'

He scrambled out and Mi and Reve followed him; and then Demi led them at a run through a cut, then along a wide street.

They heard sirens wailing, tearing across the city towards them. Right to them – that was the way it seemed. Mi gripped Reve's hand as they ran, keeping on Demi's heels as he ducked this way and that, cutting through alleys and over railings, avoiding the main streets as much as he could.

Twice they had to dive for shelter: once in the doorway of a closed cafe and another time they just threw themselves flat on the wet road and held still as the cars drove by, more slowly now, lights sweeping over them as they lay face down.

Demi jumped up first, shaking himself like a dog. 'They lookin so hard but they can't see nothing,' he said. 'Baz say I got magic in me, cos I'm so quick no one ever see nothin, you know.'

'Magic?' Reve gently detached Mi's hand from his. 'Nothing magic in this place. How far you takin us?'

'Takin you nowhere. This is it.'

He pointed to a tram stop over on the other side of the road. 'Tha's the one,' he said, and gave them the number of the tram that would take them to the edge of the city. 'Number nine to end of the line.' He wiped the wet from his face and bobbed up and down on his toes. 'Last tram run at midnight. You a'right, but you on your own now. Fay tell me to wait till you catch one.' He didn't look like someone who ever liked to wait for anything. 'But you don' need me, and you not goin to go telling Fay nothin, so I'm gone.' He glanced up and down the road. 'Stay back in that doorway there, on this side. Run when you see the tram comin. Watch police all the time. They goin be lookin. Looking for the car you stole.' He laughed. 'That first time you go stealin a police car, country?'

'You the thief, Demi.'

Mi touched Reve's face and then dabbed at the cut on his cheek with her thumb. 'You got red tears, Reve.' She said, wiping away a little smear of blood.

'That don' mean nothin,' he said. He was thinking about the Captain with his oiled-back hair and his too-tight uniform, and the way he had looked at Mi, all hungry to wrap a coil round her, drag her down . . .

'Thief someone who get caught,' said Demi dismissively. 'Me, I'm too fast for anyone catch me.' He looked curiously at Mi. 'This girl don' say much,' he said, jerking his head like an old guy. 'She got less word than Baz.'

'Maybe you steal words right out o' her mouth.' Reve said, touching Mi's arm.

Demi laughed. 'That what Baz say! Say I'd steal the air right out of her lung if she let me.'

Then he was all business again. He looked up and down the street, shrugged, suddenly looked older, smarter, like someone who knew the streets half an edge sharper than the police who stayed safe in their vans and patrol cars. 'I'm gone.'

'Hey, wait,' said Reve, instinctively holding out his hand, wanting to thank Demi. 'We owe you, I reckon.'

Demi glanced down at his hand and shrugged. 'Reckon you do, but you don't got any dollar in that hand of yours.' He stood there for a second, the rain pouring down, his T-shirt clinging to him. 'Who you to Fay she give so much trouble for you? She never give trouble for anyone, 'cept maybe me and Baz.'

Reve didn't know what to say. 'Maybe she tell you one time, Demi.'

A police siren wailed somewhere in the night.

'Sure.' He gave a little bounce on his toes. 'She tell me

most things. Tell me more than she tell Baz anyhow.'

And he was gone.

A car pulled round the corner and Reve edged Mi right back into the doorway, keeping her head down against his shoulder so the light wouldn't catch her eyes, his arms wrapped round her, holding her tight, as if that could keep her safe, keep them both safe.

They stayed like that for a while. Reve didn't know how long. Twenty minutes. Half an hour. Cars passed. Sometimes a truck. A police van came by, first time fast and second time slow, shining a powerful torch on doorways by the tram spot, not bothering with their side of the road.

'You a'right now?' he asked.

She pushed away from him and squeezed up her face, like she was scrunching up a bad thought, and then said, 'Where you learn do all that? Theon, was it, or Tomas, he do that?'

'What? Drivin a car? Tomas don't know one thing 'bout cars. Theon show me gears on the truck . . . Wasn't so hard.'

'Not that,' she said. 'Who tol' you how to hold a gun and go point it like you done? Tomas show you that?'

Reve hunched up his shoulders. 'No one show me.'

She put her head on his shoulder. 'We near lost our way back there,' she said. 'Near got pull down the devil hole. Seen him down the devil hole.' She shivered.

'That where yo' yellin come from? Cos you feelin you down in that place?'

'Did I go yelling?'

241

'Yes, you did, Mi. Think you put fear in them.'

'Think you did too. Maybe we make a gang, you an' me, put fear in this place. Put the devil back in his hole. What you think, Reve? We special people, you an' me?'

'Sure.' A truck pulled by. A tram had to come soon. How late was it? Maybe it was after midnight . . .

'Reve, you stay with me if I go some place else?'

'What you mean?'

'Just that . . .'

Then there was the tram slinging along the road under its hanging wires, lit up like a steamship, and the moment for asking her what she meant had passed.

CHAPTER TWENTY-SEVEN

Reve was already out on the road's edge, ready to dart across, when he realized Mi had hung back. 'What you mean? Come on!' He ran back and took her arm, but she shook him off.

'No.'

'Mi, please!'

The tram squealed and its doors hissed open. He tugged at her but for all that she was skinny she was like a rooted tree when he tried to move her. 'It's not safe.'

'What? They all in their beds, Mi. No one's come looking down this place for more than . . . I don't know.'

The tram pulled away. A man, hunched up against the rain, hurried back towards Agua.

'Look at at that!' Reve threw his hands in the air in frustration. 'You make thing so hard. You know that?'

She didn't move.

The tram was about a hundred metres down the street and there was nothing to see. 'Mi, this our one chance of a dry ticket out of here and you go . . .'

He was drowned out by a siren, a blaze of lights, brakes squealing and two, no, three cars blocking the road. Police spilt out and ran to the tram while Reve and Mi huddled back in the doorway.

'How you know that goin happen?' breathed Reve. 'You think they lookin for us?'

She didn't answer.

Moments later they watched the uniformed men stand back and impatiently wave the tram on. It disappeared with a rattle and a hiss down the dark shiny street. The policemen conferred, one of them spoke on the radio, called the others, who then ran back to their cars and drove off.

Mi exhaled. 'How much reach that man got?' she said.

'Him and the Captain,' said Reve. 'Seem they throw a net round the city.'

She shuddered. 'And they know where we from.'

They did, and Moro had unfinished business in Rinconda. The spider would take his time, but he would track down whoever had called in the coastguards – the cellphone number Theon had been so keen for Reve to pass on to Moro, that had been the squeal-pig's. Some night, some day, Moro would appear in Rinconda, and there would be another killing, another body snagged in a net, left out in the middle of the village for everyone to see.

Mi stood close to him and held his arm tight. 'They goin follow us all the way back, Reve. There'll be no hidin.'

She was right, but he didn't want to admit it. 'That captain never goin put a hand on you, Mi, I swear it. They're goin think we're here, somewhere in the city. It'll be a while before they decide to sniff around down in Rinconda, and by then Theon goin figure something.'

'You trust Uncle Theon?'

'Sure,' he said with a confidence he didn't quite feel. Theon said everything was a matter of business. He did business with the police, and giving that number to Moro meant he was willing to do business with him too. But hiding Tomas, that wasn't business; helping them get away from Calde, that wasn't business either. Maybe there were some people who you couldn't ever figure out, but did that matter? Theon would never sell them to someone like Moro, never sell them to anyone.

'Sure,' he said again, more forcefully this time. It would be dangerous, but they had to go back. He had to see Tomas. He had to see Ciele and tell her about Pelo, how he had saved them. He wanted to see LoJo, and have Sultan walking beside him . . .

The gutter streamed with rainwater and the road glistened like a dolphin's back.

The street lights were like sentries posted down the long road, each casting a circle of white. He saw a figure, huddled against the rain, scuttle from one side of the road to the other and then disappear into the dark. In the distance a siren wailed. They were so far from anywhere.

Two days and two nights in this city and it felt like a lifetime.

'We goin to have to walk, Mi. We can't risk taking the tram.'

'I can walk any place,' she said. 'You know which is the way out of here?'

'See the lines, the wires.' He pointed to the tram wires. 'All we got to do is follow the lines and they take us to where we want to go.'

That's what they did.

They walked through the night, trailing the tram line,

checking each stop for their number, nine, having to backtrack a couple of times when they took the wrong track out of a junction.

The rain eased after a little while, but they were so wet it hardly made any difference. It was a long, hard night. The air was clammy and warm. Mi's hair was flattened and plastered down around her face; her fancy dress clung to her and made a slapping sound against her legs as they walked. They slogged through puddles and running drains but they kept pushing on, and all the time they were careful, stepping quickly back off the road and out of sight each time they heard a motor coming their way.

Black rain. Splintered diamonds suddenly glittering in the darkness when cars passed or when they skirted the street lamps.

Ghosts, thought Reve as he stumbled along, silent ghosts, heads bowed, lining the road away into the distance, showing them the way home.

CHAPTER TWENTY-EIGHT

Around four o'clock, a couple of hours before dawn, there were suddenly more cars and trucks and then the trams started running again and early workers were hurrying along the pavements; they felt less visible.

They cut away from the main street looking for a place to rest, somewhere they wouldn't attract notice. They were in an old part of the city now, where the houses were tall and skinny, with rusting balconies and peeling shutters and trees throwing down shade. Then they came across a little church on its own like an island guarded by iron railings. It was perfect.

They climbed the locked gate and found themselves a corner out of sight. Mi laid herself down on top of a stone with letters carved in it, laid down flat on her back with her legs straight, arms by her side, palms turned up.

'They dead people under that?' asked Reve.

'They just resting,' she said, 'like me.' She didn't open her eyes. 'I can almost hear them breathin.'

'No, you can't. The dead don't breathe; any fool know that.'

She ignored him.

He was so tired that everything ached, even his eyes. He sat down but pulled his feet up so they were well away from the stone Mi was lying on; he didn't want any part of himself touching something that belonged to the dead. The sun warmed his face and he could feel his

T-shirt already beginning to dry. He closed his eyes but he didn't sleep, too many things flitting across the inside of his eyelids.

Around noon a man in a funny square-shaped black hat and buttoned up in a black coat came and shouted at them. 'You do your business some place else!' He was so angry his eyes were bulging and there were little bits of spit on his mouth.

'Don't think he like that fancy dress they put you in at Moro's,' said Reve as they moved on.

She shrugged. 'I don't care what he think. Priests. Only good at shouting at poor people.'

'How you know that?'

'People tell me thing,' she said, 'when they come to my meetings. They tell me I got more right words coming out of me than any priest they ever heard.'

They headed up to the main road and bought bread, sausage and a big bottle of water. Reve also bought a man's shirt for Mi to wear, knotting it at the waist so that it covered up the outfit Moro's girl had squeezed her into. She looked a bit strange, but Reve reckoned that now the city was up and busy no one was going to notice them, tell them apart from any other children out on the street, so long as Mi covered up her hair. He found a cap on a street stall, and Mi, after a bit of a struggle, piled her hair into it, leaving a tangled-up ponytail sticking out of the back.

No police were going to be stopping trams now, so

they used up the last of their money to buy a ticket to the end of the line.

They were getting near to the last stop, just about where streets gave way to stores that weren't anything more than shacks with awnings pulled out over their fronts, shading cheap goods. Reve was looking at Mi.

'You look different,' he said.

'Course I look different. This what they wear in the city. Don't you got eyes?'

'I don't mean that cap,' he said, wondering what it was that seemed changed. She had her head half turned away from him, gazing out of the window, the sunlight flickering across her face just the way light flickers through clear water, down on to rock and sand and shifting weed.

'Maybe you lookin more old.'

'Old? You sayin I getting wrinkled up like a witch woman?'

He smiled. 'People pay you good money if they think you got witch power.'

'Don't need witch power; got my own.' A moment later she said, 'You think I lookin old?' She turned away, looking out of the window again. 'Don't feel so old. How old you think our mother was when she give birth to me?'

He thought of Fay in her smoky den, red hair, pale face, the black cigar. It was hard to imagine her as she might have been fifteen years younger, but she could have been about the same age Mi was now. He shrugged. 'I don't know. Why you worryin?'

She didn't answer.

He closed his eyes, but now, having conjured up an

image of Fay as a young mother, his mind wouldn't let go of the idea and one picture tumbled into another: Fay holding a baby, Fay with Mi at her knees, Fay with a smile like Mi's, but smiling not at her children but at a man in a uniform . . . that policeman, that Captain. Was that man really his birth father? The thought was sickly, like a stain.

Reve opened his eyes and stared out of the window. People going about their business, ordinary people, ordinary people with families. How many of them, he thought bitterly, walked away from their children? If a mother doesn't want her child, then the child doesn't owe that mother anything. Not one thing.

He put his hand on Mi's arm. She turned her head and smiled and then looked away again.

They got out at the end of the line and then argued as to what they should do.

Not having any money to pay for a bus ride down along the coast, their only choices were walking or hitching a ride. 'I ain't walkin any more,' Mi said flatly. 'Anyhow, die of hunger before we get halfway to anywhere. And I'm not hitching a ride with nobody.'

'Well, what idea you got? If we don't catch a ride, we got to go back into the city and wait five more days till Theon come back. You wanna do that?'

'Steal,' she said, as if it was the obvious thing to do. 'That Demi make a living out of it, picking pockets. Can't be so hard.'

'Steal! What you thinkin'? That one way to get

snap up by police. You wait here.'

He left her sitting by the roadside while he went into the stores along the road asking if there were any jobs he could do, earn himself and her a bus ride back home. But they were hard-faced the people who lived on the edge of the city and didn't have any interest in helping out a boy who talked with a country voice and who'd spent the last couple of days and nights out on the streets and was all grimed up and sour.

Then with a squeal and a cloud of dust and diesel, the bus came. They tried talking the driver into letting them ride for free but that didn't get them anywhere and when it pulled away, churning up more dust, Mi shouted and threw down her cap, releasing her wild halo of hair. She was so angry she started to shake, and before Reve could step in and calm her down she had the juddering so bad that people from around the stalls started to gather round. Just idle curiosity, but then somehow Mi wasn't quite so lost in her juddering as Reve had thought; she started waving her hands and drawing up that rough voice that came from somewhere down in her belly, and she was pronouncing this and pronouncing that and her eyes were rolling and she was running on the spot, her skinny knees pumping up and down, and she was jerking her head this way and that, her eyes rolled up in that way Reve hated.

People clapped in time to her calling out. 'She got the spirit! She got the spirit in her,' they said. One woman threw her a question about the little store she had right there, and Mi's other voice told the woman to move her store back from the road cos a storm was coming that would tear up the road and if she didn't move she'd get torn up along with everything else. Then someone said, 'How this girl know they goin be widenin this road? How she know that?'

Suddenly there were more questions and more questions until Mi began to stagger and Reve stepped in and held her up and told people to back off as he pushed through them till he could find a place to set her down.

'Tell them the spirits leavin me,' whispered Mi, barely moving her lips and speaking so quiet that no one could hear her.

He tried not to act surprised. 'You called down a storm again,' he murmured.

'Just a small one.'

He tried not to smile and laid her down beside a stall selling clay pots, plastic bowls and tins of white beans; three years older than him, but she still weighed hardly anything at all. There were people pressing around, but he told them that those spirits were all gone away now and she needed sleep. They could see she was all worn down and with a fair bit of muttering and nodding they backed off. He wondered what spirits had been visiting her this time, coming just when she needed them, and keeping better time than the bus service too.

Some of the people threw down coins as they were leaving, and Reve quickly scooped them up. One old man stopped by and said he had only heard that voice coming out of the dancing girl, heard it one time before when he was a young man, living down on the coast. He pulled a ten-dollar bill from his pocket and ceremoniously handed it to Reve. 'You give it her when she come out of wherever that spirit taken her, and you tell her to remember Joseph when she do her pray-dancing again. You tell her that.' Reve promised he would and the man went away, leaving Reve counting up the money in his hand.

That ten plus the small coins people had thrown down was enough for the fare, and for some food too. They were almost home.

CHAPTER TWENTY-NINE

Reve used some of the money to buy two raffia mats and they bedded down beside one of the stalls near the road and then waited the best part of the next day for the bus that would take them down the highway to home. When it hauled up it had Paraloca written on its destination plate, and that made Reve think of LoJo's father, Pelo.

He could tell Mi's mind was on something else. She didn't respond at first when he wanted to talk about Pelo, and then, after a moment, said, 'Everyone got their chances. Tha's what happen. Happen to him, happen to our mother. Happen to us too, and we got to be ready when it come.' She sounded different, thoughtful.

She was frowning. He could see she was not really thinking about Pelo at all. She kept looking at a neat-looking boy with pointy sideburns who was sitting across the aisle talking into his cellphone. He was about her age and he wondered whether she had taken a sudden fancy to him, in the way she'd sometimes take a sudden fancy to a pretty shell or a piece of coloured glass on the beach.

He looked out of the window and watched the road streaming by. Poor, quiet Pelo. The way Reve remembered it, Pelo had had little choice; it was like something put a twist in his life, pulled him away from his family and stood him in the door of the Slow Bar. That was it. Except at the end. He'd made a choice then. Pelo was a hero. That's what he would tell Ciele.

It was a long journey, the bus stopping here and there, men smelling of salt and cigars shuffling up and down the aisle, women with baskets and cotton-wrapped parcels of food. He fell asleep and dreamed of Calde, broad as a mountain and holding a long knife in his hand, looming up over the village, one foot on the harbour wall and the other on the burying hill, and in his dream Reve saw Sultan dancing about the strand, hackles up, barking at the giant and darting at his feet as if to bite them. He woke up anxious, his heart beating and sweat running down his back.

Mi's seat beside him was empty, and the bus was just pulling away from a stop on the highway.

He panicked, sure she was gone, had suddenly changed her mind about coming back. It was his fault: the burning car – he should never have told her about that. Hevez. Calde. Everyone hating her or fearing her. Poor Mi! He scrambled out into the aisle. 'Hey!' he yelled at the driver. 'Stop the bus!'

The driver slammed on the brakes, and Reve staggered, gripping the back of a seat to steady himself. Heads turned . . . and there she was, just two rows down the bus, talking to the boy with the cellphone.

'Mi!'

'Hey,' the driver shouted at him, 'you want to get off this bus or what you want to do?'

Reve muttered an apology, while Mi turned and gave him a puzzled look. 'What you playin at, Reve? Go back to your seat. I don't need no protecting, you hear.'

An older woman sitting across the aisle from Mi cackled and looked at Reve and shook her head.

'You the man in the family?' she said. 'How 'bout you come protecting me and I give you sweet cake!'

Some people around laughed and he felt embarrassed and stupid and cross. He went quickly back to his seat. They didn't know Mi, didn't know how she could get in trouble.

'Who was that?' he asked when she came back to her seat.

'Just a boy. He done me favour, that's all.'

'What favour?'

She shrugged and looked out of the window. 'Why you care so much 'bout everything?' she said after a moment. 'You all the time running this way and that: Tomas, Arella, Theon –' she pulled a face – 'an' me too, eh. But you don' see what maybe comin roun' the corner.'

'An' you do?'

'Maybe.'

'Well, how 'bout tellin me then.'

'You think everythin' go an' fall easy when we get back? You think Uncle Theon know all the answer.'

'No but—'

'Who goin keep us safe? You got answer to that, Reve? Cos tha's what I want – I want safe.' She pulled the sleeves of her man's shirt down over her hands and then crossed her arms tight as if she was cold, even though the bus was hot and airless.

He wanted to say that he would keep her safe, that that was what he had always tried to do, but now he realized that it wasn't something you could promise. 'I don' know,' he admitted.

They sat without talking for a while, and the bus rumbled on, stopping every thirty minutes or so, letting people get off. They looked like they were going home from the city. Hardly anyone boarded the bus.

The view from the window was beginning to be familiar now. The long shore, sandy fields, dunes and the wide sea. From time to time they spotted clusters of houses and shacks down by the shore, little villages, some bigger. They weren't so far from Rinconda now. Sometimes he saw the triangular print of a sail out on the ocean and he wished he was out there, free, nothing and no one pressing in on him.

Mi broke in on his daydreaming. 'Why he want me?' she asked.

'Who?' He thought she meant the boy with the phone, but he can't have wanted her so much because he had got down at the last stop, and sure he had given her a friendly wave, but that was all.

'Who you think?

'Two-Boat?'

'His given name's Enrico. Did you know that?'

'No.'

'He ask me to marry him.'

'You just a girl, Mi. What you know about marryin?'

'Know some things. Having a mother would've helped. Thought she might have told me all I need to know.' She gave a half-laugh. 'Didn't turn out that way.'

'She had nothing to tell you, Mi; she lost whatever

mothering feeling she had when she ran with the policeman.'

'Maybe. She look sad when we saw her in the rain. Did you think that, that she looked sorry?'

'Yeah, maybe she did, but tha's all gone. '

'You think I'm too young for marrying?'

Reve didn't know how to answer. What was a right age? How could he know that?

'There's no hurry on you marryin anyone, Mi. Maybe we go see him, you an' me, like family, you know . . .'

'Tha's San Jerro there!' she said interrupting him, pointing out of the window. A cluster of houses, it was like Rinconda but bigger, a wide sprawl of huts and houses down by the ocean, but it seemed so different because the shacks were painted blue and pink, and there were white houses made of stone. Solid. Then it was gone. Mi sat back and closed her eyes. 'You know what I really keep wantin to know, Reve? That woman you seen, down in the water – what was the meaning in that? What was the meaning in you seeing her and not me? That bother me all the time.'

'You said it was our gone-away mother.'

'I know tha's what I said, but that's because that what I *wanted* it to mean.'

They lapsed into silence, lost in their own thoughts, until, out of the blue, she said, 'I'm coming back with you now Reve, but don't think I'm stayin in that place.' She sounded almost matter of fact.

'What you sayin?'

'It's got too much bad. You got Calde. You got Moro.

You got that police captain. They all goin be buzzin at me like dirt flies.' She flapped her hand as if she was swatting them away. 'But you know what I want? I want you with me when I go.'

'Rinconda's my place, Mi.'

'I think you come with me.' It was as if he hadn't spoken. 'But I want to see Tomas before we go.' He remembered the way she had ignored him, face tight as a clam when he had tried to talk to her. 'I always been thinkin,' she said, 'that it's Tomas makin our mother go away; thought Tomas the one kill our father, tangle him up in that net.' She rubbed the fug from the window with the sleeve of her shirt, then frowned. 'But I was wrong, wasn't I? That woman, our mother, did those things. Maybe she had her reasons, but we never goin know what she was thinkin. She did her choosing long time ago. She choose that policeman. She choose that place in the city.' She put her forehead against the steamy window. 'You know what I feel like after my meetings when all the voices are gone away. I feel like I'm an empty place.' She closed her eyes. 'The voices seem all gone from me. I hear nothin tellin me what I want to know . . . You think me an' Tomas can be friends?'

'Bein friends isn' so hard, Mi.'

'No?'

Three days in the city and it was strange how things felt different between Mi and him. He wasn't sure what it was. She was always changing, her mood flitting back and forward, but this was different. There was something more settled in her. He looked at her but she had her head back against the headrest and her cap tilted over her eyes.

The road curved a little and then he saw the village. The straggling line of black-clad shacks winding down to the shore, and the harbour wall like a lobster claw hooked out into the sea. Rinconda. They were home. He should have felt happy or relieved, but instead he felt anxious. What if Tomas wasn't any stronger? What if the village hadn't quietened down? What if Calde pushed his way up on to Theon's roof and found the Boxer lying there . . .

He should have borrowed that boy's cellphone. He should have called Theon. He should have checked that it was safe.

CHAPTER THIRTY

The sun was a blood-red ball in the sky behind them; their shadows stretched out spidery thin down the bank from the highway and towards the long torn ribbon of houses and shacks.

'Can you see my place?' said Mi.

Reve shook his head. 'No.' He couldn't see any boats out on the ocean either, nor anyone down on the harbour wall, which was unusual. But there was a crowd down below the cantina ten people, maybe more. There was no sign of a car anywhere so Señor Moro hadn't tracked them yet. He couldn't see anyone else at all, no one in their backyard or at the fish store. 'You think it's safe to go down, Mi?'

'Got no feelin' one way or another, Reve. Got no feelin' for this place at all – never have.' She started down the track and he followed after her.

Faces peered at them as they passed by, but no one offered a greeting, even people that Reve knew, men he had fished with. They just watched them from their doorways and let them pass by in silence. It unsettled him, but he didn't want to say anything to Mi.

They would go straight to Theon's cantina, he decided. They would find Tomas and then, if there was still trouble in the village, they would slip away when it was dark and walk down the coast to San Jerro; if Two-Boat was serious about Mi, then he would help them out.

A dog stood at the corner of one shack and barked as they walked down the middle of the track. Crickets buzzed and sawed the thick afternoon air. A black-bellied pig trotted across the track, right in front of them, head low, snout forward, busy going some place.

'Not even the pigs are bothering with us, Reve.'

They rounded a bend in the track and there was the cantina. The crowd he'd seen from the roadside had moved off, though he could hear someone shouting further down towards the shore. They slipped in through the door and Reve called out, 'Hey! Theon! We come back!'

Silence.

The tables were cleared, chairs tucked in and out of the way. The floor was swept but there was a pot of water boiling on the hob. Reve took a cloth and lifted it off. 'Making himself coffee. Must have just stepped out.'

'Thought you said Tomas was here. Where is he?' Mi asked.

'Unless he learn to fly, he's up on the roof. Come and see him.'

'There's no one here, Reve. Can't you feel it? They all gone.'

'No!' They had to be there. He took the stairs two at a time and Mi followed behind. She was right: there was no one there. No Tomas, no Theon, no Ciele and no baby. Just like below, it looked as though they had just stepped away this minute. Tomas's sheet was scrumpled up at the foot of his pallet, a jug of water beside the bed, half full and tepid from standing out in the sun; and his Bible was lying open. 'Maybe he's all right,' he said, even though nothing looked right. 'You know Tomas is strong. Maybe the cut he got wasn't so bad. What you think? Maybe Theon took him and Ciele. Down the coast . . .' His voice trailed into silence.

'Maybe.' Mi didn't sound convinced. She was over by the corner of the roof, looking back the way they had come, up to the highway.

'You see anything there?'

She shook her head and then bent down and rummaged in a deep basket over in the corner where she was standing and started pulling out long torn strips of cotton. 'This look fresh.' She held up a cloth that must have been used as a bandage; the dark stain was blood. A gull floated above them, looking down, and then tilted its wings and drifted off to the coast. 'You think Tomas strong enough to walk out of here, and him bleeding still?'

Reve stood staring at the pallet as if it could tell him what had happened, but all he could think about was how Tomas had lain there, his face grey, his voice a hoarse whisper and Ciele's white bandage tight round his middle, and the dark stain of his blood seeping through. Three days to recover? No. No hope of that at all. There was only one thing that could have happened.

This was why no one they had passed had spoken to them. The villagers knew and they wanted no part of it. He should have seen it straight away.

'Calde got him,' he said abruptly. 'Calde got him right

now! Come on!' He turned and ran down the stairs. He'd been dreaming to think for one moment that Calde would let it all blow over. Calde would have kept looking and sniffing and rooting, and someone would have heard or seen something up on the cantina roof. Maybe the baby had cried . . . and then Calde's men would have hauled Tomas down, and Theon and Ciele, dragged them out so that everyone could see what he was doin to his one-time partner. Calde would want the whole village to know that if you stood against him something bad would happen. The crowd he'd seen from the road – had that been them bundling Tomas and the others down towards the harbour?

'Wait!' said Mi, pulling at his arm. 'You don't know what's happening, Reve! You don't know what they doing down there.'

He stopped and turned round. Fear made him angry. 'What you think, Mi? You think we do nothing? You think we jus' keep out the way, keep our eyes squeeze tight so we don' see what happen? Tha' what you want?'

She frowned, then glanced back up at the highway, the same as she had done up on the roof.

'What is it? You see something?'

'No.'

So he ran; she followed, and people stared at them from their shacks as they went by. They passed the cold store and then Ciele's place and then they were almost down at the end of the track: the remains of Tomas's hut on the right; Arella's hut on the left. Arella was standing on her porch, her blank eyes staring straight ahead at the gathering right there in the middle of the track, her face worn down with grief.

There were at least ten men, all Calde's people, and Calde was in the middle. Reve didn't see Tomas or Ciele or Theon, but he wasn't going to stand there looking. He yanked Mi off the track and they made their way through the backyards of the last few shacks, stopping when they got to Arella's. Cautiously Reve peered from the corner. No one had spotted them. He closed his eyes and leaned his head back against the salty planking.

He needed to think, to be clever, clever as Theon. But how do you suddenly get to be clever? What would Theon do in their place? Make a call, that's what you do. But who? Who do you call? The police? The police would just bring the Captain and kiss Calde on the cheek, and let him kick Tomas to death. Then he would snatch Mi and take her back in the trunk of his car, lock her in his house some place. He felt like banging his head against the shack's back wall. Clever? When had he ever been clever? They had run from one nightmare, and he had led them smack into another.

'Wha's happening?' whispered Mi. 'What they doing?'

He puffed out his cheeks and peered round the edge of the shack again. He saw the brothers Cesar and Escal standing over a body they had down on the ground. Escal had a rolled-up fishing net on his shoulders, and Reve saw Cesar say something to him. Escal swung the bundle down and the two of them strung it out between them and then there was grunting and a muffled cry as whoever was down on the ground was trussed in the net.

265

Reve watched in horror. It was Tomas. Was this how it had been with their father, snagged up in a net and then what? Thrown off the harbour wall to drown?

He scanned the crowd.

He saw fishermen who owed Calde favour one way or another, or who reckoned it was safer being on the inside of the ring. He knew them all. And Hevez and his pals, Sali and Ramon. No one who might help. There was no sign of Ciele . . .

He spotted Theon though.

He was right beside Calde, and Calde had his hairy hand on Theon's shoulder, gripping it tight, like they were pals, like they were partners! And Theon was pulling off his glasses and rubbing them on the edge of his shirt and looking round the crowd, not looking at Tomas but back round at the village, and then he was looking their way. He blinked. A moment of recognition.

Instantly Reve pulled himself back out of sight. He looked at Mi. Her face was tight and her eyes screwed up. Her hands were trembling.

'Do something, Mi! Do some of your magic thing. Do your voice! Call down a storm like you done before.'

Her lips were moving and her eyelids flickering. Maybe she was trying. She was starting to tremble. But he couldn't help her. He realized with a feeling of despair that he couldn't help anyone. 'Oh please, Mi, do something . . .'

Calde raised his voice. He was speaking so loud all the people cowering in their shacks and hiding their heads away would hear him. 'You all about to see what happen

266

when someone do a bad thing in my village.' He sounded hard. 'This man here is the squeal-pig. A'right? You all heard that. You know what it mean: he brought the police burning down homes in this place.' The men around him were silent, waiting for Calde to finish. 'And,' added Calde, 'he's a runaround after another man's wife. This is not a man we want in Rinconda . . .' He paused. 'If no one goin to speak for him, I take it you all are easy about the punishment I'm goin to put on this man.'

'Take his head off,' shouted Escal, his voice ugly. 'Take it off with your cutting blade, Calde. Take his head off and put it on a pole, like in the old times.'

There was laughter and a couple of the men jeered.

Reve pulled his head back. He didn't want to see any more. 'They've roll him up in a net, Mi.' He took a shaky breath and pressed his head against the shack wall. 'I think they goin drown him . . .' He closed his eyes tight and through clenched teeth said, 'Mi? Can't you call down something . . . some of your magic . . . now, please.'

He turned his head and looked at her. Mi was trembling very badly, her eyes staring, not rolled-up white but staring hard straight ahead, not at Reve but at some point he couldn't see.

She grunted, trying to make a word. Her hand was a claw on his arm. 'Ohgh!' she grunted. Or maybe it was 'Ohd!' Nothing that made sense.

'Make him ready,' called Calde.

This was it.

Reve prised Mi's fingers from his arm. Better to do something, even if it is the wrong thing. When you step in the dance you got to know the steps. But there were no steps to this dance. 'Stay here, Mi. Keep still, OK? Stay quiet. Don' let anyone see you.' She was rigid, lost in some dark place again. He touched her cheek. 'Whatever happen, a'right?'

He ran round the corner and shouted at the top of his voice, 'Stop! You got no right, Calde! I witness what you doin! You murdering Tomas! An' he done nothin 'cept stand against you! Tha's all he done!' He took a ragged breath.

He saw Ramon looking at him, not sneering in his usual way but puzzled, an eyebrow raised and looking behind Reve as if expecting to see someone else. And Hevez, his face glazed and stupid-looking – he'd been stoking up his courage with beer.

The small crowd parted a little and Reve could see a shapeless snagged-up bundle with Tomas's face visible through the netting, and the white of his vest that looked drenched in sweat and a darker stain over the wound. He wasn't moving. He couldn't move. Was he still breathing? Reve couldn't see.

'Tomas never call anyone,' he shouted again. 'He got no cellphone. He got no interest in what you doin. Calde tellin a lie!'

Arella, up on her porch, suddenly called out, 'Reve! What they doin? What they doing to Tomas?'

He wanted to reassure her. Poor old Arella, with nothing in her life but a bit of company with Tomas, standing up on her porch, her head tilted up as if she could somehow see with her head that way.

'What they doin?' Her voice quavered.

Calde swung round and lifted his panga blade, pointing the tip at Reve's throat. 'You come back, eh! Well, you next if you step in my way. Be careful, runaround, or you find you lose a leg or an arm.'

Theon cut in. His voice was icy. 'You don't know what you're sayin, Reve. Go back out of this. You can't do anything here. Not now.' The sinking sun caught his glasses and the flash blanked out his eyes, made him look inhuman.

Reve felt as if he was trembling almost as bad as Mi. He forced himself to walk forward, past the two brothers, up to Tomas. He wished he had a knife to cut the net biting into Tomas. He wished he had a knife in his hand, give him courage, give a chance to put up some fight before they finish him.

He turned and faced them again, planted his legs apart, as if he were keeping steady on his skiff and, ignoring all the faces of the men staring at him, looked straight at Calde and said, 'You got no right! You got no right steppin on anyone, Calde!' His voice shook a little but they all heard him, every one of them.

Calde grunted with surprise. 'You got some nerve, boy. Maybe you got some of Tomas's rum runnin in your belly.' A few of the men smiled. Then Calde's tone hardened. 'Move out the way. This not the first time a squeal-pig gets done in this place. Tomas know what comin to him. Your father was—'

'Murdered,' said Reve. 'You going to do the same?' He caught Theon's eye. 'What happen, Theon?

How you let this happen?'

Theon shook his head. 'Some things you can't fix.' He had promised them it would all be safe when they got back.

There was a heartbeat when no one moved and everything was so sharp. Every sound, every breath was distinct: the crunch of a sandalled foot shifting on the track, the sea flopping up on to the sand, a gull crying, the cicadas buzzing, an engine changing gear.

Calde pulled a face. 'What is this? None of this talk interest me. Someone get him out the way.'

Reve clenched his fist. One hit. At least let me land one hit on this ugly man. One hit for what he done to us all.

There was the sharp squeal of tyres on a hot road. A few heads turned and Reve saw a black car pulling down from the highway, bumping fast along the track and into the village.

Suddenly Reve realized what Mi had been trying to say: 'The road!' She'd somehow known someone would be coming.

CHAPTER THIRTY-ONE

'You got more witness now,' Reve said. 'Look who coming for you.'

A stay of execution.

That's what it felt like, though when Reve saw the squat figure of Moro and two of his suited men getting out of the car, his throat tightened. Instinctively he stooped down, trying to get Calde and his men to block him from Moro. If Moro saw him or Mi, they were dead. He wouldn't care one way or the other about Tomas.

Why in the name of heaven and hell had he insisted Mi come back to the village with him? To be family? Dead family.

Calde's men moved towards the señor. Maybe if Mi kept really still he could swear to Moro that she wasn't with him. Maybe Moro hadn't come for them at all. Maybe he had come for the informer, trace him down with that number that Theon had insisted Reve pass on. Reve edged back towards Tomas. 'Tomas,' he hissed. 'Tomas?'

He thought there was a faint movement, a finger hooked through the mesh. Tomas was alive!

Moro put up his hand. 'Not so close,' he said to Calde's men.

'This is it,' said Moro, 'a village gathering. I like this. Everything in the open. Calde, I see you got business. Tell me what's happening, eh. And Theon . . .' he said, spotting him. 'You here too. That's good. Now, why you got that man like that. Someone been fishing?' No one laughed at his grim joke.

Calde started to tell him about Tomas – that he was the one who had informed on the smugglers and that he and his men were about to punish him, when suddenly there was an excited yell.

'I got the witch girl!' It was Hevez, his voice crowing with delight. He and Sali emerged from behind Arella's, dragging Mi kicking and struggling between them.

Reve didn't even think. He abandoned Tomas, sprinted straight at Hevez and threw a punch that landed hard, smack in the middle of his face, right on the button of his nose. Hevez's head snapped back and he fell, landing with a thud on the track, his nose bloody. In the same instant Mi wrenched her arm away and swung her free left hand round in a claw-hammer blow that caught Sali a ringing smack on his ear that made him grunt with surprise and pain. He clutched the side of his head, and she broke away from him and stepped in beside Reve as Hevez struggled back to his feet. For a moment it looked as if the two boys were going to make another move, but she just raised her arm and pointed at them, and that stopped them in their tracks.

Reve was so astonished that it took him a moment to register that no one else, none of Calde's men, had done anything to help the boys. He took Mi's arm and edged her back towards Tomas, everyone watching them, and glancing at Moro as if expecting him to give an order.

He felt oddly calm. At least the three of them were

together, like they had been all that time ago when Tomas had peeled away the net from their drowned father.

He felt for Mi's hand and gripped it.

'Ah,' said Moro, and gave three claps. 'I hoped for this. Very good. The little bull and his sister. That moves me, it does, but . . . you,' he said to Reve, 'should have been smarter. Found yourself another town, stayed free. But here, this place, this is mine now, eh. And you got serious problem.' He smiled, but his small eyes were cold and angry.

Reve kept his head up, but he felt lost. This was it. This is what it must feel like to be scooped up in the net. All three of them in the one catch. Jackfish. No running away.

'Now,' said Moro, 'my business.' He pulled out his cellphone. 'I got a number here,' he said. 'This the number of someone who think calling the helicopter coastguard a smart idea.' A few of Calde's men moved away from Tomas. Moro's suited men, Reve realized, had guns, heavy snub-barrelled weapons, pointing casually at the crowd. 'And whoever got a phone that ring when I call this number, that man got a problem.

Calde was impassive. He glanced at Theon. Theon shrugged and wiped his glasses again, but a moment later Reve noticed that he stepped sideways, leaving space between himself and Calde.

Moro tapped the numbers into his cellphone, making a performance of it, slowly, mouthing each number to himself.

Silence.

A phone started to ring. Everyone shuffled nervously and looked this way and that. Calde grunted and patted his pocket, then took out a phone, which chirped at him till he pressed a button with his thumb. He frowned. 'This is not my phone . . .' he began to say.

Moro nodded at his men.

Calde didn't even have time to look up before the first bullet took him in the chest and the second in his throat, flinging him back on to the sandy path, about a metre away from Tomas's feet.

Everyone else froze.

CHAPTER THIRTY-TWO

The silence was sudden and heavy. Even the cicadas seemed to pause their endless scraping and sawing. Maybe they were holding their breath too.

Reve studied Uncle Theon's face for a clue, but it was impassive. He'd figured this, hadn't he? Done something clever. Clever Theon. Switched Calde's phone maybe. If anyone else thought the same, they weren't saying.

'All right,' said Moro, looking up from his phone. 'I come along to do this. So now we all know: you play a game, you got to be sure the rules work for you; but you play a game with me, the rules always work for me. That fat man nothing when he lived, and he nothing now. Anyone goin step in his place?'

Reve saw Hevez keeping his head down, his hand cupping his bloody nose. He tried not to look at the body lying on the ground like a beached whale, the shirt ridden up a little, showing some belly.

Theon glanced down at Calde, then stooped, picked the phone out of his hand, clicked it off and slipped it into his pocket. Reve kept his face still and his mouth shut. Theon had figured out the whole play.

'Well,' Moro faced Theon, 'you got any business with this man? You got problem you going to give me for this?'

'No,' said Theon. 'He played his game. I got different business.'

Moro nodded. 'Yes, of course. The boy, this one

here, was your messenger. Good. I like things to be tidy. Everything in its place.' Moro looked around the crowd, seeing, perhaps, if there was anyone else he needed to identify now, anyone who might challenge his authority. There was no one. Cesar had his hand gripped round the back of his brother's neck. Maybe he feared he would make a fuss. Escal had never been smart.

'Good,' Moro said again, briskly this time. 'We do business another time. This is a long drive to make to kill a man, but some things you got to do.' His eyes found Reve. 'All right. You and your sister come now and you get in the car.'

Mi's grip tightened in Reve's hand. 'No,' she said, her voice barely audible.

'What's that she say?' Moro sounded surprised.

'She said No,' said Reve. 'She not going with you. She not going to that police captain who murder our father. She not doin any of these thing.'

'No?'

'No,' said Mi, her voice light and clear now. 'You should leave this place.'

'I think you make a mistake about me, princess.'

Princess?

The strange thing was that was exactly how Mi looked. It didn't matter that her legs were scratched or that she was wearing a crumpled man's shirt over a crumpled and stained green dress. She stood somehow taller, stronger; her hair, free of the cap, blazed round her serious face. She didn't looked like the crazy girl who scraped around in a sand garden and lived in a dead car.

276

Calde's men couldn't take their eyes off her. It was as if they had never seen her before; and not one of them made a move towards her or Reve.

Even Theon seemed surprised to see this girl stand tall before the señor.

'Put her in the car,' said Moro. 'You and you.' He jerked his head at Cesar and the man beside him. 'You can leave the boy. Hold him, eh.'

For a moment Reve thought the men would disobey him, but it was just a moment. Then three quick strides and they had their hands on Mi. A brief silent struggle, with Reve kicking until someone, Escal maybe, had him lifted off the ground with his arms pinned tight by his side, and Mi, silent too, being dragged to the car.

Why couldn't she? Oh, why couldn't she call down a storm? Why couldn't the sky darken and the waves rear up, tall as rolling cliffs, and thunder down on them, like the sea on the Egyptians in Tomas's story. He wouldn't mind; he wouldn't care at all if he got swept away, if they all got swept away together, but not this helplessness, seeing Mi, her head pushed down, being shovelled into the back of the car. Not this!

Reve jerked and snapped his right heel back hard and high, catching Escal in a place that sure enough hurt him so badly that the burly fisherman gave a loud 'huff' and let Reve drop as he buckled over, clutching his groin.

The car door slammed shut as Reve ran towards it. He could see Mi's face through the window. Moro was getting in at the passenger side. Moro's man, Secondo, was standing beside him, holding the door with one hand

and his gun, casually pointing at Reve, in the other. His expression was impossible to read under his dark glasses, though the corner of his mouth lifted. He could have been smiling.

From either side of the track people were coming out of their shacks, the women, one or two of the men, but mainly women, five, ten, more. Maybe they thought they were safe now; maybe they wanted to watch. He saw Tomas's neighbours, the whole family and the family next to them and the fisherman who lived two up from Arella.

Moro's window whispered down. 'You had your chance, young bull. You could have worked for me. I showed you the city, eh. You didn't want it.' He sounded almost regretful. 'This is how it is. Now I take the girl because I need her.' He lifted his shoulders a little, making his neck almost disappear. 'It's business.'

Reve didn't look at him, this devil. He looked at Mi. She smiled at him through the glass, the sunlight flickering across her face, and he saw her lips moving. What was she saying? Her smile was so sad. She seemed so much older somehow, a woman now, and she was going away from him. She raised her hand as if to wave.

He clenched his fists. There was no point saying it out loud; she wouldn't hear him, but he wished the words with all his heart: 'Call down a storm, Mi. Call down thunder!'

His eyes burned and stung.

And when he blinked furiously to clear away that stinging feeling, he suddenly saw it was *her*! Without any mistake, this grown-up Mi was the woman he had seen smiling sadly up at him through water that had seemed so clear and clean that it was like looking through glass. And now here she was, looking through the glass of this rich man's car.

What Reve had seen was the future, but that future was now. This moment. His sister being stolen away.

CHAPTER THIRTY-THREE

Moro's car engine purred into life and the car rolled backwards, jolting slowly on the broken ground, making its unhurried three-point turn. Why should he ever hurry? He had everything in his pocket: the village, the Barrio and the Captain himself.

He just come in so easy, thought Reve. Take what he want; take a girl; take a boy maybe; take a life and then all he got to do is glide out, the heavy wheel of his car grinding the sand and stone, leaving nothing that the wind won't blow away, and people forget.

And then a strange thing happened.

Miracle maybe.

When the rich man's car had turned and was just starting to drive off, five, six, seven women suddenly surged out across the track and blocked the way. There were more hurrying down from the shacks further up the village.

'Let her go!' one shouted. Reve saw that it was sharp-faced Maria Scatta, who had lost her own child a while back. She was always visiting Mi, asking her things, asking what it was like on the other side and was her little girl all right.

'You let her go!' Another woman shouted the same thing. Then another. A row of angry women, like a living fence.

The car stopped and blasted its horn.

They jeered at it while Calde's men stood around like sheep, not knowing what to do.

Moro's window hissed down. 'Get out of the way, or I run you down!'

Reve looked around for Theon. At first he thought he had disappeared, but then he saw him crouched down on the ground beside the poor bundled-up shape of Tomas.

The car's engine revved and the driver blasted the horn again.

'Filth!' they screamed. 'Pig!' They shook their fists as they shouted. One picked up a rock and threw it at the car; it hit the bonnet with a tinny pop. The car lurched forward but the track was so uneven that it couldn't accelerate properly and all the women did was take a step back; someone else threw another rock, and this one cracked against the windscreen.

If the car got past the women, and then up on to where the track ran smoother, Reve would lose Mi for good. Now was his only chance.

He sprinted.

He yelled, 'Let her go, Moro!'

He reached the limousine and banged on the roof. 'Let her go! Let her go!' He banged again. Another stone smacked into the windscreen just as the car began to pick up speed. The women scattered. One of Moro's men was so angry he leaned right out of the window, cursed and loosed off a wild shot towards the running women. Reve didn't see whether it hit anyone or not because, instinctively, he hurled himself forward, catching the man's arm with all his weight, bringing it down hard, so the man yelled in pain and the gun suddenly hammered off five, six shots in a violent burst that sent bullets flying and hissing out into the edge of the track or ricocheting off stone. Someone gave a sharp cry.

Reve hit the ground hard, snatched the fallen revolver and was then jerked, twisted, tumbled over this way and that. His leg felt as if it had been jammed into the jaws of a mako shark, and he was being dragged along the track. The rear bumper had snagged his leg, and although the car was going no more than a smart walking pace, Reve's vision blurred. He got a jumbled impression of a hand, the back of the car, dirt, a foot, orange sky. All the time there was yelling and the horn blaring and his back burned . . .

He tried to twist himself free but the car swerved, swinging him sideways. His head whacked against something hard and he felt the iron taste of blood in his mouth and his eyes hazed.

Then, he realized with relief, his foot had wrenched free and he wasn't being dragged any more.

And then, behind the shouting and the blasting of the horn, Reve heard another sound: the roar of trucks and gears grinding. He managed to tip up his head and look to where the sun was dipping down, resting like a red-hot dollar on the tip of the hills, and there he saw the trucks, three of them, pulling down from the highway, one after the other. They were painted blue and gold and red, flags and bunting fluttering from the cabs, and the backs of the trucks loaded up with men.

He struggled dizzily to his knees, clutching the gun,

a vague thought that he should shoot out the tyres of the car, but the gun was heavy in his hand and wobbled badly when he tried to aim. He squinted and then felt a hard grip, pushing his arm down. 'You don't need this,' said Theon. 'Leave it, Reve.'

'They takin Mi . . .'

'No. You don't got need for that, Reve. Look.'

The car had stopped. The driver had tried to turn off the track, and now its back wheels were spinning in the sand, sinking in deeper as the driver furiously gunned the engine and then in frustration switched it off.

Moro got out, his men flanking him, one of them with a right arm hanging limp, Secondo gripping Mi and holding a pistol to her head.

Moro glanced at Reve, quite expressionless, as if he had never seen him before, never taken him up to the roof of the Slow Bar and shown him his city. Then he turned to face the new threat.

The trucks rattled past the cantina and slewed across the track, blocking the way, just as the women had tried to do before. Men vaulted down from the sides clutching an assortment of clubs and wicked-looking knives, and Reve saw some of them holding guns – nothing fancy like Moro's men, not snub-nosed and oily grey but more like old hunting shotguns. Women who only a few moments before had scattered out of the way were now hurrying back.

Climbing down from the cab of the first truck was a stern-faced man in a baseball cap. Two-Boat.

The two men faced each other.

'Who're you?' said Moro. 'You're in my way.'

Two-Boat tipped his cap back. He studied Moro and then he looked around him, at the women and their families who had been blocking the route. He took in Calde's men, still waiting it seemed for someone to tell them what to do, and Theon. Finally his eyes rested for a moment on Reve.

'You don't look like a man who's goin any place,' said Two-Boat eventually. 'Not unless you put some manners on your asking.'

Moro nodded, as if this was a reasonable comment. 'Maybe you don't know who I am.' He shrugged and glanced back at Mi. 'All I need do is—'

'I don't give bishop spit who you are,' said Two-Boat, interrupting him. 'You got something that don't belong to you; and you don't let her go now, this moment, you goin be fish bait. You hear me?'

Moro held the fisherman's gaze for what seemed like a long time. 'This is my place here,' he said, still keeping his voice level, but anyone could tell he was angry. This was the señor who planned to control the Captain of police, this was the man who wanted to feed off the whole city; and then here was some fisherman telling him what he could and couldn't do. 'You cause me trouble here, you got no idea what I bring down on you.'

'No,' said Two-Boat. He had a different kind of authority from Moro. It didn't come from the men ranged up behind him but from the heavy certainty with which he spoke. 'You listen. You got a nothin share of nothin here. Who you got to call down and help you? No one.

284

So if you want to go back to your city, you let the girl go right now.'

Moro looked around, as if counting the number of men ranged against him, checking the odds maybe. But he didn't have any choices. 'You let me drive out of here?'

'You got my word.'

Moro nodded to Secondo, who lowered his gun and released Mi.

She walked away from Moro and his men towards Two-Boat and then she stopped. Her head was high, her shoulders straight, and she waited for him to come to her.

There she was, a girl and a queen at the same time; and she didn't seem to need anyone to tell her how to be – didn't need her mother, didn't need Reve either.

Two-Boat smiled for the first time and strode to her and took her in his arms; and although he wasn't a tall man, she seemed tiny against him. He bent his head and kissed her forehead, and the women clapped and laughed. Reve thought he should smile but his leg hurt too much and there was a feeling in his chest that he didn't recognize, a different kind of hurt, and he didn't know what it was.

'I'll take this, yes?' said Theon, unlocking Reve's fingers from the revolver and then gently helping him to his feet. 'You don't need to go shooting anyone now.'

'He's still here,' said Reve anxiously, keeping his voice low so only Theon could hear him. 'No one safe with him here. He could do something.'

'I don't think so.'

Moro and his men hadn't moved. When Two-Boat released Mi Moro said, 'My car needs digging out.'

Two-Boat nodded. 'Paolo,' he called out, 'give this man a spade.'

A couple of spades were thrown down from the truck and carried across to Moro and Secondo, and then the two city men sweated and dug into the sand around the rear wheels of the car while everyone else watched. The third man sat in the shade, barely conscious, cradling his broken arm.

When the rear axle was clear, and the driver had bumped the car up on to the track, and the third man had been helped into the back seat, Moro turned to Two-Boat again. 'You think I forget this?' he said.

'No,' said Two-Boat, 'you remember. You remember how lucky you been this time.'

Moro looked at the fisherman for a long time and then he turned and stepped into the car, which immediately rolled up the track towards the highway.

Everyone watched till it reached the road and turned north, and then it was as if a soft wind had picked up, because the air seemed somehow fresher and people eased their shoulders and started to talk. The women came down and chatted to the men by the trucks, and Theon helped Reve limp slowly back to Tomas, each step sending a spike of pain up from his right ankle.

'You think that man goin come back?' he asked, gritting his teeth and leaning on Theon. He couldn't help it, but he had a vision of Moro and his men tearing up the village because of the way he had been shamed.

'He's a businessman. He'll come back if he think he can do business. That's the way it is.'

'And you'll do business with him.'

'Reve, you gone to the city and you learn nothing? Everyone got to do business with everyone. That's the way it is.'

'Even do business with the devil?'

Theon paused, letting Reve take a breath. 'When he come knocking on the door, sometimes you don't got a choice.'

Although Reve's mind was muzzy with hurt, he thought that Theon, for all that he was clever, didn't have this right, but he couldn't argue it now; maybe it was one of those things that you can't argue anyhow. And it didn't seem important, not now that Mi was wrapped up with Two-Boat, and Tomas was maybe dying, and Pelo was dead too, had to be.

The sun disappeared and the darkness, as always, fell suddenly and there was a moment or two when it was pitch black and you couldn't see anything at all, and then the headlamps on the trucks were switched on and lamps and fires were lit and the village seemed to breathe again.

CHAPTER THIRTY-FOUR

It should have been dark down at Tomas's end of the village, because Arella never had a light in her place, never had need, and now that Tomas's shack was burned away there was no light coming from that direction. But someone had set a brazier burning, and someone else had hung lamps on Arella's porch, so when Theon brought Reve close enough to see what was going on he was half dazzled by the light and the giant shadows stretching and bending with the soft inshore breeze and people hurrying this way and that to tend Tomas.

Reve stopped a little back from where Tomas was lying up on Arella's porch, suddenly unwilling to come any closer. He gripped Theon's arm. 'Tomas was safe in the cantina. What happen?'

'Tomas come down from the roof,' said Theon. 'Couldn't stop him. Calde know Tomas some place in the village; goin come a time when he get roun' to my place . . . And Tomas fretting. He know if they goin find him, they goin find Ciele and her baby. So he come down; call out Calde. Then,' he said flatly, 'while Calde's men beat him, I get Ciele out the back, across the field, tell her to keep walkin till she make San Jerro. Life for life – that's what Tomas say to me. The old way.'

The old way? Tomas giving up his life for Ciele. What kind of a way was that if it left you beaten dead and wrapped in a net?

'That business with the cellphone?'

'Best you don't talk about that.' He looked at Reve and the lights glinted off his glasses blanking out his eyes. 'Sometimes you make a long-term plan, you know, set things moving and hope the pieces fall out right; we got lucky Moro roll up when he did . . .'

Reve frowned. 'Were you the one call the coastguard?'

Theon acted as if he hadn't heard. 'You a'right?' he said. 'You want to stop here?'

'But that chopper could've finish them all off: Calde, Moro . . .'

Theon nodded. 'An' would that have been a good thing?'

'Yes,' said Reve quietly. 'An' when it didn't work, you tried something else . . . an' all the time, until things fall the way you want, you do business . . .'

'You're learnin,' said Theon.

One of the women tending Tomas, straightened up and Reve saw that it was Maria Scatta, the woman who'd always gone out to Mi's meetings. The other figure beside him was Arella, wiping his forehead with a cloth and with such tenderness that Reve realized something he hadn't ever really recognized before; this old blind woman loved Tomas; the rum she might have liked but that wasn't the reason she picked her way across the track to his shack every evening. She'd be lost without him.

'Is he dead?' Reve asked Maria.

'He's livin,' she said, pushing a strand of hair away from her eyes. 'Take more than that animal Calde to put him down.' Maria sounded weary. 'Oh, that you,

Theon . . .' She hesitated. 'Come see for yourself. Only thing going kill this man is his rum.' She took a step back and wiped her hands down her skirt. 'We need to put him inside.'

'Take him up to Pelo's,' said Theon. 'Ciele be happy to have him stay there.'

'A'right.'

Tomas was laid out on a blanket, his head tipped up a little, resting on a wad of the net that he'd been snagged up in. His eyes were closed and the colour of his skin was grey as rock. He looked dead to Reve; but she'd said he was living. So it was all right. It was all right.

Maria startled him by patting his cheek. 'You don't look so good, Reve, you and him both. You some pair, eh. What you think, Theon?'

'Looks like they been hit by a hurricane,' he said.

Then Maria bent down and spoke quietly to Arella. She picked up the bowl she and Arella had been using to wash clean Tomas's hurt, tossed away the water, tucked the bowl under her arm and went off with Theon to get some help, Theon saying he would tell Mi where Reve was. 'She'll be looking for you,' he said.

Reve wasn't sure; Two-Boat had hold on her now, arms wrapped round her for all the world to see. Reve let himself buckle down beside Arella. 'Let me do that, Rella,' he said.

'Who that? That you, Reve?' A skinny hand on his wrist. 'Knew you'd be back.' She smiled her blind smile, released her grip on his wrist and went back to dabbing at Tomas's forehead. 'You know who come see you,' she murmured to the unconscious man. 'Your boy, back from the city. How about that, Tomas?'

Reve looked down at the new bandage Maria had wrapped around Tomas's middle; it was staining orange. The knife wound had opened up again. His face was messed too: a puffed eye and a split lip. 'He's not so handsome now,' Reve said.

'Handsome enough,' Arella said.

A few moments later Maria was back with helpers who gently rolled Tomas on to a makeshift stretcher and carried him up the track to Ciele's and, though she protested, Arella was led back into her own place. Reve was left sitting outside with his back to the fire, his arms wrapped round his left knee, his right leg which throbbed all the way down to the ankle stretched out in front of him, hoping for Mi to come down but trying to tell himself that it was all right if she didn't because that was the way she was. He missed Sultan settling down beside him, and he worried about what he would have to say to LoJo and to Ciele when he caught up with them. From up the track he could hear shouting and celebrating. Some of those San Jerro men must have pressured Theon into opening the bar. Reve felt as alone as if he had been set adrift in the dark.

Mi found him like that, holding his good knee, his head down, eyes closed. 'What you doin dreamin all the time?' Her voice was bright and rippling with excitement. Everything bad washed away.

'Where's your man?'

'Why callin him that? He got a name, Reve. Phoof! You burnin up sittin so close to that fire.' She glanced over her shoulder and then turned back to him. 'You comin with us, Reve.'

'Us?'

'Enrico's waitin on me.' He saw Two-Boat up the track a little way, talking to one of the men that had come with him. Mi shrugged, tilting her head to one side, trying to be casual but not quite managing it. 'Come on. He got a place we can stay. We be gone out of here and we won't get trouble. No more trouble, Reve. None of that. And our own place,' she rattled on, repeating herself, her words skittering like shingle when you walk on it.

'Mi.' He stopped her. 'It's a'right. You go on.'

She stepped forward and touched the side of his head where he'd cracked it against a stone and looked at her fingertips and frowned. 'You got blood on you,' she said, and then, 'You think you got to stay for Tomas? He got half this place lookin' out for him now. He don't need you, Reve. You come with me.' She kicked her toe into the sand.

'I can't.'

'Why?'

He hugged his knee tight. 'It's not just Tomas; I don't know what to say to Ciele 'bout what happen.'

She frowned.

'How Pelo saved us, Mi. Are you goin be the one to tell her? One of us got to tell her – how they shot him down.'

The firelight flickered, made her face waver in and out

of shadow, tinged her hair with flame. 'The whole thing one bad dream. I don' want nothin of that time now. I want it all gone, Reve.'

She took one step back as if she was about to turn and go, then a step forward. Then she looked over her shoulder and back at him; she gripped her hands together and she began to tremble. 'I don' care if I got no voices in my head tellin me things, if people don' want me for meetings; I don' need any advising 'bout what I got to do with my life; I don' ever need think about our gone-away mother ever again . . . but I don' want leave you, Reve . . .'

'Mi,' he said, all the old anxiety for her flooding back, 'don't!' He struggled up on to his good foot. 'Don't fret. You got no need. You go on. Two-Boat'll keep you safe. Maybe you stay with Ciele. You'll be a'right. I'll come an' see you when my leg mends.'

Her eyes were streaming. 'Come with me, Reve!' She flung her arms round his neck and held him tight.

CHAPTER THIRTY-FIVE

Two-Boat came and told her gently that it was time they were going. She nodded. 'I know that,' she said. Then she gripped Reve's hand and looked at him so hard he almost had to turn away. 'Where you get so strong?' she said. 'You the one who's rock steady all the time.'

He didn't know what she meant. He felt like a rag, that if the breeze picked up it would blow him down along the shore and out to sea.

'You got a place with us, Reve,' said Two-Boat, 'when the time's right for you, eh.'

'A'right.'

Reve watched them walk up the track towards the lights of the cantina.

He was wondering how he could make his way to Ciele's place with his bad leg when he sensed someone standing close to him. He turned quickly, almost losing his balance, and a hand steadied him. 'Ramon!' Reve instinctively tensed when he saw it was the hard-faced boy.

'I saw you with the gun,' said Ramon. 'I saw what happen.' His voice was level but there was a hint of something else. Reve wondered whether there was almost something he found funny in what Reve had done, or maybe respect. 'Here,' he said, and took Reve's arm. 'You want go up to where they put Tomas?'

'Yeah. What Hevez goin think, you helpin me?'

'He got nothin on me. I step where I want.'

There was a light at Pelo's old place and, without another word, Ramon left him there. Reve frowned. He couldn't make him out; he had always lumped him with Hevez; bitter and hard as a whip, no family, just the little brother.

Reve pulled himself up on to the porch and found Theon talking to Maria, and in the corner of the room Tomas lying stretched like a corpse. Even his lips were grey, and his breathing was shallow.

'You stay with him?' Maria asked.

Reve nodded.

She made him sit, and looked at his swollen ankle. She wrapped it tight in a damp cloth and made him as comfortable as she could, and then she and Theon left.

Reve stayed awake a long time, thinking and listening to Tomas's breathing. It sounded sharp and thin, like he was pulling the air in through a tear in his chest. He wondered whether Moro would ever return to the village. Finally, when the moon was low in the sky and the door frame looked as if it had been dipped in silver, he fell asleep.

The days that followed were long and slow. Tomas drifted in and out of consciousness, seemed feverish most of the time. He didn't recognize Reve at all on the first day, seemed frightened of him and turned his head away when Reve tried to feed him clear soup. And Reve, with no skiff, no chance of working and with his leg too sore to do more than hobble down to the harbour wall and back again, spent a lot of time on his own. They had little money either, but Theon made sure they didn't go short. 'You're good, Reve. You got credit.'

Credit? It wasn't so long ago that he had thought saving up dollars was the answer to everything.

People helped, Maria mostly, but though she meant well she had spiky ways so that Reve tried to keep out of the place while she was there. Arella came up to Tomas every day and Ramon called by now and then, cut wood for the fire and carried supplies down from the cantina. He did it without being asked and didn't like thanks. He still had few words, though he asked about Mi. He wanted to know if she was going to marry Two-Boat because that was the talk in the village. When Reve said he thought that given a little bit of time she would, he had nodded. 'Tha's a good thing.' That surprised Reve. It also surprised him how he was soft with Arella too, always seemed to be there to walk her back to her place at the end of the evening.

By the end of the first week Reve was healed enough to walk the strand and he found himself by the burned wreck of Mi's car; there was little of it left: the scarred and scrapped shell, springs, a melted steering wheel and scorched sand all around, like a dirt shadow. But he'd sat there all the same and looked out to sea, watched the skiffs setting out and running home at the end of the day. Life seemed to go on much as it always had, much as if nothing had happened. He wondered if that's how it had been after the murder of his father and his mother running away; the village shuffling on, doing its business, surviving: Calde, the Night Man, police. One thing after another.

As soon as Tomas could sit up Reve moved his bed over to the door so that he could look out to the track and see the harbour wall and the blue of the sea. He asked Reve to read to him, old newspapers when Theon brought them down and from the Bible – always the Old Testament, that's what he liked. Old hard-time Job, he liked him, and Jonah too. All that running away, and where'd he go? Right in the belly of the whale. It was about the only thing that made him smile. The story stayed with Reve and he began to reckon there were different kinds of running away; some of them didn't involve running at all, just sitting still.

He told Tomas, piece by piece, all that had passed on their journey to the city, and Tomas listened, didn't say a word, didn't ask a question, just listened until Reve told him about their gone-away mother who called herself Fay. Then Tomas nodded and said, 'Santa Fe,' in a voice that was about as thin and whispery as wind across the marram grass. Reve found it hard to tell him about her because he still didn't understand why this woman had turned them away, as if he and Mi were some kind of nightmare to her, or why, having done that, she had come out in the storm to save them from Moro, and piled up a lot of bad for herself with him. She would have known that that would be the price.

'Your sister,' Tomas whispered, 'she remind Fay of what she might have been; that what happen, Reve, and it caused her fright and that made her sour.'

'What might she have been, Tomas?'

'Queen of this place,' he said. 'But she wasn't ever happy here, wasn't happy with me, wasn't happy with your father, and I reckon she wasn't happy with that policeman in the end . . . Still,' he said softly, 'I hoped she come back, eh.'

'We're a'right without her,' said Reve.

Tomas didn't say anything for a while and then eventually, with his eyes closed, he said, 'Maybe. Time to let go these things. She got a different life now.'

Yes, thought Reve, and not one that he wanted for himself or Mi. He picked up the story again. He described how they had escaped and Pelo's fall and how they had left him there on the rain-wet pavement, and the rain falling so thick it was almost like smoke.

Tomas put his hand on Reve's arm. 'Pelo . . .' He sounded the man's name so softly it was almost a sigh. Then he said, 'Comes a time when you got a choice, Reve: you go one way, you go another. Know what I'm sayin? Pelo make a fine choice; you remember that. All the time. An' that's what you tell Ciele. Tha's what she need to hear.'

Reve looked down at the large hand with its scored and sore knuckles from all his fighting and he said, 'How can you be so sure she want hear 'bout it?'

'Cos not knowing goin twist a person up so they got nothin but pain. That's one thing. An' not doing a thing that you know you got to do, tha's the same; it jus' goin twist you up, Reve. An' one more thing.' His grip tightened on Reve's arm. 'You know, you already done so many thing, and every one of them make you shine in my eyes, Reve . . . that's how it is.'

CHAPTER THIRTY-SIX

Reve had spoken to Mi on Theon's cellphone. It was so strange talking to her and not seeing her. She told him that she was staying in a stone house with Two-Boat's mother, just the two of them, and the mother told her all the things she wanted to know, and when Reve asked what were these things, she laughed as if he had made a joke, but he hadn't. She told him about what she could see from where she was standing: the sun coming down on a little tree by the house, a tree with red flowers, and when the sun touched them it made them flame. 'Like your woman you seen, Reve,' she said. 'You rememberin' that?' As if it was something from a long time ago.

Of course he remembered.

He let her talk, and it eased him to hear how happy she sounded, all that bad time washed back out into the ocean; that's how it seemed. She told him about Ciele and Ciele's baby, told him how they had walked all the way from Rinconda and that the first person they had seen when they had come to San Jerro was LoJo carrying the furled sail from the skiff up the street to the little place Two-Boat had given him to stay at the back of the village. They were there together. Safe.

He asked her if she had said anything about Pelo. The phone went silent. 'Mi? You there? Something happen?'

'No.'

'Will you tell her?'

'No.'

He stared at the edge of the table he was sitting at and traced his finger in a cross someone had carved into the wood.

'You seen it, Reve; you do whatever tellin you need. But you come and see me, Reve. Tha's what you got to do.'

The day after he had spoken with Mi he went to see Theon, borrowed money for the bus fare, washed and scrubbed himself clean under the standpipe, ignoring the girls joking at him while he washed, and then walked up to the highway, sat down on the edge of the road and waited for a bus to take him north.

The same coast, the same ocean, the same sandy land, and yet San Jerro seemed to breathe a different air to Rinconda. The place rippled with colour and made him think of the church window he had seen up in the city. There wasn't just one track but streets threading this way and that and paved almost all the way down to the bay, where a few skiffs rode at anchor. He wondered which was his, or whether LoJo was out fishing with the rest of the fleet. He could see sails dotting the horizon.

The village was busy: there were the sounds of building and even traffic; twice he had to step out of the way as trucks came rolling down from the highway. There were even stalls selling fruit and vegetables, and clothes, pots and tools brought in from the city, he supposed. Such a short way, and yet it was so different to Rinconda, and he wondered why Rinconda couldn't be like this. Maybe this was something he could do. Why not? Take away the bad things.

He wanted to find Mi. He wanted to see her and tell her what he was going to do now. He wanted to see her in her house and meet Two-Boat's mother and make sure that she knew what to do if Mi got one of her fits. But he knew if he did that he would lose his courage and not go see Ciele at all. So he asked where he would find the woman who had come from Rinconda, and he was shown to a little white house, on the edge of the village and back from the sea. He knocked on the door and stood back.

She opened the door, and when she saw who it was she smiled and made as if to embrace him, but he took a step back. 'What is it? You lookin like a ghost.'

'I got something to say,' he said.

Her smile faded. He didn't know how to put it other than how it had happened, so he told it to her plain and her face seemed to shrink in on itself.

When he was done she said, 'I am sorry,' which is what he had meant to say, and she shut the door on him. He stood for a moment, thinking she might open it again, but she didn't and so he walked away.

He walked fast. He didn't want to see Mi any more, or LoJo, or even his dog. He didn't want them to see him, someone who had just come into their village to dump a whole sack of pain, because that's all he'd done.

He made his way back up to the highway and waited four hours through the heat of the day to catch the bus going south. When he got back to the Rinconda he cut straight down to the shore and walked, and collected plastic bottles and didn't go back up into Pelo's old place until it was dark, and even then he didn't go inside, just looked in at the door and saw Tomas was sleeping and then stayed out on the porch and fell asleep out there.

The next day Tomas asked him how it had gone, but he didn't want to talk about it. He just said, 'I told her. Tha's all.' Then he made himself busy and went off as soon as he could, down to the pier, did some work for one of the older fishermen, mending nets. When that was done he walked up to Mi's old place and sat down under the accacia tree, trying to make up his mind what he was going to do with his life, because that bright thought that maybe in time he could change things, make the whole village a better place, seemed too far away.

Then three things happened. Two of them on that day, the third a while later.

The first thing happened while he was sitting there, staring at Mi's burned old car, trying to be practical, trying to think what to do. He heard a shout and a dog barking and there, right below him, running in towards the shore, was his skiff with the small figure of LoJo in the stern and Sultan up in the bow, paws up on the gunwale, barking at a gull.

He stood up, hardly believing it was possible.

Sultan ran straight up the beach and hurled himself into Reve's arms, almost knocking him on to his back and then sniffing his eyebrows and licking him. When Reve pushed him back, LoJo was standing there.

'He pinin all the time,' said LoJo, 'an' I reckon he so

smart he even know what we sayin half the time. Heard mother say you call bring that news, and start up howlin' so bad I didn' have no choice but bring him right on back to you 'fore the neighbours up and drown him!'

Reve fussed the dog a little and settled him down. Then, after a moment, he said, 'You blame me for your father?'

LoJo shook his head. 'No.' His face was sad but set firm. 'No. We don' know why he was in that place, why he didn' call us or anythin, but he did a right thing helpin' you and Mi. Like a hero, hey?'

'Old style,' said Reve. 'Only way.'

'Tomas and him. They both the same.'

'Maybe.' He thought for a moment. 'Yes, Tomas too.'

Second, Ciele and the baby arrived in the evening, walking down the track to her old house while the two boys were out on the porch and Tomas was upright in his bed, rolling a cigarette. He didn't smoke them any more, just rolled them up. 'Keep my hands busy,' he said. She moved right back into her house and took over the care of Tomas, which rankled Maria Scatta a little but there wasn't any negotiating; and everyone in the village knew that Tomas had taken the fall so Ciele and the baby could be safe. She never said anything to Reve when she moved back in, just set her baby down and wrapped her arms round Reve, held him tight and then let him go, saying: 'This your place now.'

A whole year went by before the third thing happen. Mi was happy and settled in her mind. Two-Boat was steady and kind and Reve knew him well now, knew he was right for his sister. Everyone had known that this wedding was coming, rolling in like good weather from the south. Mi came up in a truck to collect them all, and although she was excited there was no spin or dip in her, she seemed more steady than he could remember. They talked a little before all the celebrating began, down on the beach at San Jerro, with the waves curling in on the sand and behind them the band beginning to play.

'It was some miracle,' said Reve, 'Two-Boat coming. Making Señor Moro give you up, like that.'

'Makin him huff an' puff a little, eh.' She hitched her brown knees up under the bright blue skirt Two-Boat's mother had made for her.

'He did that, and the devil's old car getting stuck in the sand! How 'bout that!' She laughed.

'How'd it happen, Mi? Was that you callin down a storm, wishin so bad for Two-Boat that he hear you in his mind and come for you? That what happen? Because that the most magic thing, you ever done.'

She tipped her head to one side. 'That wasn' magic. I used a cellphone. The boy on the bus, you recall? You were sleepin and so I sat up next to him and I call Enrico, because he gave me the number and I got that number in my head all the time we were in the city. He said to call him any time I want him, so I call him. Told you we goin get trouble when we hit the village, know the devil goin come lookin. Just a cellphone, Reve. Borrowed it from that boy.' She giggled and then fell silent. 'I think my magic all done now,' she said after they'd sat there for a few moments listening to the waves keep easy time with the music of the band.

'You got magic all the time, Mi,' he said. 'You goin keep holdin your meetings?'

She shrugged and hummed a snatch of the song the band was playing. Hummed it like she'd got the tune in her head. He'd never heard her do that before.

'Maybe,' she said. 'If it's what people want.'

'When you ever do what people want? You the most walk-alone person I ever known.'

She didn't answer that, just smiled a little. 'You cross with me, Reve? You still chewed up 'bout somethin?'

'No. I'm a'right.'

'What you goin do, Reve? You goin find some girl and go marryin?'

He smiled and put his arm round her. 'You just got marryin on your mind.' But he did try to tell her what he wanted. How he wanted to put a change on Rinconda, make it something better. Maybe one day he could take on all the fishing boats Calde had owned, make a business like Two-Boat, maybe make a partnership with Two-Boat. Then there would be work in the village and not so many boys like Ramon would go drifting up to the city and get lost; and families like Ciele's, instead of getting broken up, could keeping on living together . . .

'You could do that,' she said, 'so long as you don't go living under somebody's hut with your dog; you out in the air now, Reve, you an' me both.'

'Yeah,' he said. 'You think Uncle Theon goin help me?'

'You worry 'bout him?'

'Some. He always tellin me sometimes you got to do business, even if that man is someone like Moro, and I never doin that.'

She looked at him, head tilted on one side, but said nothing.

'But you know, I don' figure him, cos you know he the one who bring the coastguard in. He got no love for Calde or Moro, and he done what he could for Tomas and Ciele—'

'I know,' she said, 'but this is it, Reve; you the one goin show him the way. Tha's your business now.'

He nodded slowly. 'A'right.' He took a deep breath of the salt air and stretched his shoulders. 'I can try.'

A voice called for Mi to come up from the shore. Two-Boat's mother, it sounded like, and there was clapping and singing and a drummer driving up the music, and there was firelight and candles and the air was soft and warm on their faces. 'You goin to come dancing, Reve?' she said.

'I wish Tomas was here,' he said.

'He is,' she said. 'I got Two-Boat go back and fetch him and Arella.'

'You did that!'

'Yes, I did that,' she said. 'So you goin to dance at my weddin, or you goin to shuffle like some old fishing man?'

'I can dance,' said Reve. 'That's not such a hard thing, so long as no one goes laughin at me.'

They walked up the beach together and he felt a lightness in himself that he hadn't ever felt before.